IMPERIAL HIGHNESS

This is the true story of one of the most
remarkable women who ever lived,
Catherine the Great. Gifted with beauty,
boundless ambition and intellectual
brilliance, she suffered the misery of a
loveless marriage to a demented imbecile.
Persecution, jealousy and intrigue, dictated
by the unpredictable and neurotic Empress
Elizabeth and her half-witted nephew,
threatened her freedom and in the end her
life . . .

IMPERIAL HIGHNESS

EVELYN ANTHONY

A New Portway Large Print Book

CHIVERS PRESS
BATH

First Published 1953
by The Museum Press Ltd
First published in Large Print 1974
Reissued 1982 by Chivers Press
by arrangement with the author
at the request of
The London & Home Counties Branch
of
The Library Association

ISBN 0 85997 091 4

Originally published in the U.S.A. under
the title *The Rebel Princess*

IMPERIAL HIGHNESS

CHAPTER 1

THE peace of a snow-driven December night in the year 1743 was shattered by a horseman galloping along the road from Berlin, his mount slipping dangerously on the icy surface, the rider urging him on relentlessly, for he rode to the orders of one who would brook no excuse for delay.

He paused only once during that night to rein in at a wayside inn and swallow a cup of wine, not even waiting to dismount.

"Is this the road to Zerbst?" he asked.

"It is, Sir, about three miles distant, and a Merry Christmas to you," answered the innkeeper, but his traditional salutation fell upon the empty air, for the horseman had dug spurs into his beast and was already speeding on his way.

The small German city lay grouped about the central pile of the castle, its towers half hidden by the veil of thickly falling snow that clothed the rider and his mount in phantom white.

By a window in the castle tower a young girl, muffled to the tips of her ears in a counterpane, knelt on her bed, looking out into the night. Princess Augusta Fredericka should have been asleep, but she was far too restless to lie there in the darkness without even the cheerful comfort of a candle. So it happened that the first person to see the horseman clatter into the castle courtyard was she whose destiny he carried with him in the despatch case strapped to his body.

The Prince of Zerbst was at table in the banqueting hall when a lackey announced that a messenger begged admittance. He was a big jovial man, fond of women and of wine, and the occasion was one of double celebration for him, for he had just succeeded to the Principality of Zerbst. As a gesture he had invited his poorer relatives to spend Christmas with him.

A long table piled high with dishes stood in the centre of the huge room, whose walls were hung with faded tapestries that moved gently in the draught. The faces of the guests were illumined by the light of many candles, faces flushed with wine and the rich food they had eaten.

At their head sat the Prince, laughing with great good humour and surveying the scene with comfortable satisfaction. In the soft candle-light the cups and platters shone like silver and the uniforms of his lackeys gleamed with tarnished braid; it was difficult to notice the threadbare shabbiness of the family seat of Anhalt Zerbst.

The feast had been in progress several hours

and in accordance with the customs of the age most of the diners were drunk, their powdered wigs askew, while some lay sprawled asleep across the table, undisturbed by the talk and shouts of laughter that grew in volume as the wine flowed freely.

The floor at their feet was littered with bones, and wine-spillings dripped unheeded from the board, while the stolid German servants stood like statues behind their master's guests, refilling empty cups.

It was one of these who approached the Prince and murmured something so that he turned to his younger brother Christian and roared jokingly:

"Come, Christian, lay down your inward Bible and fill that empty goblet! There's a messenger outside, perhaps he's from Heaven in answer to your prayers? What if the King has given you a province at last?"

It was a tactless remark to make, for the comparative poverty and obscurity of Christian and his family was too sore a point for any of them to appreciate the joke. Christian raised his head and looked about him with angry, sombre eyes. The extreme piety that afforded him comfort in his misfortunes had become a standard jest among his more pleasure-loving, feckless kin and a source of impatient irritation to his wife, whose freezing,

3

contemptuous glance met his across the table, and caused him to wince involuntarily.

"My lady wife has enough to say upon the matter without your jesting," he muttered, half to himself, for the dark, quick-tongued Princess Johanna was of nobler blood than himself, an advantage which she had never allowed him to forget, and was impelled by an ambition that her cautious, slow-moving husband had utterly failed to understand or gratify.

In the midst of the general din of conversation the Prince of Zerbst addressed the messenger, travel-stained and shivering, who bowed before him.

"Whom do you seek?" he enquired grandly. The answer was both unexpected and unwelcome.

"The Princess Johanna of Anhalt, may it please your Highness!" the courier replied.

The Prince frowned suddenly, all his boyish, blustering humour gone. "She sits over there," he directed sullenly.

Johanna of Anhalt was a small dark woman in the early thirties, her carriage was upright and her expression sourly disdainful. Married at seventeen to the uninspiring Christian, disappointment had blighted her vivacious looks and destroyed those scant virtues possessed by a nature at once shallow and conceited.

Now she regarded the messenger with an indifferent hauteur, belied by the red patches of excitement that burned on either cheek.

She was poor and unimportant; no messages ever came for her. . . . But her hated relations must not see that the delivering of a letter had come to be an event in the monotony of her life.

"I am the Princess," she said sharply.

The man dropped to his knee before her, unfastening the leather satchel which was strapped to his waist. He handed her a scroll.

Johanna took it from him with hands that trembled, for she recognized the emblem on the messenger's case and, as she broke the heavy seal, saw the same cypher repeated on the head of the document. There was a sudden silence at the table, and the Prince of Zerbst put down his wine-glass to stare at her while she read.

He too had seen the seal that dangled from its crimson ribbon—the dreaded double-headed eagle.

"What news, sister?" he demanded. "You look as if your letter contained something that we should be interested to hear."

Johanna lowered the parchment into her lap so that her brother-in-law's sharp eyes should not notice how the paper wavered in her shaking fingers, and despite her efforts at composure, her voice was uneven with excitement as she replied.

"It is a message from my kinswoman . . . the Empress Elizabeth of Russia," she announced. "It is a most cordial message, most cordial. . . ."

"Naturally," the Prince answered impatiently, "but do not keep me in suspense, my dear Johanna. What does the message say?"

Johanna looked at him, remembering how he had sneered so often at her pitiful boast of kinship with the great. He would find out what the Empress had said soon enough. Insolently she ignored her husband; already she had determined what stand must be taken against him if necessary.

"I am summoned to go to Russia," she announced boastfully, "and I am to take my daughter Augusta Fredericka with me. We are to leave without delay."

There was an immediate babble of comment, but neither the Prince nor his brother felt the need to question the meaning of the summons; for they knew that it was the usual procedure with the Imperial Court to decide upon a bride for one of their number, and then to send for the girl without any previous warning.

Johanna's brother-in-law ventured one more question:

"And is there anyone in particular who desires

to see Augusta, besides the Empress?"

"She is most anxious to present my little daughter to her nephew, the Grand Duke Peter," replied Johanna venomously, for the Grand Duke Peter was none other than Elizabeth's heir.

In those few words she told them all that her daughter might well become the next Empress.

She herself had not quite realized the full import of her own words; excitement, vindictive satisfaction, and a sense of unreality vied for full possession of her feelings.

It was surely not possible that her daughter, the unremarkable Augusta Fredericka, should be called to such a destiny. But the parchment scroll still clasped in her hands gave the lie to her doubts; it was true enough.

Johanna could not endure that smoking, shabby dining hall another moment.

"I must waken Augusta. I must tell her this news without delay. With your Highness's permission . . ."

The Prince of Zerbst nodded his dismissal, while Johanna swept him a proud curtsy and hurried from the room. She had to relate her story into a sympathetic ear, or at least into a submissive one, and the person least likely to interrupt or question was the fourteen-year-old Augusta who was upstairs in bed.

7

Discussion with Christian would be difficult, for she knew well that the roots of strict Lutherism went deep in him and that the ridiculous conscience of which he made such boast might not be blinded by the brilliance of his daughter's future. His hatred and distrust of all things foreign was the only strong emotion, besides his long-dead passion for herself, that Johanna had ever known to possess him.

As she mounted the stone stairs to Augusta's room, the Princess marvelled at the choice of Russia's Empress. Of all the eligible royalties in Europe, why had she chosen the least important, a half-educated, precocious creature, who concealed her infuriating obstinacy beneath a manner at once brow-beaten and trusting?

Others, like her husband and that impudent French governess, might protest that her daughter exercised both charm and intelligence, but these qualities had never revealed themselves before Johanna.

Augusta Fredericka had long been a convenient butt for her ill-tempers and innate spite; it was no fault of Johanna's vigorous methods that the girl retained a spark of gaiety or spirit, and her mother's jealousy found vent in a half-recognized resentment that her child must share in the good fortune which had befallen them.

As she paused at the door of Augusta's room, her hand touched the miniature of Elizabeth of Russia which was pinned to her breast. The diamonds surrounding it were large, and the Empress's gift to her distant relative was the finest piece of jewellery that Johanna possessed. Soon there would be other jewels, other gifts. . . .

She delivered a pat of satisfaction to the painted features of her benefactress, and lifted the latch of the heavy door.

"Wake up, Augusta! Wake up this instant!"

The girl in the bed sat up obediently, drawing the covers around her for warmth, and regarded her mother's dim figure with misgiving.

Johanna seated herself upon the bed and, forgetting the dislike her daughter always inspired in her, related her story with a wealth of detail. Augusta was to go to Russia, there to meet the Empress Elizabeth and her nephew, heir to the throne. If she pleased them (and God help her if she failed), then she would be married to the boy. She would become a Grand Duchess, eventually an Empress. . . .

Sitting there, shivering despite the covering of bed-clothes, Augusta remembered the horseman whose arrival had relieved the long sleepless hours of Christmas Eve, and knew then that the messenger she had glimpsed from her window had carried this summons that was to change the course of her life.

*   *   *

Augusta woke at dawn the following morning, and still in her night-gown ran down the castle's icy passages to find her French governess, Mlle Cardel. She was a kindly woman, though strict, and a strong bond of affection had grown between the young Princess and her instructress.

Augusta knew better than to attempt to question her mother, but Mlle Cardel might perhaps know something about the Russian court, its Empress and, more important, the Grand Duke Peter.

She had heard rumours of the fabulous Northern Empire, and strange things had been whispered about the woman who ruled over it, but the stories were vague, intangible scraps of gossip, half forgotten until now. It was said, of course, that the Empress was very beautiful, and the lovely face on her mother's ornament would seem to bear that out. But Augusta, with an insight beyond her years, felt that those surrounding Elizabeth could hardly say otherwise.

There had been talk that she was even a little mad and given to the eccentric tyrannies that seemed to amuse every ruler who sat upon the throne of the Czars, but the girl's excited mind refuted the idea. She must find someone to whom she could talk about her future, someone who could satisfy her curiosity.

But the room occupied by her governess was empty, the bed unmade. Johanna had obviously wasted no time in rousing her entourage; it behoved Augusta to go back and get dressed as quickly as she could. Passing down the corridor on the way to her own apartment, she noticed that the door of her parents' bedroom stood half open, and she peeped guardedly inside lest the occupant be her mother. Christian sat propped up, in the huge four-poster, its shabby curtains drawn aside to let in the morning light.

For a moment his daughter stood quietly watching him as he read the heavy Bible that she recognized so well. What would be his feelings on this great matter of her travelling to far-off Russia? Augusta did not think that he would share her own enthusiasm, and she sighed so audibly that Christian raised his head and beckoned her into the room. "Good morning, child," he said gently.

"Good morning, papa," she replied, kissing the hand he held out to her.

Seeing that she shivered in her thin night-gown and that her feet were bare, Christian dispensed with ceremony and bade her creep under the bedcover. He had scarcely recovered from a biting argument with his wife, and now the object of it sat beside him, eager eyed and excited. How much impression had his frequent lectures and Bible readings made upon her mind, he wondered uneasily, and would her soul be asked as forfeit for the undreamed-of worldly eminence now offered her?

Johanna had dismissed his religious qualms with savage scorn, reminding him angrily that for a trifling change of creed her daughter was not going to risk the loss of the greatest imperial throne in the world. He would not be there to meddle in affairs above his understanding, Johanna had announced finally, for the Empress's letter expressly forbade Christian to accompany his wife and daughter. Only Augusta could set his conscience at rest, and he held out the leathern Bible for her to hold.

"You are going away, Augusta," he said solemnly. "Far away into a foreign land, where I fear you will find customs practised that are very different from those of Stettin. Do not be swayed by wealth or strangeness, my daughter, nor by the promise of greatness in this world. Remember the good Protestant faith that you were born in, and I ask you to promise me, by the Bible, that you will never change it! Do you promise, Augusta?"

The girl dropped her eyes that her father might not read the disappointment in them. She reflected that such promises were easy for those whom life had left in a forgotten back-water of the German States like Stettin, or even Zerbst. Her decision was prophetic of the years to come. "If I refuse, it might be in his power to prevent my going," she thought quickly, and her natural affection added that her reply would set his mind at rest.

Augusta smiled back at him. "I promise, papa," she said. Christian sighed with relief. Doubtless, as Johanna said, his daughter's character had many faults, but to his knowledge lying was not among them, and he never doubted her sincerity.

In the midst of his reflections it occurred to him that it might go hard with his daughter at Elizabeth's court, with no one to protect and guide her but the self-seeking and incautious Johanna. Looking at her with more than usual interest, he noticed that she was quite a pretty girl, she had her mother's dark hair and his blue eyes, but her face had a vividness of expression foreign to either parent. She promised, in fact, to be a very handsome woman.

Since there could be no question of refusing the Empress's request, he salved his uneasy conscience with the promise he had just extracted from her and tried to dismiss the affair from his mind. After all, he considered, the courier that had arrived last night, almost on the heels of the Russian emissary, bore a message from their King, Frederick the Great, endorsing Elizabeth's invitation and even sending for Johanna to attend an audience with him before she left for Russia.

Christian was not a clever man, nor was he a coward, but he knew enough of the age he lived in to realize that, in sending for Johanna, something of further significance besides the marriage of Augusta was in the mind of his wily sovereign.

"It is time that you dressed, Augusta," Christian observed awkwardly, somehow unwilling to look at his child. "You had best return to your own room."

Augusta slipped to the floor, bobbed a quick curtsy and ran to her apartment, while her father opened his Bible and continued reading.

Once in her bedroom, she shut the door and climbed back into her own chilled bed, shivering with cold and excitement. The thought came to her that if the cold of Zerbst nipped her so cruelly, what of that land of furious ice and blanketing snow that was to be her home for the future?

Russia. She said the word aloud and then laughed in sheer delight. The morning before she had greeted the world as plain Princess Augusta

14

Fredericka, daughter of a poor and unimportant prince, whose future appeared as bleak and uneventful as the flat marshes and barren lands of her native Prussia. Tolerated by her father, despised and bullied by her mother, without wealth or family connections, there had seemed but small chance that she would ever change her lot even by marriage, for who, as Johanna had enquired acidly in her hearing, would want to marry *her*?

Yet she was mature for her years, tall and high breasted, her complexion radiant with health; there was grace in her carriage; humour, intelligence and animation in her conversation as she never failed to prove when out of ear-shot of her maternal critic. For these, perhaps, some German princeling might eventually have married her, and until now the prospect had always represented conflict in her mind.

Marriage should be a source of pleasure, an experience of those romantic and sensual transports that had been described to her in books and through the less cultured medium of the kitchen-maids at Stettin; the marital relationship was no secret to Augusta, for it was not a squeamish age.

But her innermost heart demanded that it should offer something else. All her life, she had cherished one strong, secret ambition; her childish mind had brooded over it, peopling her drab world with riches and fantasy, and her adolescence had strengthened the half-formed desire. She wanted to be a queen. She, the humblest princess in Germany without a dowry large enough to warrant marriage, longed and dreamed of power and the possession of a crown.

Now, as if by some miracle, Fate had provided her with the most eligible prince in Europe as a husband, a youth destined to wear an emperor's crown, and what was more, to share it with her. . . . She was not to know that in the eyes of the Russian Empress her very obscurity was her greatest asset. A princess of importance might prove difficult to tame, but not this little nobody, Augusta.

Suddenly she sprang out of bed, tearing off her nightgown, aware that the hour was late and that she had lain day-dreaming and wasting time.

Augusta splashed her face and hands with water in which thin wafers of ice floated like transparent fish, and dressed hurriedly. Standing before the small, spotted mirror, she brushed her black hair and pinned the shining mass on her head, pausing to regard her own reflection, a new, disturbing question in her mind.

Supposing that she was not to this Grand Duke Peter's taste?

The image in the tarnished looking-glass stared back at her with large thoughtful blue eyes; it was an arresting face of brilliant complexion and gifted with a high broad brow, the nose was very straight and her jaw a little square; but when she smiled the reflection showed perfect teeth set in a soft mouth.

Augusta turned from the glass, her question answered.

The Grand Duke would find her pleasing, and he would find her loving also, for she would owe him much.

*   *   *

Two days later Johanna departed alone on her journey to Berlin in obedience to the summons of her King.

Frederick received her graciously, bade her be seated, and passed a few minutes in formal enquiries as to her health and her family's well-being, while he examined her with a look that held none of the amiability of his words.

Despite herself Johanna averted her eyes from that penetrating stare; Frederick of Prussia was a thin, dry man, whose presence filled his subjects with an awe out of all proportion to the mere physical aspect of their sovereign.

His voice and manner bore unmistakable traces

of the restraint imposed upon him in boyhood by the maniacal hatred of his father, and his cold blue eyes regarded Johanna of Anhalt with an unblinking, hostile stare which weighed her character and intelligence and found small merit in either.

He judged her vain and hasty, of a jealous and overbearing temperament without the personality powerful enough to inspire either confidence or fear, and even as she spoke he mentally regretted the necessity which forced him to employ a tool at once so garrulous and so conceited.

The purport of Frederick's summons, and indeed of many things, was made clear to her during the audience, while she fidgeted upon a straight-backed chair, and Frederick's dry voice explained that the House of Anhalt owed its change of fortune to his offices. He had recommended Augusta to the Empress, having noted her evident intelligence and pleasing looks during their last stay at court.

He wished to impress upon Johanna, he remarked at length, that she owed first allegiance to him, and as proof of that allegiance she would send secret reports to him from Moscow and undertake to influence the Empress Elizabeth against her Vice-Chancellor Bestujev, who was, the King added, a bitter opponent of her daughter's coming marriage and of Prussian interests.

The future Emperor was his young friend and disciple, it only needed an Empress of similar sympathies to ensure that peace and security which was the natural outcome of Prussian domination. He felt sure that Princess Augusta Fredericka would remain loyal to the land of her birth. . . .

Fortified by promises of rich rewards should her espionage prove successful, Johanna returned to Stettin. To her husband's questions she answered nothing, and he decided that for his part it was safer not to know.

The person least consulted in these momentous days was the central figure in the drama about to be enacted, the Princess Augusta. No one had bothered to tell her anything beyond her mother's bare outline of the Empress's message, so she had to fall back upon her imagination to fill in the gaps.

It was not difficult, but sometimes, especially at night, her day-dreams faded and she felt afraid. Russia was a strange land where terrible, violent things happened every day. Gossip painted a terrifying picture of the Czars and their courtiers. Elizabeth was a Russian, daughter of Peter the Great, the Emperor who had flogged his own son to death. . . . Augusta shuddered when she remembered it. But people said that she had never executed anyone. One would have to be wary, no doubt, not to displease the Empress, but as long as she obeyed, Elizabeth would favour her.

And the Grand Duke whom she was to marry, he was German like herself, a nephew of the Empress, adopted only because she had no heir. He was not even a foreigner, she reassured herself over and over again. He was a young man, and gossip declared him very fond of soldiering and an admirer of Prussia. She determined that she would make him fall in love with her.

To Augusta the image of the Grand Duke Peter was that of the handsomest of men, endowed with all those qualities of charm and wit that she had admired secretly in some of Frederick's courtiers, and the inherent generosity of her nature responded to the mirage she had created.

"I shall love him," she declared to her governess Mlle Cardel one day. "I shall devote my life to pleasing him and making him love me! Even now, Mademoiselle, I can hardly believe that I am really leaving Germany; that I shall never go back to Stettin; that I shall soon be married . . . and living away from mama!"

Mlle Cardel turned from her charge, avoiding those bright, candid blue eyes. With a hand that trembled slightly she stroked Augusta's black hair.

"I am sure that he will love you, in fact I think

many men will . . ." she said.

Poor little one, so eager to escape from one prison into another, the Frenchwoman thought sadly. To exchange the execrable Johanna for none other than His Imperial Highness Peter of Russia. God help her! But she managed to smile and send her pupil away on some pretext.

It was not for her to shatter the illusions of the bride. . . .

Augusta lay in her bed that last night, but sleep refused to come. She was too excited, too disturbed by traitorous qualms of homesickness. She passed some of the time in prayer, but the stiff, formal phrases failed to bring her comfort and never had her cold Lutheran God seemed so far away as in those last hours before daybreak.

At dawn the next morning, two carriages waited outside the castle, one for the Princess Johanna and her daughter, the other smaller one for their little retinue of servants, a proper escort having been forbidden by the Empress for reasons of her own. The Prince of Zerbst, his wife and family, stood with Christian to bid the travellers farewell.

Johanna bade her husband a dutiful good-bye, promising to keep him informed of their progress; then Christian turned to the daughter he would never see again and embraced her for the last time.

"God protect you, Augusta," he said gently. "Conduct yourself well, and above all with caution, and you will have nothing to fear."

These were not the parting words she would have wished to hear, and her father's solemnity cast a cloud over her spirits. Surely she had nothing to fear? In the morning light, the terror of the darkness put aside, her future seemed to hold nothing but happiness and success. She kissed her father and her uncle and for a moment the tears started to her eyes, for this was her last sight of them all. Then she turned quickly and followed her mother, the newly recruited spy, into the dim interior of the carriage.

She looked out and saw the figure of Mlle Cardel at an upstairs window. Etiquette had barred her from this final gathering in farewell. Bravely Augusta waved to her, choking back sudden tears, then the door was slammed shut and with a shout the coachman whipped up the horses. With a great clatter of hooves the procession began to move out of the courtyard, the clumsy vehicles swaying as they gathered speed.

Within a few minutes they had passed out of sight.

★　　★　　★

Throughout the long hours of that first day's

journeying, Augusta occupied her mind with thoughts of Russia and the Grand Duke Peter, while her mother stared out of the window.

When Johanna glanced at her daughter she noted the expectant happy look upon her face. She shrugged inwardly and dismissed Augusta's feelings from her mind. They were not of the least importance.

As they travelled towards Stargard the roads became increasingly bad and the two passengers clung to their seats as the carriage lurched over potholes and ruts. Their nights were spent at inns and posting-houses on the way, often in great discomfort, and the indignant Princess was sometimes forced to share the landlord's quarters, for there was no fuel to warm the freezing guest rooms.

When they reached Memel the weather became so severe that they had to wear masks to protect their faces from the icy air; weeks of travelling under such conditions, with little sleep, tormented by cold, cramp and fatigue, reduced the future Grand Duchess to terror and despair.

On the 6th February, 1744, the battered procession entered Riga, where the emissaries of the Empress of all the Russias awaited them.

They were magnificently received and Johanna found herself lodged in sumptuous rooms in the castle, a train of servants placed at her disposal, the attention of the whole Russian garrison centred on herself and her daughter.

Elizabeth's advance reception promised great things, and Johanna accepted greedily the superb furs that were presented to them with the Empress's compliments.

But too much delay was not encouraged, and the last stage of their journey began. In the few days at Riga Augusta had been bewildered by the extravagance and splendour she had witnessed, but the most fantastic sight of all awaited her when she accompanied her mother from the castle.

A train of sledges stood drawn up in the snow, piled high with baggage. A mounted military escort pranced about them, and at the head of the procession stood an enormous golden sledge, covered in crimson. Even Johanna's haughty airs could not take this complacently, and she was led to the vehicle with eyes as wide as Augusta's own.

The sledge was designed as a huge bed, piled with mattresses and cushions upon which the two princesses lay at full length, wrapped in silken coverlets lined with sable.

Their journey to Moscow was carried through with the maximum speed, but in perfect comfort, and in the last stage, when the city lay seventy versts distant, sixteen horses were harnessed to the royal sledge and it flew over the ice at a tremendous speed, arriving in Moscow within three hours.

They were driven straight to the Wooden Palace, where Elizabeth and the court were then in residence. It was eight o'clock in the evening. Snow was falling steadily from a dark, leaden sky as the Princess Augusta alighted from the sledge.

She gazed at the great palace, its hundreds of windows ablaze with light, and shivered despite the furs that enveloped her. It reminded her of a picture-book fortress, seen and remembered through nights of childhood fear.

The interior of the palace dispelled the momentary shadow of oppression that had come upon her, for gracious figures, gorgeously dressed, hastened to welcome them in the Empress's name. The great staircase was thronged with men and women, extravagantly jewelled and clothed, who stepped aside as they approached, staring at them with open curiosity. With great ceremony they were conducted through the palace to apartments specially prepared for them, lofty, firelit rooms, magnificently furnished. Gratefully Johanna approached the great fire that burned in their bedroom and spread her hands to the blaze. The courtier who had first welcomed them bowed courteously.

"I hope you find these rooms comfortable, Your Highness," he said.

"They are charming," replied Johanna condescendingly, anxious not to appear overwhelmed by her surroundings. The smiling Russian bowed again, but there was just a hint of mockery in his voice as he answered:

"Her Imperial Majesty will be gratified at your approval. . . . Now, Highness, I have orders for the Princess Augusta to accompany me elsewhere! If you will excuse us!" Without another word he motioned Augusta to the door, and with one startled glance at her nonplussed mother, she obeyed and walked into the corridor.

"Where are you taking me?" she asked. "To the Empress?"

"No, Highness," came the answer. "To the Grand Duke Peter."

*   *   *

It seemed an age to Augusta as they walked past many doors, each guarded by a huge uniformed lackey, and her legs were trembling with weakness and excitement. The Russian seemed to sense her nervousness, for suddenly, without a trace of ceremony, he turned to her and remarked, pleasantly: "It is not far now, Highness, and do not be afraid. He is expecting you."

Dumbly she nodded in thanks, her mind busy with frantic thoughts. "He will not like me. . . . Oh, I know he will not. . . . Please, God, make him pleased with me. I must look awful, my hair is not even dressed properly and I am still bundled in these furs. I should not have come when this man said. . . . Oh, what shall I say to him, I have forgotten everything. . . ."

Suddenly, faced with the reality of her future husband and the importance of this first crucial meeting, all her courage deserted her and in her desperate need for support she put out a trembling hand and clutched Elizabeth's courtier by the arm.

Instantly a warm hand patted her cold one with a friendly, comforting gesture. "I am Leo Narychkin," he whispered. "Courage, little one, we are almost there."

As they approached a great archway, barred by a massive door, Augusta heard strange sounds; she could hear the muffled tread of marching feet and the yelling of commands in her own German tongue; there were curses too, foul, barrack-room language overheard in the military stables at Zerbst.

Before she had time to ask a question the door was flung open and she stood on the threshold of a long, high room, which at first sight seemed to be filled with an army of marching men. The whole place shook with noise as three lines of uniformed giants paraded up and down with military precision.

For a moment Augusta stood motionless, until, slowly, her gaze rested upon a figure standing at the head of the room nearest the doorway. A small, stunted, ill-shapen figure, dressed in a baggy green uniform, wearing an outsize wig on its large head, the face below contorted with rage. It was the figure of a youth, callow and undeveloped, but the expression in the staring eyes was the ageless glare of madness.

She had no need of Leo Narychkin's cautious whisper. This was Peter. She knew it. This was the Grand Duke.

Like a person in a dream she allowed herself to be guided towards the future Emperor, and, as if it were from a great distance, heard Narychkin's voice ring out above the din.

In a moment the noise ceased, the sweating, gasping men stood at attention and there was an utter silence, through which her betrothed's voice cut like a knife.

"How dare you halt them! They were just getting it right. Clumsy fools, I've been drilling them for hours, they're so stupid. . . . But what can you expect from Russians! What? Who?" She saw the dilated blue eyes turn upon herself and automatically she dropped a trembling curtsy. When she raised her head, Peter stood before her.

"You're Augusta Fredericka, the one whom my aunt says I'm to marry?"

"Yes," she whispered.

"Well, I bid you welcome," he said rudely. "How was your journey, are you well? No, don't answer, because I've not the least desire to hear. I only say what I've been bidden. And now, Princess, excuse me! These are my servants and I have to teach them military drill, the God-forsaken, Russian louts! One thing"—Peter looked at her narrowly for a moment—"you're not as ugly as I expected anyway." With that he turned his back, and, guided by Narychkin, Augusta stumbled from the room.

As the door closed behind her, she heard a shrill voice raised in furious command, and the exhausted servants commenced their "military training" once more.

Blinded by tears, she walked beside the silent Russian courtier till he stopped before the apartments the Empress had assigned her. He bent down and picked up something dark and soft. "You've dropped your muff, Highness," he said gently.

"Thank you," Augusta sobbed, and, thrusting past the lackey who opened the door, she ran into the room and fell into Johanna's arms.

The Princess of Anhalt was not surprised at the tears and hysterics that followed, for she was far from ignorant of the character of the Grand Duke; but ambition had long since destroyed any squeamishness or sympathy, and her reaction to Augusta's misery was swift and brutal.

Gripping her daughter by the shoulders she shook her violently. "Stop it . . . stop it at once. How dare you cry and complain? What did you expect besides a crown, a handsome lover? Control yourself, you little fool, or I shall beat you. This is no time to waste on tears and weakness. The Empress has sent for us! Take off your cloak and furs. Go wash your face and cease that wailing!"

Still sobbing, Augusta got up and did as she was told. Then Johanna surveyed her appearance with hard eyes. "Very well, now come," she ordered.

With dragging steps she followed her mother from the room. Now it was the mighty Empress herself that she had to face. God knew what that would mean. . . .

CHAPTER 2

A MEMBER of the Grand Duke's household, the Prince of Homburg, escorted Augusta on her second journey, while none other than Peter himself appeared to offer an unwilling arm to her mother. He neither spoke to, nor looked at, his future bride.

For the most part of their progress Augusta walked with her eyes on the floor, nodding absently to the polite comments of her companion, whose shrewd glances perceived very quickly that the young Princess of Anhalt had already been in tears. Wisely he guided her along the route to Elizabeth's apartments in diplomatic silence so that she had time to recover herself, for a weeping bride would scarcely find favour with the Empress, and it was vital to the plans of the whole Prussian faction at court that Frederick's protégée should make a good impression.

At length he turned to her and smiled.

"His Majesty King Frederick bade me deliver this message to you on your arrival. He sends his most cordial wishes to you and reminds you, in all earnestness, that the way to the Empress's heart lies through meekness!"

31

Augusta looked up at him with wretched eyes and nodded. As they approached the carved portals of Elizabeth's state bedchamber, the Prince of Homburg added his last word:

"Remember our King's advice, Highness, if you would one day sit upon the throne of Russia!"

With that injunction still sounding in her ears, Augusta made her deepest curtsy on the threshold of the Empress's chamber.

Many years later she was to recall that first glimpse of Peter the Great's daughter, when injustice and bitter persecution had clouded the memory of the Empress whose beauty and grandeur surpassed anything that Augusta Fredericka had ever seen.

Her mother's miniature had not lied; the woman who sat upon the raised scarlet and gold throne was far lovelier than her image, for no painter's brush could capture the delicacy of feature, the brilliance of colouring, or the indefinable touch of the Oriental that marked Elizabeth apart as a beauty at once fragile and voluptuous.

Diamonds glittered on her throat and arms and winked from the folds of her enormous hooped gown. A single magnificent jewel fastened a sweeping black ostrich feather to her powdered head.

At that moment the majesty and wealth of a

Russian Empress ceased to be a symbol as Augusta advanced towards the throne; it became a fierce reality and a burning desire. One day the obscure princess from Zerbst would share that power, and somehow even Peter seemed to be worth enduring for such a prize.

Elizabeth's reception was typical of her emotionally unstable nature, and she greeted Johanna and Augusta with extravagant embraces and tears of sentimental joy. The two German princesses were overwhelmed with her graciousness, and the Empress expressed herself delighted with the looks and demeanour of her nephew's future bride. Augusta blushed under such unaccustomed praise, and her shyness melted in a genuine glow of warmth towards Elizabeth. Surely there was no need for all the hinted warnings of her father, and the Prince of Homburg's cautionary words?

As she stepped back from the throne, her eyes saw a remembered figure, conspicuously small and twisted among the splendid towering Russians, and, in spite of all, her heart filled with a strange, momentary pity for the callow, shiftless youth whose glance rested upon his imperial aunt with a look of loathing and fear that his scowls and posturings did nothing to conceal.

In the midst of that great assembly the terrifying lunatic, who had greeted her less than two hours previously, appeared only an ugly, feeble-minded boy, ill at ease and strangely nervous. Who would be cruel enough to oppress a youth whose wits were obviously none too stable and whose pallor and physique proclaimed him delicate and miserably immature? Augusta looked once more at the Empress, engaged in pleasant conversation with the voluble Johanna.

Surely the tyrant could not be Elizabeth. But a small frightened voice inside her asked persistently, if not the Empress, who else? And Augusta could not answer.

Long after they had been dismissed and lay resting in their own apartments, Augusta relived the audience in her mind while the Prince of Homburg's words echoed in her uneasy brain.

"The way to the Empress's heart lies through meekness." Lying there in the darkness, while Johanna snored, Augusta thought of the vast, snow-covered land that Elizabeth had seized for herself one night less than four years ago, marching at the head of her devoted Russian Guards to overthrow the Regent.

It was said in Germany that the throne of the Czars had always been occupied by means of bloodshed and revolution. With God's grace and her own good sense she would succeed to it peacefully by marriage, and for this end she determined to be meek indeed. . . .

And upon that resolution the future Catherine, whom history would style the Great, fell into a weary sleep.

*   *   *

At midnight the sleeping princesses were roused by an army of waiting women and lackeys bearing gifts from the Empress and a command to attend the state banquet which was to begin during the small hours. Elizabeth's presents were magnificent: dozens of beautiful gowns, heaps of embroidered underclothes and innumerable pairs of shoes were laid out for Johanna's approval, while a whole wardrobe was placed at Augusta's disposal.

Johanna, finally gowned in purple satin over an immense hoop, paused to look at her daughter and felt a pang of envy at the picture of loveliness that met her critical eye. Augusta had chosen a dress of pink brocade which gleamed with silver thread, and a necklace of rubies out of Elizabeth's own jewel box glittered round her throat.

Johanna's suppressed jealousy gave vent to an angry summons and her hand itched to box her daughter's ears as in the old days at Stettin, but too many pairs of Russian eyes were upon her and

35

she promised herself that satisfaction another time.

Not less than a thousand guests sat in the vast Banqueting Hall of the Wooden Palace, and the scene that greeted the princess was a strange mixture of Western luxury and barbaric splendour. She had never seen such myriads of candles, such a glitter of gold plate upon the long tables burdened with elaborate dishes; even Frederick's stately Berlin court paled almost to shabbiness before the magnificence of Elizabeth's imperial setting. The very lackey who pulled out her chair wore a uniform more gorgeous than any possessed by Christian of Anhalt.

Immediately opposite her sat the Grand Duke, weighed down with jewelled orders, and he returned her greeting with marked ill grace, glancing constantly at the empty chair that stood at the head of the table. The furtive hatred in his expression alarmed Augusta more than ever.

Elizabeth had not yet appeared, and something of Peter's unease crept into her as she played with the spicy Russian food and sipped at the wine in her golden goblet. She watched the Grand Duke push his platter to one side and drain his wine cup again and again, till at length he began cursing the impassive servants and shouting for good German beer as the alcohol loosened his discontented tongue. Suddenly the spectacle of Peter drunk revolted her, so that her poor pretence of gaiety fell to pieces and she turned away, sick with disgust.

Farther down the room, a thin-lipped, expressionless Russian regarded the German interlopers with cold dislike, and his hostility was not lost upon Augusta, for she knew him to be none other than Count Rjumin Bestujev, Vice-Chancellor of Russia, and bitter opponent of her coming marriage. She might have been afraid indeed, had she known that this was the man whom her foolish mother had undertaken to bring down in disgrace.

At three o'clock in the morning a blast of trumpets resounded through the great hall, and instantly the hundreds of courtiers rose to their feet as the Empress entered, leaning on the arm of a superbly handsome Russian.

Elizabeth's vanity was insatiable and her toilette occupied hours while she shouted and aimed blows at her luckless waiting women, but the result was dazzling.

Out of the fifteen thousand dresses that comprised her wardrobe, Elizabeth had chosen a heavily jewelled gown in the French style she copied so slavishly, and she walked slowly down the huge room smiling graciously, only to scowl suddenly at some unfortunate who had incurred her displeasure and doubled his offence by catching her eye.

Augusta smiled eagerly in the Empress's direction, and Elizabeth presented her to the handsome Rasumovsky, who sat by his royal mistress's side. He spoke little, this son of poor Ukrainian peasants and former church singer whom the Empress had chosen to solace her lonely hours. His adoration for Elizabeth was open and unfeigned; fortunately for Russia, his passion for the woman left no room for ambition at the ruler's expense, and so it was to remain to the end of his life; love of the Czarina filled his simple soul to the exclusion of all else. He had many rivals but few enemies at court.

At that moment the Grand Duke began to laugh; the sound was shrill and grotesque, and Augusta saw the Empress frown with anger. She snapped a few words in Russian to her nephew in a voice of fury, but the wine had done its work too well and the wretched youth rose to his feet, swaying helplessly, his sallow face flushed with belligerence and a courage denied him in sobriety. When he spoke it was in German, and the words came out in a bellow of defiance.

"I'll not be silent! Why should I not laugh,

Madame, as the whole snivelling court does behind your back! Is he not a good joke, that pretty peasant of yours? I'll bet he leaves lice in your bed, for all the gold braid you may pin on him!"

Peter leaned farther across the table towards Elizabeth and leered at her.

"Permit me to advise you, my most gracious aunt. If you want a worthy lover, forget your serfs and oafish guardsmen. Take a German!"

There was complete silence at the imperial table, while Augusta paled with terror; then Peter spoke again. This time his bloodshot eyes paused for a moment on Johanna, before they rested maliciously upon the shrinking figure of his betrothed.

He flung out an accusing hand that suddenly became a fist and descended with a crash among the table ware.

"See what has been chosen to wed me," he shouted. "See that vixen and her daughter! Nobodies, miserable beggars that lick at your hands, Madame, but not fitting for the Prince of Holstein! Not fitting, I say!"

He ceased on a hiccough, breathing heavily from the violence of his outburst, then a sudden shade of fear passed across his fuddled brain and his arrogance shrivelled away visibly as Elizabeth raised herself slowly and stood facing him.

Augusta watched the Empress's countenance contort with fury. For one brief second nephew and aunt resembled one another, as the demon of Romanov insanity showed on the faces of both.

Then the Empress lifted her wine cup and flung the contents directly at Peter's head. The liquid struck him full in the face and streamed over his wig and upon his coat like blood.

A torrent of profanity in Russian and French poured from Elizabeth's painted lips, and the Grand Duke cowered under it, suddenly brought to his senses by the terrible anger his drunken insults had aroused. Wiping his streaming face on his sleeve, he burst into tears and, with a look of mortal hatred at the Empress and Augusta, rushed from the banqueting hall, crying out to be returned to Prussia. His last words rang out in a wail of defiant entreaty:

"Send for Ivan! Make him your heir, I want none of this damned country or your throne! Send for Ivan, Ivan!"

In the midst of her rage Elizabeth paled under her rouge and sank trembling upon her throne at Peter's challenge, while Rasumovsky tried to comfort her. Watching them, Augusta forgot her own humiliation as she sensed that in that innocent name lay Peter's talisman of safety from his aunt.

Who was this Ivan, that the mere mention of him could make the Empress of Russia tremble?

It was almost dawn as Augusta confronted her mother in the privacy of their own apartments, aware that the scene had left its mark upon Johanna, for she was pale and restless.

For a few moments the mask of charming benevolence had slipped from Elizabeth's lovely face, revealing a furious barbarian beneath the trappings of Western dress and manner. Despite herself, Johanna shivered; suddenly the task set her by Frederick of Prussia seemed both difficult and dangerous. She turned impatiently upon her daughter, that innocent bait that she had helped to thrust into the merciless trap of imperial politics.

Augusta's voice was only a whisper as she asked the question that thousands of humbler people had suffered torture and banishment for voicing.

"Mama, who is Ivan? What did the Grand Duke mean?"

Johanna gripped her in fierce anxiety.

"Hold your tongue, in God's name! Did you not see the Empress at the mention of him? Do you want us to be banished, perhaps imprisoned, for your foolish curiosity? Were it not for the succession, I'll swear she'd have Peter's head as satisfaction for his words to-night. . . ." The Princess of Zerbst glanced fearfully over her shoulder, then bent down to the shrinking Augusta and whispered quickly:

"For all our safety I must warn you never to speak that name. Ivan is but a child, yet a child anointed and crowned rightful Czar of all the Russias! The Empress seized his mother, the Regent, and dethroned him; the boy is confined in some fortress, but already rebellion has broken out in his name. 'Tis said that a lady-in-waiting had her tongue torn out for being implicated in the plot. Let that satisfy you, little fool, and remind you that it is safest to forget what you have heard!"

But Augusta did not forget and, during the long hours of the night when sleep eluded her, hideous images besieged her bed. This then was the true nature of her changed estate; a cruel young imbecile, himself haunted by fear, was the man to whom she must give her heart and body, and the prize for this fearful bargain was to be a usurper's crown. Somewhere in the blackness of a dungeon the rightful lord of Russia lay captive, and the shuddering Augusta recalled that her mother described him as only a child.

For the second time within twenty-four hours of her arrival in Moscow, Princess Augusta Fredericka wept, baptizing the embroidered pillow on her strange bed with a flood of unhappy, hysterical tears.

*　　*　　*

During the days that followed the young princess found herself involved in an endless round of pleasure, the recipient of almost daily gifts from the Empress Elizabeth who overwhelmed her with favour, and the subject of universal attention at court.

Her early pleas to Johanna to return to Germany had been savagely refused, and it came to the Czarina's ears that on the morning after her arrival in Moscow, the elder German princess had begun it by slapping the future Grand Duchess.

Elizabeth, who struck her own servants and intimates for the slightest fault, was filled with indignation, for the open admiration of the young Princess of Anhalt had flattered her vanity, and something of the girl's warm-hearted charm had touched her own childless heart. On the instant the Empress had approved her, and with the single-mindedness of her nature she pursued this new enthusiasm, lavishing affection upon Peter's future bride, unable to be without her company for a single hour.

At night Elizabeth Petrovna turned to that other occupant of the gaps spinsterhood had left in her emotional life, so that the time of the most powerful woman in Europe was divided equally between her humble lover and the fourteen-year-old Princess of Anhalt Zerbst.

In return for all this favour, Augusta responded to her protectress with a whole-hearted love and loyalty which would admit no wrong in the magnificent Elizabeth.

Whatever her fears on that first night, her disappointment in the Grand Duke, her horror at the story of Ivan, Augusta absolved the Empress from all blame. What Elizabeth had done was best forgotten, the past must not be permitted to overshadow her future or betray her into cowardly misgivings about her marriage. And at first that marriage did not obtrude too much into her mind, for the Grand Duke was confined to his apartments as a punishment for his behaviour at the imperial banquet, and not for some time could she bring herself to ask the Empress's permission to visit him.

The request was a diplomatic one, dictated by the policy of obedience which Augusta had determined upon following before she left Germany. The slur which Peter's drunken insults had cast upon her birth and status had been a public one, made before his aunt and the whole court; for that she could not yet forgive him, and the prospect of an interview with him in private filled her with aversion.

He was ugly and hostile, twisted in mind as he was illformed in body, but their destinies demanded that they should be joined together as one flesh, and whatever her feelings in the matter, Augusta stifled them and asked Elizabeth if she might see him.

The Empress consented eagerly, for she counted on the girl's fresh, vital charm to rouse her nephew's sluggish blood to manhood. The sooner Peter Feodorovitch could be weaned from his childish pursuits of drilling lackeys and apeing Frederick of Prussia like an infatuated adolescent, the better Elizabeth Petrovna would like it.

"Dear God, Holy Virgin of Kazan," begged Elizabeth in her fits of frantic religious devotion: "Let him marry this healthy, docile girl; may they bring forth a child, a strong child that will live to reign after me should Peter die of his frequent illnesses. Then perhaps the spectre of Ivan and revolution will not disturb my nights. . . ."

So the Empress prayed, kneeling for hours in her bedchamber until the first light of dawn assured her that the dangers of a night-time coup were over, and Rasumovsky entered to soothe her fears in his passionate embrace.

Regardless of her weakness for Rasumovsky, or

indeed any handsome man who attracted her senses, Elizabeth's nature was at the same time deeply religious; all the contradictory scruples, devotion, superstition and hopeless remorse peculiar to the Russian people were symbolized in the person of their Czarina.

Weeks of pleasure and debauchery were followed by periods of wretched repentance, when the mightiest woman in Russia retired to a convent cell and spent her days in prayer and fasting or trudged the dusty road to some shrine, like any humble pilgrim. No one could say how long Elizabeth's retreat from all things wordly would last, but her people knew of their Little Mother's piety and worshipped her for it. In the meantime state papers piled up, unread and unsigned, and the affairs of the land were at a standstill while the Empress expiated her sins, only to emerge, refreshed in mind and body, to commit them all over again.

On the day named by the Empress for her visit, Augusta was once more conducted to her future bridegroom's rooms, not this time by the friendly Narychkin, but by a gross, blunt-featured Swede whom she discovered to be Peter's tutor, Brümmer. This gentleman answered her questions in monosyllables, remarking that the Grand Duke was as well as could be expected after being shut up in his rooms for nearly three weeks without fresh air or exercise. This explanation did nothing to prepare her for her second sight of Peter.

The heir to the throne of Russia was sitting alone in a corner in his big bedroom; he seemed smaller, more shrunken, his clothes were creased and his hair undressed. As Augusta advanced towards him, he raised a pallid face, drawn and swollen-eyed with unmanly tears, and, horror of horrors, he clutched a doll to his breast for comfort.

The sight was suddenly too much for her, and the girl who had long since scorned such playthings for herself, burst into tears at the sorry spectacle of Peter's cowardice and effeminacy.

For a moment the Grand Duke regarded her distress and then began weeping with her in an agony of nerves and self-pity.

Such was their first meeting alone, a meeting reported by spies to the Empress, who hesitated whether to double her nephew's punishment as a reminder to play the man with his betrothed, or to release him and hope that the relationship might progress properly of its own accord. Under the advice of Peter's physician, Elizabeth sacrificed her inclinations and removed the ban upon his freedom.

On his return to court life the Grand Duke became instantly aware that the impossible had happened; his aunt, the beautiful despotic Elizabeth by whom all women were regarded with the jealousy and suspicion of feminine autocrats towards their own sex, had become infatuated with his future bride. Augusta of Anhalt, the "miserable nobody" of his unhappy description, was the most popular person at court, the spoiled darling of the Empress, fêted and flattered by the greatest nobles in Russia.

They had found him a wife, he who dreaded women and wedlock, and she had become a rival, admitted to a favour with Elizabeth which his own conduct had denied him from the start.

But even as he hated her, so did another.

The Chancellor Bestujev stood by, watching and silent, while the girl sponsored by his enemy Frederick of Prussia seemed to have all Moscow at her feet. It appeared that he, Elizabeth's most powerful minister, had lost this battle to a chit of a princess, that the German influences at work had triumphed.

For the moment he was well content to let it seem so, and if sometimes he was observed to watch his enemies and smile, none guessed the reason for it, least of all the principal object of the Chancellor's silent mirth.

Frederick, wily, cunning Frederick, with his plans for creeping domination over Russia, had made one bad mistake. He had trusted his intention to a fool, whose first amateur attempts at spying on his behalf had immediately been revealed to Bestujev.

Johanna had entirely failed in her efforts to influence the Empress against her minister, for Elizabeth hated discussing politics at any time, and flatly refused to be engaged in tedious conversations about her own affairs with a mere foreigner. The Princess of Anhalt was as indiscreet as she was treacherous, and the letters penned by her and intercepted were found to contain enough evidence of treason to have her executed on the spot.

It only remained for him to choose the moment when Elizabeth Petrovna's eyes should read her guest's descriptions of her person, manners and armours. If he knew his Empress, and sensed her growing dislike of the Princess Johanna's conceited, overbearing personality, that should ensure the return of Peter Feodorovitch's affianced bride to the land of her fathers, unhonoured and unwed, if nothing worse befell her.

*   *   *

Meanwhile Christian's daughter was learning

the Orthodox faith. One of the foremost theologians in the Church, a priest named Simon Todorsky, undertook the conversion of the future Grand Duchess, and reported to the Empress that his pupil was as submissive to its doctrines as she was intelligent in understanding them.

The oath she had taken to her father was forgotten; Augusta cared as little for Lutherism as she did for this new faith, and she abandoned her childhood creed without a scruple.

By day her every hour was filled with gaiety, with dancing and feasts, with sledging parties and incessant card-playing, which the Empresss taught her; she laughed often and without restraint, aware that here her mother held no power, the shadow of Elizabeth protected her from Johanna and almost from Peter. But not quite.

The image of Peter crouching in a corner, hugging a doll to his breast for comfort, was a phantom that returned again and again to haunt and sicken Augusta during the long night hours when the imperial court, worn out with pleasure, had sought rest at last. Then the princess would lie tossing in her great bed, sleepless and wretched, until she put an end to these waking nightmares by pacing the icy floors, barefoot and in her night-gown, murmuring Todorsky's lessons.

The Empress had retired to the Troitsky Convent in one of her fits of melancholy penitence when the news reached her that Princess Augusta of Anhalt had fallen ill with a high fever. Instantly Elizabeth forgot her devotions and raced back to Moscow, as distraught as if the sufferer were her own child.

Gazing down at the sick girl, scarlet-faced and tossing in delirium, Elizabeth Petrovna's heart contracted with fury and despair. Here lay the answer to all her prayers; a wife for her nephew, a mother for her unborn heirs. Who had permitted this thing to happen, this tragedy that would most likely disrupt all her cherished plans? Who indeed but that unnatural mother whom her sudden entry had surprised arguing shrilly within earshot of her suffering daughter? The next moment the Empress had swung round on the astonished princess, her face crimson with fury.

"Get out!" she shouted. "Outside with you, and leave the girl to me! Only put your foot inside this chamber door and I swear I'll have you arrested!"

Without a word Johanna fled, trembling with terror and resentment.

Seated at his desk in his private writing-room, Chancellor Bestujev made a careful annotation in his neat, crabbed handwriting:

51

"The Princess Augusta Fredericka has contracted a malignant fever and her condition is causing grave disquiet."

His plans for dealing with her and her traitorous mother could well be shelved for the time being, for it seemed that death, so often the willing instrument of Russian politics, would remove Augusta of Anhalt Zerbst from the path to the imperial throne.

CHAPTER 3

"I THINK," said the Empress lazily, "that I shall name her Catherine. . . . Catherine Alexeievna, after my own mother. Do you approve my choice, beloved?"

Rasumovsky pressed Elizabeth's soft hand to his lips and mumured in agreement. He was alone with his adored Czarina, and it mattered little enough to him what she christened her nephew's German bride.

Elizabeth sighed in contentment; lying at ease in her darkened bedroom, soothed by her lover into a languid state of mind, for once the future seemed secure and free from fear.

Death had almost spoilt her plan by making off with the Grand Duke's betrothed, but since the girl had begun to recover nothing must stand in the way of the wedding.

"Catherine," she whispered, and for a moment her thoughts raced back to the beautiful Estonian peasant girl who had been a camp follower to the Russian Armies, finally becoming the mistress of the Czar himself, and bearing him a daughter out of wedlock. She, the Empress of all the Russias, had been eight years old before her mother had been lawfully wedded to Peter the Great and raised to consort's rank.

The first Catherine had been a simple woman, easily led by characters stronger than her own, a gentle plaything whose simplicity had pacified and endeared her to Elizabeth's ferocious father.

Catherine. It would suit Augusta of Anhalt admirably. Elizabeth determined that she should accept the honour and assume the nature of her namesake at the same time. Upon that resolution the Empress closed her eyes against the first faint light of dawn and fell asleep at last.

In a wing of the Annehof Palace, the object of her deliberations lay wide awake, watching the early daylight seep through the curtains in her room. Augusta waited until the chamber had become sufficiently light, then she reached out for a silver hand mirror that had been placed beside her bed in recent weeks.

Anxiously she studied her own pale reflection, and the glass showed her a very different person from the plump, radiant princess who had left her native Germany with such high hopes all those long months ago.

Sickness and disappointment had ravaged her face; the childish contours had melted away while the fever and delirium had run its course. A stranger stared back at her with wide, dark-ringed blue eyes, surprisingly high cheek-bones, and a chin so square that it betrayed will-power of a terrible degree in one so young.

She was certainly not beautiful now, and her dark, abundant hair had fallen out in handfuls. It would be weeks before time had repaired the damage to her face and figure, and that meant peace and respite from Johanna whose presence, even during her daughter's convalescence, had been forbidden by the Empress.

During the critical weeks of her illness, the story of the foreign princess whose love of Russia's language and religion had driven her to study barefoot in the middle of the night, had transformed the feeling of the court from watchful politeness to real enthusiasm.

Little by little the tale spread across the country, from Moscow to Petersburg, carried by the boatmen whose craft sailed the broad waters of the Neva, through city and town, hamlet and village. The nobility talked of it and the simple serfs believed it; gossip painted a glowing picture of the unpopular Peter's bride-to-be, and the prayers for her recovery were recited fervently from end to end of Holy Russia.

The Chancellor heard the news of her recovery from the lips of her personal physician, and he received the tidings without comment. Fate had cheated him of the solution he had hoped for, and now it seemed that other means must be employed to prevent this marriage from bringing his beloved Russia to a state of German vassalage.

Peter Feodorovitch, with his insane devotion to the Prussian King, was an evil for which there was no remedy, since the Empress refused to marry; but a bride of different racial leanings might perhaps hold the balance when Elizabeth Petrovna surrendered her power.

The time had come when he must place the evidence of Johanna's treachery before the Empress, and doubtless the Princess Augusta would also fall victim to the imperial wrath. . . .

Bestujev arranged the documents in order and then rang for his most trusted clerk.

*   *   *

That very afternoon Augusta was to leave her bed for the first time and sit up, and in her latest rôle of maternal affection, the Empress supervised the event herself. Bestujev's messenger was waved impatiently aside as Elizabeth embraced the thin, emaciated figure of Augusta, leaning back weakly in a chair, while Leo Narychkin, he who had first welcomed her to Moscow all those months ago, kissed her hand in congratulation.

On the fringe of the crowd, as usual, stood

Peter, his illformed body clad in the inevitable uniform, an outsize wig perched on his bulbous head, fingering the gilt buttons on his coat with dirty, shaking fingers, a prey to hatred, jealousy and despair.

Ever since her arrival in Russia, the sight of her vivacious beauty and eager charm had filled Peter's heart with inexplicable dread. In the darkness of many a sleepless night, he had acknowledged with bewildered anger that Augusta frightened him.

He had insulted her, snubbed her mother, avoided her whenever possible, but however he might try to wound and break her spirit, as his had been broken by Elizabeth, he could not feel at ease. Somehow her personality always emerged the stronger . . . that was it, he thought, and in spite of the stuffy atmosphere of that overcrowded room, he hunched his shoulders up and shivered.

There was strength in her ready smile, her eagerness to please; unlike him, everything she did drew admiration, even his aunt's savage despotism had succumbed to her charm.

In the midst of these reflections his eye met Augusta's, and she summoned a dutiful smile; as always her amiability made his flesh creep, and he looked down, scowling.

"God damn her," he muttered savagely under

his breath. "How I hate that bright, terrible look of hers! How am I to lie in her bed, as everyone expects me, when I cannot bear to touch her? Why didn't she die? If only she had died I need not marry till I wished, and then to a wife of my own choosing. . . ."

For the only time in their lives the Grand Duke and Bestujev were in complete agreement. Contrary to all their hopes the grave had not closed over Augusta of Anhalt Zerbst.

Within the month she made a short appearance at a court ball given in her honour, and all over Russia the church bells pealed in thanksgiving. A magnificent necklace of brilliants was added to her jewel casket by Elizabeth, and a ruby watch was Peter's unwilling gift.

It was a brilliant season, and the future Grand Duchess recovered rapidly. She was taller now, and quickly maturing into a lovely girl whose witty company was increasingly sought by the young and gay at court, particularly Leo Narychkin, whose harmless devotion to her was a general joke.

Through narrow eyes the Chancellor watched Augusta, noting that her shyness had given place to a poise and practised charm capable of winning many hearts. But there was something a little too boisterous for a girl, despite her outward meekness. Bestujev felt that he was in reality watching a young lioness who had escaped her cage and was too busy roistering in her new-found freedom to try her claws.

And she had claws. The Chancellor, like Peter, saw her more clearly through the eyes of hate, and he promised solemnly that she should never use them in Prussia's interest.

From April until the end of May the court exhausted itself with gaiety, and Augusta entered wholeheartedly into a breathless whirl of pleasure. Watching her, the Empress approved her choice anew. If Peter could resist the lure of such a creature, then Elizabeth's long succession of lovers had taught her nothing about the weaknesses of men. . . .

With an easy mind the Empress abandoned her pleasures and, dressed in sober garb, set out for her annual retreat to the Troitsky Convent, there to fast and purge her soul in the peace of its ancient cloisters, while the court amused itself at Moscow in her absence.

Two days after her departure on the 1st of June, a furious summons arrived at the palace, and an extremely agitated Johanna was bundled into a coach, together with her daughter and the Grand Duke, and the party was driven off at speed to the Troitsky Convent.

Bestujev had gained his audience at last.

The next hours were a nightmare of anxiety for Augusta, played out in the long cold room of the convent where she and Peter sat waiting, listening to the sound of Elizabeth's voice raised shrill with anger, and the muffled pleadings of Johanna who was facing her ordeal behind the door of an adjacent room.

There was the short glimpse of Bestujev's figure outlined in a window as their carriage stopped; then the ordeal of Peter's stupid, curious conversation, maliciously light-hearted in the conviction that no danger threatened him, and still the terrible waiting, until it seemed as if Johanna would never emerge alive from that inner room.

Augusta's mind writhed with uncertainty and dread.

"What has happened, what has my mother done?" The question repeated itself fruitlessly.

"God in Heaven, don't let me suffer for my mother's folly! Don't let them send me back to live with her again!"

In her agony she turned to the smirking Peter, desperate for comfort, even from him.

"Your Highness," she said, unable to restrain her tears, "I beg of you, plead with your aunt on my behalf. Whatever has offended her I swear to you that I have committed no crime. My only thought has been to please, and my mother's faults are not my doing. Peter, remember that one day I shall be your wife, and show me a little kindness I beseech you! Do not let them send me home. . . ."

For a moment the Grand Duke stood there, pondering the spectacle of the proud, successful creature who had so completely overshadowed him until this moment and now knelt in tearful supplication at his feet, catching his hand in hers.

But even as he looked at her his feeling of malicious triumph changed to revulsion and hate, while the old sensation of uneasy dread clutched at his heart.

Savagely he snatched his hand away and drew back from her.

"The only plea I'd make of my aunt would be to send you back to Germany, as no doubt she will! Ask nothing from me, Madame, my only wish is to see the last of you, and by God as soon as I rule this heathen country I shall put you where you'll never trouble me again, and marry whom I choose!"

As his shrill voice rang through the long room, Augusta heard another sound; the sharp click of the communicating door behind which her fate had been decided.

Hurriedly she stood up, a crumpled, tearful figure, her cheeks scarlet with shame at Peter's brutal rebuff, and turned to face none other than the Empress. One glance at Elizabeth's flushed and angry countenance froze the words of entreaty on her lips. She had humbled herself unbearably once, and the hurt of the Grand Duke's words gave her unexpected courage.

She was a princess born, and her ominously square jaw set hard with resolution. She would not beg.

There was absolute silence as Elizabeth advanced into the room, while a shaking, weeping Johanna leant against the doorpost for support.

The Empress's dilated eye rested upon Peter, who looked down and kicked sullenly at the floor; the sight of him inflamed her with irritation.

He was another Prussian, an ugly, graceless German imbecile, as treacherous to Holy Russia as the deceitful, spying Princess of Zerbst. Only let him father a child, said an evil whisper deep inside Elizabeth, then perhaps he need never succeed to the throne at all. Still without speaking, the Empress swept across the room to where Augusta stood.

Whatever Johanna had done, the marriage must go through. Elizabeth could not endure the strain of another choice, another courtship. She bent and kissed the astonished girl, and patted her arm reasuringly.

"Dry your tears, my little Catherine," she said

gently, and the Grand Duke started at the name.

"You are not to blame for your mother's crimes. She returns to Germany as soon as you are married; for your sake I will not punish her as she deserves. Come now, it grows dark and you must return to the palace."

The Empress favoured Johanna with a withering glare of rage and contempt.

"As for you, Princess, for your own sake spare me the sight of you as much as possible until you leave the country. Your King and your husband are assured of my sympathy, but I have no doubt that the former will know how to deal with you. I hear he does not suffer fools or shrews with patience!"

With a final nod to Augusta, Elizabeth walked out of the room, and the sparsely furnished chamber echoed to the slam of the door behind her. It seemed to Johanna that with that sound she heard the knell of all her hopes; the door of opportunity had closed upon her for ever and the future held nothing but a terrifying picture of Frederick of Prussia, that cold, merciless man, sitting in judgment upon her, demanding explanations. . . .

As the carriage sped away from the Troitsky Convent, Johanna wept nervously and Peter sulked in a corner.

She had won again. There was no escape from

63

her, and he looked at Augusta's dim profile with something like horror. She had come to Russia and some malignant fate had determined that she should remain.

*   *   *

On the 29th of June, the day after her baptism into the Orthodox Church, Catherine Alexeievna knelt before the High Altar in Moscow Cathedral and heard the Archbishop of Novgorod pronounce her formal betrothal to the Grand Duke Peter Feodorovitch, at the same time conferring the rank of Grand Duchess upon her.

Dazzled by the light of hundreds of wax candles, her senses bemused by the heat of the church, which was filled to overflowing, and the mingled smell of perfumes and incense that hung heavy upon the air, Catherine's thoughts flew back many hundreds of miles, far across Russia over the border to Zerbst . . . Zerbst, which she had left as a penniless, brow-beaten little creature all those months ago, her foolish head filled with romantic notions concerning the repulsive youth who knelt at her side.

Part of the dream had come true: wealth, grandeur and eminence were now hers indeed, as the Archbishop's words sent Augusta, Princess of Anhalt Zerbst into eternal oblivion and summoned Catherine, Grand Duchess of Russia in her place.

Closing her eyes, she bent her head as if in prayer, and a fierce determination welled up in her, born of Peter's unforgettable threat in the Troitsky Convent.

Everything desirable in life was within her reach, and surely love in some form or another would not be for ever denied to her. Fate would not withhold that from her when it had bestowed all else with such a lavish hand.

And no one in Heaven or earth should take away what Fate had given.

On her knees, Catherine swore that in her heart, though she did not call upon the gentle, painted Christ that watched her from the jewelled ikon on the altar.

Elizabeth, with her cruelty, treachery and immorality, spent hours in prayer, while the boy Ivan rotted in a dungeon, black and silent as the tomb. . . . Catherine remembered him and shuddered.

The God of Holy Russia was no more her God than the fierce German divinity who had been addressed by her frantic pleas for help and guidance on the eve of her journey from Zerbst. She swore by none of them; her touchstone was herself alone, and on her own life, with all its aspirations, she made that vow.

Many among the hundreds in the church, noting that bowed head, remarked upon the humble piety of the young Grand Duchess.

Only Bestujev, watching the defeat of his plan, doubted these qualities. He knew a deal too much of human nature to trust that charming, bright-eyed foreigner who had wormed her way into everyone's favour. She was far from humble, only careful because her position was still insecure; her conversion left him entirely unmoved, for the mark of the voluptuary was in his judgment stamped all over her, and he suspected that the change of creed had been an easy matter.

But she was yet too young to be of any danger, and her mother had been exposed and rendered powerless.

There was still time to build a cage about her, a bright gilded cage suitable for a Russian Grand Duchess, but with bars of iron beneath the gilding.

*   *   *

The celebrations that followed the betrothal lasted day and night until even the Empress's appetite for pleasure was appeased, and Catherine's strength exhausted.

Then without warning Elizabeth sank into one of her moods of abysmal melancholy, convinced of the ultimate damnation of her soul as punishment for her sinful excesses at the table and in bed. Her gorgeous dresses were put away, Rasumovsky retired discreetly, and the whole court was ordered to prepare for a pilgrimage to Kiev.

The journey took three months, for the pace was set by the Empress, who walked at the head of the procession, murmuring endless prayers, covered from head to foot with dust, while her courtiers rode in comfort. It was an extraordinary sight, that vast procession of carriages and litters crawling in the wake of the weary, footsore Elizabeth, and her company of chanting priests.

Watching the endless landscape, the hundreds of villages and towns, Catherine gained an everlasting impression of the vastness of Russia, of the sweep and power of Elizabeth's domain, broad and barrenly magnificent, like its ruler, indelibly marked by the Oriental; neither truly East nor West.

The people fascinated her; they came in droves to do homage to their Empress, kneeling in an endless line along the roadside, and the sight of their rags and faces gaunt with hunger stirred Catherine with strange tenderness and indignation.

Elizabeth did public penance for her sins, an exhibition which struck Catherine as foolish and undignified, when the Empress thoughtlessly squandered millions of roubles, paid for by the sweat of those dumb, nameless crowds who worshipped her.

Again and again Catherine turned to Peter, hoping for some sign of interest or enthusiasm similar to her own, but the Grand Duke spent his time quarrelling with his tutors and jeering loudly at the whole affair. Otherwise he made fun of the luckless Johanna, whose disgrace with Elizabeth made her a safe target for his malicious tongue. Catherine found herself wondering what evil star had chosen to deliver Russia into such hands as Peter's.

On their return to Moscow there followed months of comparative quiet, pleasant enough for the young Grand Duchess, for all contact with her erring mother was discouraged by Elizabeth and the only trial put upon her was an hour or two each day of Peter's presence.

These interviews were compulsory, and their object was to prepare the way for the more intimate relationship that the two young people would soon share.

Day by day Peter sat sullenly in her room, gazing morosely out of the window, while Catherine worked at her embroidery frame, miserably aware that the atmosphere between them was going from bad to worse.

Steeling herself, Catherine determined on a last

effort to gain his friendship. He had a weakness, and one which was heavily punished by his aunt if she discovered its indulgence. Catherine knew that weakness; she had seen it to her horror, and the memory served her purpose now.

During the Grand Duke's daily visit they were left diplomatically alone, and one afternoon she got up from her embroidery frame and walked over to the window where he slouched in boredom.

"Peter," she said quietly. He continued to stare out of the window as if she had not spoken.

"There is little to amuse you here, I know," she went on, "but since you are kind enough to visit me, perhaps . . perhaps you could bring your dolls and we might play with them together?"

It was her only bribe, and she waited anxiously for his reaction. Peter turned round and looked at her, his protruding eyes sharp with suspicion.

"We would be punished," he stated cautiously.

"Only if we were found out!" amended Catherine coolly. His expression changed to one of almost feminine longing, and her hopes rose as she watched his face register that temptation had won.

"I should like to play with them," he muttered wistfully, and for a moment Catherine glimpsed the utter pathos of his unhappy, twisted nature, feeble-minded and warped by the weight of his destiny. "If I could smuggle them in tomorrow. . . ." He looked broodingly at her in mixed uncertainty and delight. "You will not tell anyone?" he demanded.

Catherine held out her hand. "I promise not to say a word."

Gingerly, Peter touched her fingers, for he disliked all physical contact with her, but she would make his favourite pastime possible.

"Very well then, I will bring them to-morrow. Perhaps I may let you play with them also," he added loftily.

Catherine swept him a silent curtsy, and when he had gone she remained by the window in his place, looking out with heavy eyes while the manly, dashing Grand Duke of her imagination strutted mockingly away into space.

She was growing up; every nerve in her body proclaimed her advancing womanhood; and now that the bargain was made, her whole soul rebelled against Peter and his dolls, and the hideous immaturity they represented.

Every day the Grand Duke visited his betrothed, the forbidden playthings stuffed in his uniform pockets, and spent carefree hours in her apartments till his good humour even included Catherine in his games.

Never in his regimented life had he known the

luxury of a playmate or been free of adult company, and for a time his instinctive fear of Catherine lessened as they laughed and romped on the floor together. His twisted mind saw only enemies about him, but there were times when he could forget that the willing companion of his childish games was also to be his wife, and then there was almost friendship between them.

Catherine looked up in surprise one day when suddenly he dropped his puppets and shaded his eyes with a hand that trembled slightly, for the afternoon had scarcely begun. She noticed with alarm that his face was livid and that two harsh patches of colour burnt on each cheek.

Pushing the dolls to one side, she slid across the floor on her knees towards him.

"What is it, Peter? What ails you, are you ill?" she asked in a whisper. The Grand Duke shook his head and began rubbing his eyes like a fretful child.

"I don't know," he answered. "My head aches and my eyes are sore. 'Tis only a chill though, and you are not to tell or I shall be physicked again!" He looked warily over his shoulder and then leant nearer Catherine.

"One day I know they will try to poison me, and I must never be taken unawares or their plan may succeed! When I am Czar I shall have a food-taster," he added.

Catherine gazed at him in astonishment. Who would try to poison him? It was impossible, a figment of his disordered brain, yet the wretched youth shook with fear before her eyes.

"Hush, Peter," she said quickly. "No one would harm you. You mustn't think such things. But rest easy, I will not tell that you are unwell. . . ."

Peter picked up his favourite doll, a little soldier dressed in the uniform of Frederick's Prussian Guard, then laid it down again. He looked at Catherine with strange simplicity and directness.

"I believe that if I were not going to marry you, I would not hate you so," he remarked calmly.

Despite herself, Catherine blushed with disappointment.

"Tell me, why do you hate me?" she asked suddenly.

Peter frowned crossly. Often enough he could not understand his actions and feelings properly himself, let alone explain them to someone else. "I have just told you . . . because I have to marry you, and I do not fancy marriage, least of all to you! You are my aunt's choice, remember, I did not want you. Now she prefers you to me. Indeed everyone does," he continued with growing resentment. "You are a mere nobody, yet you come here and try to displace me. Oh, do not think

I have not noticed! Believe me, I notice everything, and I knew from the first that you would be my enemy like the rest of these damnable Russians!"

Catherine had not yet learnt the folly of trying to reason with a lunatic.

"But I am not a Russian," she reminded him. It was an unfortunate remark, for Peter turned on her in fury.

"You remember that a little late, Madame," he shouted, his sallow face suffusing with rage. "For a German and a subject of His Majesty King Frederick, you take surprising well to this God-forsaken country and its heathen Church! You learn their hideous language, pray before their idols. You fawn upon my aunt and make free with her courtiers. Have you so soon forgotten Prussia that you must copy these barbarians?" Peter clenched his fist and shook it angrily. "Well, you may have forgotten, but I have not, and when the time comes I shall show them all that a Prussian is worth a hundred of their dirty moujiks!"

Catherine stood up, then she looked down at him and her bright blue eyes were flashing with rage. For once her caution and perseverance went to the wind as Peter's taunts and insults over the last eight months mounted up in an unbearable surge of humiliation.

"I am sorry that the thought of me fills you with

73

such distaste," she answered, and her voice shook with anger. "I did not ask to wed you, and I was as little consulted as yourself! But do not speak to me of Germany, and jeer at me for lack of loyalty. I owe Prussia nothing, and I was glad, with all my heart, to leave it."

Contemptuously she kicked one of Peter's dolls out of her way, and with a cry of protest he snatched it up and hugged it to his breast with the old feminine gesture that belied his feeble show of militarism.

"Perhaps your court was rich, your parents kind; I do not know," she continued. "But have you ever been to Stettin, Peter? Do you know what it means to be poor, a nobody indeed, just as you described me?" She gestured vehemently towards the door. "What of my mother? Imagine living under her authority. She has hated and bullied me since I can remember. Must I long to return to her also?"

Peter grimaced and hung his head, while the flow of her pent-up feelings swept her on.

"Oh, I am German-born, but this is the land which has taken me in, showered me with gifts. . . ." She walked swiftly to the window and flung out her arms towards the dark landscape of the palace gardens, fringed by the city's roofs and towers. "It is a wonderful place, Peter! It is so large, it might be the whole world under your domain!" She turned round to him in exasperation. "Would you make war? There will be great armies at your command. You could win power and glory. Does it mean nothing to you that you will be the mightiest king on earth? Well it means a deal to me," she added, and her eyes glowed at the thought. "Germany! Stettin!" Catherine almost spat the words. "I have forgotten what they mean. Russia is my home."

Peter looked at her through eyes that were narrowed with hate and suspicion, until the sight of her tears reassured him that the storm was over.

She might give way to feminine weakness now, but he would never forget the passion that she had displayed, or the terror she had inspired in him. All the old sense of intangible menace from her person overwhelmed him more strongly than ever.

"I am glad, Madame, that the grandeurs of Unholy Russia should ease your conscience of its burden of disloyalty to your homeland," he sneered. "But if you imagine that you have no enemies among those who fawn upon you, then you are simple-minded and not I, as people say! Do you suppose that my aunt's promise never to sign a death warrant has transformed these Russian devils into saints? How many die from a thousand lashes of the knout? How many prisoners perish under the torturers' knives in my aunt's dungeons? But you do not know about such things, of course."

Peter sniggered derisively.

"You bask in my aunt's friendship; you think because she smiles that you are in favour? Well, heed my words, Madame, and do not trust our gracious Empress too far, for there is something else you did not know—did no whisper of it ever reach you at Stettin? Ah, perhaps not, few men live to fly with tales across the Russian border.

"Well, I will tell you. A bridegroom should have no secrets from his bride, eh? My imperial aunt is mad . . . mad as her father before her! I have seen her, kneeling before a statue of the Virgin Mary, asking for guidance on who should share her bed that night! Ha, ha, is it not humorous? I tell you she is mad, they are all mad here; one day you are on her right hand, the next morning finds you stretched on the rack in a dungeon, charged with some crime you have never committed."

Peter gave a ghastly laugh.

"You think the bitch of Anhalt is a tyrant? Before God, wait until the gentle Elizabeth takes a dislike to you, then you will know what oppression means!"

Panting, the Grand Duke wiped his streaming face on his sleeve; he seemed to be shaking from head to foot with fever. Without another look at Catherine, he ran to the door and dragged it open.

"Brümmer, Brümmer," he yelled, and his Swedish tutor came hurrying down the corridor.

"Take me to my own apartments. Why are you so late in coming for me?"

Peter cast a malignant glance over his shoulder, pulled a savage grimace, then slammed the door behind him. Catherine stood rooted, her brain afire with the picture of horror that Peter's furious tirade had painted for her.

Elizabeth . . . her nephew's blasphemous assertion was unthinkable. Cruel, capricious and indolent she might be, but she had been kindness itself to Catherine, and she resolutely shut her ears to the allegation that had been whispered throughout Europe.

Peter was spiteful and jealous, he had only tried to frighten her; because life was a hideous mad house of fear and suspicion for him, he could not bear that it should be otherwise for her.

Catherine poured herself a cup of water and tugged at the silken bell-rope for her women; it was time to begin dressing for the evening's ball, the last before the Empress's migration from Moscow to Petersburg.

★   ★   ★

The next morning Elizabeth's huge sledge bore her out of the city, and the whole court prepared to follow her. After four days' journeying, the slower vehicles stopped at the village of Chotilovo.

Johanna and Catherine were to spend the night together in an inn, as Elizabeth's sledge had sped on ahead to Petersburg.

That night Catherine sat alone in her room, huddled in furs by the small stove which had been opened to give the greatest heat possible. She felt low-spirited and strangely uneasy; depression closed over her, while the snow fell outside in a thick, freezing curtain, and a bitter wind howled through the village from the steppes.

She had scarcely seen Peter since that last afternoon, though he, too, was lodged in the inn.

As the hours went by she began to wonder why no one came with supper; somewhere in the house doors were banging and the corridors echoed with hurrying feet.

Catherine got up and walked about the room, suddenly restless and aware that the evening was far advanced for such activity.

There was something wrong; she knew it and, unable to bear the company of her own uneasy thoughts, opened the door and called out.

The passage was empty and freezing; a single candle guttered dimly in a wall sconce, and after a few minutes Catherine retreated shivering into her own room and resumed her place by the stove.

It was almost midnight when the slamming of the chamber door roused her from a fitful sleep.

Johanna advanced towards the fire, and the expression on her sharp features, which the flames illumined, brought Catherine to instant wakefulness.

"Get up and make way for me at once! I'm frozen to the bone," the princess ordered, and her tone recalled the old days at Stettin when a downcast little girl had fled before her vindictive scolding.

Catherine stood up, but she did not move.

"What is the matter? No supper was served me to-night, and I have heard such sounds and scufflings. Is something wrong?"

Johanna snorted angrily; she was quite mistress of herself and the situation, but her daughter's unconscious manner irritated her.

"Don't play the Grand Duchess with me, Madame! Out of my way, and cease these airs and graces." The princess smiled at her daughter with slow, revengeful spite. "Prepare yourself for bad news, my dear. Peter lies sick, sick near to death at this very moment." Johanna paused, that her words might sink in and take effect. "He's caught the smallpox," she announced deliberately, "so be ready to return to Germany with *me*, my fine Catherine! By God, I'll dispel your pride and punish your insolence towards me! That is, if you don't catch his sickness and share a grave with him instead of a marriage bed!"

Without a word Catherine shrank away from the stove as her mother elbowed her way to the blaze, then suddenly she ran from the room, heedless of Johanna's angry detaining cry, and sped down the corridor and up the stairs to Peter's room.

"It's a lie!" she gasped aloud. "It must be a lie. Not smallpox, he could never survive that! He was sick yesterday afternoon, the fever was already on him. . . ."

Frantic with dread, Catherine hammered on the Grand Duke's door, which was opened to a mere crack by his physician, Boerhave.

"Let me in," she demanded. "I hear he has the smallpox! Tell me it is not true, it cannot be true!"

The Russian doctor answered in an impatient whisper:

"I fear it is so, Highness. He has been sickening for some days and would not be tended. Now the rash has covered him. I beg you, go to your own room and keep away from infection! As it is, my head will be the Empress's price for his life," he added gloomily. With that he shut the door and

Catherine heard him shoot the bolt into place.

Peter, weakling that he was, would be devoured by the scourge that laid thousands in their graves every year.

Her title, honours, jewels and hopes of the Crown would vanish like a snowflake on the fire when Peter Feodorovitch breathed his last.

There would be no future for her then but to return to Germany with Johanna.

Catherine cried aloud at the thought, and sank down by Peter's door in an agony of despair, weeping as if her heart must break.

If she had loved him her grief could not have been greater.

CHAPTER 4

In January of the year 1745, a very worried woman paced up and down the polished floor of an ante-room in the Winter Palace at St. Petersburg.

By nature she was carefree, and until now her responsibility of head lady-in-waiting to the Grand Duchess had never weighed upon her, but the task confronting Countess Roumiantzov was not an easy one. It required tact and sympathy, and where the good lady was an expert in dress, etiquette and the affairs of the heart, she felt that someone more serious-minded should have been sent to Catherine in her place.

She continued to walk up and down, fiddling with her jewels, repeating empty phrases in her mind only to reject them as unsatisfactory.

A mere half an hour ago she had been sent for and told to break the news to her mistress, with an injunction from the Empress to prepare Catherine to meet the ordeal correctly.

Someone entered the ante-room, and the Countess swung round in alarm. Leo Narychkin stood with his back to the door, his usually gay face clouded and frowning.

"Oh, my God!" exclaimed the Countess. "So

soon? Why I haven't even seen her yet, she is still dressing! Am I to have no time at all to speak to her?"

"The Empress said I was to fetch her," replied Narychkin. "I dared not delay. Besides, I thought you would have spoken to her by now!"

He looked at her irritably, guessing that in her distaste for the task she had not pressed for an interview with Catherine, hoping that a messenger would come, as indeed he had, to relieve her of the responsibility.

"Have you seen him?" demanded the Countess. Narychkin grimaced.

"Yes, I have seen him. Christus! What a horror! The beggars outside Kazan Cathedral are scarcely more repulsive. . . ."

The Roumiantzova threw up her arms in despair.

"I knew it! I knew it was terrible by the Empress's words to me. How am I to tell her, Leo? What a responsibility! Suppose she screams or swoons; the Empress will blame *me*!"

Narychkin abandoned his stance by the door and caught the Countess in a most ungentle grip.

"Think of your mistress for once and forget yourself! "Damnation," he exploded, "it would have been better for her if the young German pig had died. God help us, that we may help her! As for you, Countess, in with you and break the news to her this instant, and see that you do it as gently as maybe, or I'll pour a tale of your inefficiency into the Empress's ear that'll send you to Siberia!"

He thrust the Countess towards Catherine's door and watched her knock and disappear into the bedroom with a mixed expression of anger and concern.

He was a courtier and a man of the world, he reminded himself. Only a fool would have made such an open display of his feelings before a gossiping featherhead like Roumiantzova. However it was too late now. He, the clever, sharp-tongued Narychkin, hero of a hundred amorous intrigues, had fallen victim to the charms of a mere girl.

What an age had passed since he had met the nervous Princess Augusta of Anhalt and taken her to that first meeting with her bridegroom!

Now the child had gone and a woman had taken her place, a lovely, gay creature, warm and eager for life, shining like a bright star at Elizabeth's court, and her easy, friendly glances had stabbed Narychkin with a longing and tenderness that he knew must remain for ever undisclosed. . . .

"Leo," said a well-known voice, and turning, he dropped on his knee before the Grand Duchess.

Catherine smiled down at him, but she was very white.

Countess Roumiantzov coughed discreetly in the background. She caught Narychkin's eye and her expression said clearly that she had done her best.

"The Grand Duke is here," Catherine said, "and you are to bring me to him. As before," she added, half to herself.

Narychkin's courtly training came to his aid as he released her hand and straightened up.

"His Highness is waiting for you with great impatience, Madame. As soon as the risk of infection had quite gone, he came at once to Petersburg to see you."

Catherine thanked him for the lie with a wry smile, then her eyes sought his and held them with a look that demanded nothing but the truth.

"Roumiantzova tells me that he is much changed, Leo. Have you seen him; is he very —marked?"

Narychkin looked away from her as he answered.

"I fear so. You must be prepared to find him greatly altered." Still the full significance had not sunk in.

On her way to the Empress's apartments, Catherine wondered sadly why Narychkin and her lady-in-waiting should be so concerned. Did they imagine that she loved him and would weep over a few pock-marks?

He was alive, but he was still Peter, and she could not visualize how even smallpox could have altered him for the worse.

*　*　*

"Her Imperial Highness, the Grand Duchess Catherine!" announced Elizabeth's Court Chamberlain, as Catherine and her retinue sank down in homage inside the doorway.

Elizabeth sat in a raised chair, gorgeously dressed as usual, sipping wine out of a golden cup. Her delicate face was lined and puffy with fatigue beneath a generous coating of cosmetics, for in her desperate anxiety the Empress had returned to Chotilovo to nurse her stricken nephew herself.

Her nerves were frayed with the ordeal and she was still quivering with tiredness and ill-temper. She greeted Catherine with irritable haste and the girl's heart began to beat uncomfortably as she became aware of an atmosphere of extreme tension.

Where was Peter?

Then she saw him, standing with his back towards her, in a corner of the room. She noticed quite impersonally that he had grown taller.

The Empress followed Catherine's glance and set her wine cup down quickly.

After all, she had been warned. . . .

"Peter!" called Elizabeth. "Come here."

The figure in the corner turned round and walked a few places forward.

"Well," it said to Catherine, "do you recognize me?"

Suddenly the walls of the great gilded chamber seemed to close in on her, and the floor on which she stood heaved dangerously. Like people in a dream, the Empress, her women, Narychkin and the Countess swelled and swayed before her eyes, while a huge head, completely shaven under a wig that had slipped awry, bobbed up and down like some monstrous thing; the swollen features were encrusted with smallpox sores, so cruel and deep that they were still unhealed.

The horror that was Peter tried to smile, and the question came again through his disfigured lips:

"Do you recognize me?"

"Yes," whispered Catherine, and it was Leo Narychkin's strong arms that caught her as she fell.

*   *   *

It took Elizabeth's physician some time to rouse the Grand Duchess from her fainting fit; in fact Her Imperial Highness lay speechless and stony with shock upon her bed, stubbornly resisting all

87

efforts to rouse her, the tears coursing down her face, her eyes fixed unblinkingly upon the canopy above her head, while Countess Roumiantzov chafed her cold hands and ordered that her dress and corsets should be slit.

At length the Empress's doctor abandoned all pretence of gentleness and smacked his patient sharply across both cheeks; he was gratified to observe her sensibilities return and express themselves in a flood of hysterical tears. With assurances to her ladies-in-waiting, he departed to make his report to the Empress.

Elizabeth received him in her boudoir, lying in *déshabillé* on a couch with a decanter of wine at her side. She listened to his reassuring words with an impatience that the learned man could not fail to notice.

He noticed something else, though his shrewd eyes were blandly deferent, something that was already whispering its way through the palace corridors and gradually finding a place in diplomats' despatches.

Her Imperial Majesty was drunk.

She held the wine cup in hands that were unnaturally careful lest a drop be spilt, and her powdered head nodded while he spoke.

Elizabeth's eyes were bloodshot and their stare was hot and angry. She refilled her wine cup and ended his report with an irritable gesture.

"Enough about the Grand Duchess!" she said. "It was a foolish display of weakness and my idiot nephew is weeping over his scars at this moment because of it. His face will heal in time; but he is the one that concerns me, not Catherine. Speak no more about her fainting fit. Tell me, how long before I can arrange the marriage?"

The physician groaned inwardly; the question was a very awkward one and he dreaded Elizabeth's reaction to the answer he must give. He shrugged and tried to soften the blow.

"The Grand Duke is not strong enough yet, Your Majesty. Perhaps when he has gained a little flesh it would be easier to tell. . . ."

The Empress snorted angrily.

"Do you take me for a fool, with your babble about smallpox! I know very well he is weak, that is not the question. Is he a man yet? Can he give the Grand Duchess a child? Why, God's blood! My father had a trail of bastards across Russia when he was Peter's age!"

The physician folded his hands under his coat tails and said nothing.

If Elizabeth wanted the truth she must arrive at it herself. In his private opinion, the Grand Duke's virility was on a level with his mentality, but he knew better than to say so and be knouted for his pains.

The Empress drained her cup and rose unsteadily from the couch. "He plays with dolls!" she announced thickly. "Is that a man's pursuit? I have given him a girl that any man would be glad to bed with, and he had never even touched her! Oh, I have had them watched, day and night, but they might be brother and sister for all the interest they show in one another."

She began to walk about the room, holding on to the furniture to steady herself.

"They must marry and beget a child. How am I to have peace while the throne depends upon this weakling, idiot nephew of mine? Would to God there was someone else," she muttered, and the answer followed dismally. "But there is no one. . . ." She swung round and caught at the back of a chair to steady herself, while the sight of the doctor pulled her together.

"But why should I torment myself? Peter is backward perhaps, but he is still half Romanov! My sister was hot blooded enough. Once he and the Grand Duchess are married, all will be well!"

She turned to the doctor.

"How long before the nuptials? Come now, speak out; when will my nephew be ready for his bride?"

The physician made what he considered a

compromise.

"A year, Your Majesty."

"Six months!" amended Elizabeth. "And not a moment longer! You may go!"

Then the Empress seated herself once more and took a long comforting draught of wine.

Of course Peter and Catherine would produce an heir; she already saw the infant in her mind's eye and cradled it in her own empty arms. The expression on her delicate face boded ill for the Grand Duke and Duchess if they should disappoint her.

★　　★　　★

During the long weeks of his convalescence, Peter moped disconsolately about his apartments in the palace, for he was still too disfigured to appear in public.

The time passed slowly for him and he spent his leisure hours shut in with his lackeys, drilling them endlessly, or discussing his coming marriage with his tutor, Brümmer.

As a subject for conversation, his wedding opened up endless interesting conversations with the otherwise taciturn Swede, who waxed most eloquent on the theme of a husband's rights over his wife. Mindful of his own domineering spouse, mercifully left behind in Sweden, he emphasized the need for a firm hand in dealing with women.

"Always remember, Highness, the man is the master! Women are inferior creatures and they're always the better for a good beating. Use your fists and use them often; the Grand Duchess must have no will but yours, and a good blow on the head will do her no harm!"

Peter listened delightedly; the manners of servants and lackeys to their women suited him exactly.

"Very well," he thought. "Until now I have always been bullied, forced to come to Russia, to do everything I hated. Even my games at drilling are frowned upon. My gracious aunt has given me a wife for my amusement instead . . . perhaps it will be entertaining after all, if marriage is indeed what Brümmer says. . . ."

His eyes lit up with pleasure at the thought of the superior Catherine cowering under the weight of his fists, and he doubled them in anticipation.

He need not fear her, or shrink from her. His tutor had taught him something worth learning at last.

"In the meantime," added Brümmer, "look about you, Highness. These court bitches would fight for your favours, I tell you. Before or after marriage, no man's eyes should be turned always on his wife! God above, if I were in your place I

92

know the ones I'd choose," he muttered.

Peter accepted this advice too, and promised faithfully to follow it. Excited by Brümmer's envy, his imagination began to review the ladies who attended at court and whose company he would select instead of Catherine's. More than company he did not want, not yet, he thought hastily, but it made him feel strong and virile even to pretend; and, perhaps, with a woman who pleased him he might make pretence into reality. At any rate, no one need guess how far his favour went, and what a barb of spite to flaunt before his bride!

Catherine spent her spare time studying, and entered into the court's amusements with as much spirit as she could muster. But despite her natural love of gaiety, a cloud of uneasy depression hung over her which refused to be dispersed.

Peter was a hideous imbecile, but other women had risen to prominence through marriage with such men.

It was Elizabeth who frightened her most. She had accepted her favour with intense gratitude, believing that at last she had found a woman who would be what her own mother had never been, affectionate and understanding. But it was not so. She had failed the Empress by fainting at the sight of Peter, and Elizabeth's friendship for her had vanished like the phantom it really was.

She had a wretched feeling that the Empress would have been just as amiable to any other candidate for Peter's hand, provided she was obedient and virtuous. One small slip, surely excusable, thought Catherine angrily, and Elizabeth had become the haughty, unreasonable despot, whose will had been for once thwarted by a lesser creature.

Soon even Johanna would be gone and, with her, the last link with home. After the wedding she would be left alone, alone with Peter who hated her and was paying court to one of his aunt's maids of honour before her very eyes.

Quite often her ladies-in-waiting would surprise the Grand Duchess in tears, but they were tears for which she never gave a reason, and indeed no one pressed her for an explanation. Too many royal brides had wept in Russia's palaces, and vanished once their turn was served, to be shut up in some convent cell and forgotten until death released them.

It might well be that Catherine Alexeievna would be one of these.

Gradually the groups of admiring courtiers who used to surround her thinned out, and she found herself politely avoided by men and women who had fawned upon her only a week or two before.

The Empress's spies reported that Peter spent

94

as little time as possible with his betrothed, and that his language and attitude towards her grew increasingly violent, also that he was indulging in a flirtation with the Labuchkin, and boasting of his conquest of her virtue before anyone who would listen.

Instantly Elizabeth put the blame for these developments upon Catherine's unhappy reception of Peter that fateful day.

In her heart the Empress doubted his boasted seduction of her maid of honour, but his preoccupation with her boded ill for his relations with his future wife, and Elizabeth's fury mounted as her anxiety increased.

Her resentment had to find a victim, and since it was almost impossible further to restrict and harass Peter, she visited her anger upon Catherine.

It was Countess Roumiantzov who delivered Elizabeth's message to her mistress, and she chose an afternoon when the two women were seated in Catherine's favourite spot in the palace gardens, a secluded arbour screened by trees and cooled by an ornamental fountain.

The Empress was disappointed and displeased, both in the conduct and relations which existed between her nephew and the Princess whom she had favoured so generously. It seemed to her, the

Countess continued, that the Grand Duchess had shamefully neglected her duties towards her future husband in abandoning him to the company of a mere lady-in-waiting, and the Czarina expected this situation to be remedied forthwith. Peter's rumoured liaison was causing public scandal, both in Russia and abroad, and only his betrothed could put an end to the affair.

Catherine listened in silence to this rebuke, her cheeks scarlet, aware that Roumiantzova's pretty face was hard as marble, and that the lady's friendship had vanished at the first sign of Elizabeth's wrath.

Within three weeks she would be married, and the world would count her the most fortunate princess in Europe.

Yet already troubles were gathering about her thick and fast.

*　　*　　*

Some three days later Peter sat in his apartments, playing cards with Brümmer and two lackeys, when a messenger arrived announcing the Grand Duchess.

Peter flung his cards down and swore.

"Tell her I am engaged and cannot see her! Tell her to go to the devil!" he shouted.

Brümmer looked up and grinned. In one respect

at least, the Grand Duke was proving an apt pupil.

*　　*　　*

The Grand Duchess and Leo Narychkin stood conversing in the State Ballroom, watching Elizabeth lead out in a gavotte.

"Only two days before your marriage," remarked Narychkin.

"Yes," she said, her eyes following the Empress's gorgeous figure as it gyrated and trod the graceful measure of the dance.

Narychkin studied her closely while she thought herself unobserved, and for a moment his feelings penetrated the light-hearted mask he always wore.

No man was less likely to risk his head and hers by trying to make love to the Grand Duchess than the careless court humorist, Leo Narychkin. But at that moment his expression devoured Catherine's face and figure with a passion that would have astonished even those who knew him best.

Truly the loveliest woman in the whole of that great room, he thought.

Her dazzling complexion and brilliant blue eyes were set off to perfection by the vivid scarlet of her velvet gown; red was a predominating colour in Catherine's wardrobe, and, not withstanding the

Empress, she glowed like a magnificent ruby.

All her fresh, vital beauty, her courage that he had seen and admired so often, the driving energy that patience held strictly in rein; these things would fashion the girl in her teens into a magnificent woman. Others had possessed some or even all of these qualities, but they lacked Catherine's laughter and generosity, and her nature was devoid of that curious, twisted streak of cruelty that he had discovered again and again in the most fragile-seeming female.

Elizabeth and her ladies would amuse themselves by a visit to some of the palace dungeons, and sometimes pause to watch a flogging, as exhilarated by the sight of blood as a pack of she-wolves.

But Catherine was never among them, and nothing would induce her to witness these diversions. Dislike of suffering was an unusual quality in that age, but she possessed it to a remarkable degree.

All his life Narychkin had searched for such a woman and at length abandoned the ideal, only to meet it in the person of Peter's future wife, the most jealously guarded virgin in Russia.

So many women could call forth desire, but only she had ever roused him to tenderness as well, and it was this feeling that held him in check.

The prize was Peter's, and the whole court knew that Peter did not want it.

"The Grand Duke is indeed the most fortunate man in Europe," he said quietly, and the urgency in his voice escaped his listener.

Instead she smiled, and the smile was mirthless and bitter.

"Don't mock me to-night, Leo; no doubt you know that I am in trouble!"

The tall Russian opened a gold snuff box and pretended to sniff the contents.

"I have heard things, Highness," he muttered. "What is the matter? You can tell me, you know that I can be trusted. . . ."

"I know that! Of them all, only you have not deserted me. Peter was right, he told me this would happen and I didn't believe him. It seems that he knew more of the ways of courts than I!"

Catherine opened her fan and began to sway it idly as she talked.

"The Empress is furiously angry with me. You know of Peter and his affair with Demoiselle Labuchkin? Indeed, everyone knows of it and is talking. . . . Well, I was ordered to break the liaison. *I*, to whom he never speaks a civil word!

"Of course I failed; he would not even see me. So the Empress blames me, and every day her disfavour is made more obvious. The court has

99

almost deserted me. But for yourself, hardly a person has dared to linger and speak to me to-night!"

Narychkin examined the lid of his snuff box before replying.

"The Labuchkin is unwell, I hear," he said casually. "I should say that the Empress has provided her own remedy for our Grand Duke's folly. I dare say the lady will retire to the country to re-cuperate rather than face the rigours of court life when she is better. That is, if she gets better . . ." he added.

Catherine went white.

"God in Heaven, Leo, you don't think that the Empress would . . ."

"I think she would and has!" he answered quickly, and then smiled at the horror on her face.

"But do not distress yourself; I imagine the Labuchkin will live to go into exile, with the memory of a belly sickness as proof of the Grand Duke's devotion!"

In spite of herself, Catherine had to laugh. He was such an incorrigible jester and such a stand-by in times of trouble and depression.

"Dear Leo," she said impulsively. "What should I do without you?"

"You would do very well, Highness," came the answer. "You will never be without followers, my humble self among them!"

Catherine pouted ruefully. "Well I don't see them pressing round me at this moment!"

Narychkin picked up her hand and kissed it boldly.

"Wait a while. Wait until men's eyes have recognized that a new star is rising over Russia. When the time comes they will know how to follow it!"

With that he left her, and she spent the rest of the evening pondering the meaning of his words.

A new star rising over Russia.

In the right order of things that should be no other than Peter Feodorovitch, but she knew in her heart that it was not the Grand Duke that Narychkin had in mind.

The night before her wedding, Catherine sat down at her dressing-table; she had dismissed her ladies and was quite alone, for Elizabeth had excused her with the injunction to be fresh and rested for the ceremony next day.

The Grand Duchess was tired indeed; every moment had been filled with fittings for her wedding-dress, the choice of jewels, coiffeur, and repeated rehearsals of the marriage procession, until her head ached with fatigue.

Somehow the bustle and excitement had failed to move her as she had always supposed it would.

To-morrow was the greatest day in her life, yet she felt none of the breathless happiness that was the romantic prerogative of brides.

Triumph, yes; but it was a cold emotion, tinged with a vague fear.

She moved the candelabra closer, and the candle-light cast a soft glow through the spacious room, picking out the gilt furniture and the canopied bed.

Her eyes turned to the jewel casket, whose contents she would wear the next day. Slowly she lifted the lid and her fingers dislodged the bridal diadem from its velvet bed.

Standing before her mirror, she placed it on her head, and stood looking at her reflection as if watching someone else.

The woman in the glass wore no wedding veil, for it was not a bride reflected there, it was the future Empress of Russia, her brow encircled by a crown ablaze with diamonds. . . .

* * *

The sun shone down brilliantly on that day of August 25th in the year 1745, touching the roofs of St. Petersburg with gold and flooding through the great windows of Kazan Cathedral, where Russia's Grand Duke and Duchess were being joined in marriage.

The interior of the huge church was illumined by thousands of scented candles, and clouds of incense floated gently up to the gilded roof, while a hundred hidden voices sang the age-old chants of Russian worship.

Diplomats from all over Europe knelt among the congregation; Princes, whose blood and heritage were older than the Boyars who served Ivan the Terrible, bowed down in homage to Russia's God and asked His blessing on the couple who would one day rule the land.

Bestujev closed his eyes in meditation, the subject of which was far removed from the sanctity of his surroundings, while Leo Narychkin pondered on similar lines to the Chancellor, and wondered in agony what the pale Grand Duchess, a distant glittering figure kneeling at the high altar, would endure at Peter's hands that night.

While the ceremony proceeded inside Kazan Cathedral, a great concourse of people were assembled outside, overflowing into the streets and squares. It was a joyous crowd, its belly filled with free bread and its head swimming happily with the Empress's gift of wine that ran in unlimited supplies from every fountain in the city.

The people might perish of cold and hunger on every other day of the year, but on this day every man, woman and child could eat and drink their fill for nothing and scrabble in the gutter for the Empress's scattered largesse.

All the church bells in Petersburg began to peal in a swell of joyful sound as the doors of the cathedral opened and the Empress's magnificent state carriage drove up to the steps.

A tremendous roar of cheering greeted Elizabeth as she emerged from the cathedral and stood outlined in the archway. Hundreds of the devout among the pressing crowds sank to their knees, dazzled by the splendid figure of their ruler.

Elizabeth paused to acknowledge her people's homage, and then walked slowly down to her carriage. A thunderous shout told her that the Grand Duke and his bride had emerged from the church.

Every eye was fixed upon the couple who stood at the head of the cathedral steps; thousands of voices were raised in a roar of welcome to the future Emperor and his Empress; and the sight of Catherine on that day was to remain engraved on many humble hearts.

She lingered there, with her hand resting on her husband's arm, a picture of youthful beauty and grace, attired in a dazzling gown covered with silver and gold embroidery, diamonds blazing from her throat and hair.

The ceremony had lasted almost six hours, but she showed no sign of fatigue; a wave of colour rose in her cheeks at the reception given them.

She stood rooted, detaining the impatient Peter with a firm hand, looking out on to the forest of heads and waving hands that surged about the cathedral, listening to the unforgettable cry of acclamation that drowned the joyfully pealing bells.

The people approved her; the great, shadowy masses of Holy Russia welcomed her and took her to their hearts as she waited there, smiling and kissing her hand to them while tears of emotion filled her eyes and her heart beat wildly with sudden, unbearable exultation.

The triumph of that day was hers. Russia had claimed her for its own for ever, and with utter gladness she surrendered to that call.

It was not Peter the crowd cheered, for his gorgeous uniform and glittering decorations could not deceive the people; they knew him for what he was, a German through and through, ugly, sullen and alien.

It was Catherine's name they shouted, and Catherine knew it.

Once in the Empress's carriage, the Grand Duchess gazed through the windows, smiling and bowing like a queen to the lines of struggling citizens who thrust forward, braving the Cossack soldiers' blows for a glimpse of the royal party.

As they proceeded slowly towards the palace,

Catherine almost forgot the presence of her husband and the Empress; in her excitement she was not aware of the sudden jealous tightening of Elizabeth's lips as she watched the radiant Grand Duchess so readily taking the plaudits of the crowd.

Her little protégée had developed on quite unexpected lines; her personal beauty was counted as second only to Elizabeth's own at court, and her assumption of popularity with the people made the Empress's heart contract with rage.

What viper had she nourished all these months, Elizabeth wondered suspiciously, as the yells of Catherine's name came to her ears almost as often as her own.

At length the Empress leaned forward and tapped the Grand Duchess sharply on the knee with her fan.

"Sit back, Madame!" she said shortly. "You are not the Consort yet, remember; and you obscure my people's view of me!"

Catherine obeyed instantly and her smile faded as she met Elizabeth's furious eye.

Peter laughed maliciously.

"Take good care, Your Majesty," he sniggered, "or my wife will have the crown off your head before you know it! Eh, my dear Catherine?"

Elizabeth turned on him with a snarl of rage.

"Hold your stupid tongue, you damned imbecile! Conduct yourself like a prince instead of a stable-boy! Incline your head to the people and smile, curse you, this is your wedding day!"

Peter smiled, but it was a grim expression.

Only a state banquet and a few more hours of ceremony remained before his marriage night, and the prospect filled him with hidden excitement.

He had planned such a glorious revenge on these two women that he hated; his aunt, that vicious tyrant with the face of an ikon Madonna, who had snatched the Labuchkin away from him, and his wife, the clever, ambitious little Catherine upon whose greedy hand he had placed a wedding-ring that morning, symbol of a union sanctified by force and hate.

⋆　　⋆　　⋆

The coffers of Elizabeth's treasury had been rifled almost bare to provide a fitting spectacle for the imperial marriage, and the state banquet held that night in the Summer Palace surpassed in extravagance anything that had ever been seen before at court.

Every noble in the realm who was not under sentence of banishment had been invited; all the foreign ambassadors and their entourages had been bidden, while the heads of Church and State were gathered at Elizabeth's side.

The guests dined off solid gold plate, eating until outraged Nature forced them to rush from the table and relieve their stomachs into golden basins which the Empress, mindful of her own habits, had thoughtfully provided.

The company drank the health of the Grand Duke and Duchess in cups of priceless crystal, and followed Elizabeth in the Russian custom of hurling the vessels to the ground.

Throughout the banquet Catherine ate little and drank less, uncomfortably aware that Peter was drinking a great deal and that his remarks in respect of his marriage were growing more audible and insulting as the evening progressed.

Leo Narychkin sat at a lower table, and Catherine watched him steadily emptying his cup and slipping lower in his chair as the wine fuddled his brain and stupefied his limbs.

Somehow she had depended upon him for support; a look and a smile of encouragement, even from a distance, would have heartened her. But Narychkin was certainly drunk; too drunk, thanks to his own foresight, to dwell upon Catherine and Peter in the privacy of their bedroom.

At midnight the Empress glanced around her and nodded towards Catherine.

It was time to conduct the bride and bridegroom to their marriage bed.

Out of the banqueting hall, up the palace staircase flanked by lackeys bearing lighted candelabra, the Empress led the procession to the suite of rooms prepared for the couple.

There Peter and his entourage separated from them and went into his own dressing-room.

Then the ceremony of undressing and bedding down the bride proceeded, assisted by the Empress herself.

Catherine stood passively while her women removed the beautiful ball gown and released her stays; she felt numb, mentally and physically, now that the ordeal she had dreaded and put off in her mind was so close at hand.

She knew that Elizabeth was appraising her with calculating eyes, eyes that tried to assume Peter's vision and judge her desirability from a man's point of view.

Still Catherine felt nothing, neither embarrassment nor fear; for the moment her sensibilities were completely stilled and she remained quite silent, until the Empress drew on her embroidered night-gown with her own hands.

Obediently Catherine climbed into the huge bed and kissed Elizabeth's extended hand.

The Empress smiled down on her with the first

genuine kindness she had shown for some time.

"Good night, my child. We leave you now to your bridegroom. God's blessing be on your union."

"Thank you, Your Majesty," whispered Catherine, suddenly brought to life by Elizabeth's gentleness, and dangerously near to tears.

When they had gone, leaving her to await Peter's coming, she did weep, burying her face in the frilled pillow lest anyone should hear.

At length she sat up and wiped her eyes; at any moment her husband might come into the room and it would only enrage him to find her crying.

Catherine pulled back the bed curtain and looked round the room, there must be a clock somewhere, and she could hear laughter and the subdued clink of glasses from behind the wall.

Peter and his household were celebrating. She wondered unhappily how drunk he would be.

She lay back and closed her eyes, fighting the temptation to shed more tears, reflecting that outside in the streets of Petersburg people were dancing round the wine fountains and watching firework displays, making merry in her name and Peter's.

Some of them were making love; there were other brides in Russia on this night, men and women lying together for the first time in dirt and straw, while she lay alone in the gilded bed, shivering between the silken sheets, denied the joy granted by Nature to the poorest peasant girl in the land.

A little jewelled clock on the mantelshelf struck two and Catherine started. It was over an hour and a half since Elizabeth had left her.

She lay there, listening to the muffled sounds of revelry that drifted through to her from Peter's dressing-room, watching the candles burn low in their sockets and the firelight sink slowly in the marble grate.

Why didn't he come?

Torn between miserable anticipation and uneasy suspicion, Catherine tossed wretchedly, wondering whether to get up or try to sleep.

The insult to her was so brutal; Peter preferred to sit drinking with his household on his wedding night. It would be common knowledge all over Petersburg by the morning.

At a quarter to three the door opened and Catherine saw Peter standing on the threshold.

He was wrapped in a gorgeous dressing-gown, and the tasselled night-cap on his shaven head gave him the grotesque appearance of an overgrown gnome.

He kicked the door shut behind him and began to stagger towards the bed; Catherine sat up

111

slowly, aware that her bridegroom was so drunk that he could scarcely stand.

Peter favoured her with a sly, malicious grin, then he struggled out of his robe and stood there by the bedside in his night-gown.

Not a word passed between them.

Roughly he dragged the covers aside and fell on to the mattress.

Despite herself, Catherine shrank back as he leaned over her, for the smell of wine and stale tobacco that emanated from him made her feel faint and sick. For a moment they looked at each other and Peter's bloodshot eyes gleamed with hatred and some hideous, suppressed mirth known only to himself.

"Good night, Madame," he said mockingly.

Then he drew the covers up to his ears and turned his back on Catherine.

Within a few minutes he was fast asleep.

CHAPTER 5

In the spring of 1746 the imperial court was once more in residence at the Wooden Palace, and the Moscow season was at its height. Elizabeth danced and drank and gambled; it was rumoured that she intended to sanctify her affair with Rasumovsky by a secret wedding; the figure of Bestujev loomed more powerfully than ever in the political scene and relations with Prussia were consequently a little more strained.

The confidential despatches of the foreign ambassadors informed their sovereigns of all these things, and among the items of importance was a single astonishing fact.

After nine months of marriage the Grand Duchess Catherine was still a virgin.

Day by day Peter and his wife appeared at court functions; they feasted, gambled and lived like the rest, but every night the Grand Duke climbed into bed beside his bride and fell asleep.

Sometimes he would produce his dolls, carefully hidden among the bedclothes, and force Catherine to play with them; or if his temper was short, he might relieve his feelings by hitting her, as the thoughtful Brümmer had suggested. Then he would have the malicious satisfaction of falling asleep to the sound of her sobs, while Catherine lay and clenched her fists, the tide of hatred and resentment growing in her.

The Empress was well aware of the relationship between Peter and his wife, and the frustration of all her hopes was such a bitter blow that her wrath with the couple could not be concealed.

Unreasonably she blamed Catherine, supposing that the Grand Duke's ugliness had led her to repulse him in the privacy of their bedroom. It was inconceivable to Elizabeth that a young man, who could pursue the plainest among her maids of honour, should feel no attraction for Catherine's charm and sensual beauty.

Partly from anger and partly to take precautions, the Empress redoubled the watch on the Grand Duchess. Everywhere Catherine went her ladies accompanied her, and even the most casual conversation with a man was interrupted, while the courtier she addressed was afterwards warned about familiarity with one above his station.

The plan worked so well that even the most reckless gallant recognized the extreme danger of friendship with the Grand Duchess, and Catherine's position became one of supervised isolation.

Even Narychkin dared not exchange more than

a brief word or smile, and he was the least suspected of all men.

Elizabeth calculated that if masculine company were denied her, Catherine's obvious maturity would force her to seek satisfaction with her husband; and mindful of her own intemperance at that age, the Empress relied upon Nature to do the rest.

*　　*　　*

All through the long winter months Leo Narychkin had watched Catherine from afar, knowing that the girl whose unhappy gaze had haunted him at her wedding banquet was more alone than ever.

Had she been happy, his love for her might have died; the knowledge that Catherine had found tenderness and satisfaction in her marriage would have made it easier for him to forget her in the arms of one of the many attractive women who were always at the disposal of any young and handsome man at court.

But he saw that her eyes were often red with weeping and that she seldom laughed.

Instead, the gay, beautiful Grand Duchess who had been the darling of the court seemed almost crushed by the course her life had taken since she had been wedded. Always thrust into Peter's unwilling company, the constant, often public rebukes from the Empress and the humiliating fact of her continued virginity made her a tragic, outcast figure whose future began to look increasingly dark.

It was the thought of her future that destroyed the last shreds of Narychkin's caution.

He knew that the present situation would not be allowed to continue much longer and the only alternative was Catherine's divorce, which would mean her instant "retirement" to one of Elizabeth's conveniently isolated convents. It was not the Russian custom to return unsatisfactory brides to their parents. . . .

The thought of Catherine shut up for life, suffering the fate of the unhappy Ivan, determined Narychkin to show his hand at last.

The court was leaving Moscow for Petersburg when the rumour reached him that the Empress's patience had come to an end.

No one knew what Elizabeth's plans for the erring Grand Duke and Duchess might be, but Narychkin dared not take a chance on leniency; he must give Catherine the choice of saving herself if she wished.

The Empress was giving a masque soon after her arrival at the capital, and Narychkin judged that Catherine would attend and the general

confusion of identities might give him the opportunity to speak to her alone.

Masked and in fancy dress, he would approach
her and tell her of the love that had been devour-
ing him for all these months, and warn her of the
danger that threatened her, offering his protection
and the chance to escape.

Inwardly he hoped that Elizabeth would not
indulge her usual caprice by ordering the men to
dress as women at the masque, for if his plan went
well the Grand Duchess Catherine, before the
night was done, should be in his arms, driving
through the city streets to the banks of the Neva
where a small boat awaited them. . . .

The prospect of exile did not disturb him in
the least; only two things filled his mind, the
unspeakable delight of possessing the woman he
loved, of living with her for the rest of his life,
and the urgent necessity to get her out of
Elizabeth's reach in time.

He knew his Empress; he had seen that look
before, a bland, stony expression that deadened
her pretty face like a mask of marble. Very soon
the façade would be shattered by a fearful
explosion of fury, and he could only prepare and
pray that, with God's help, his beloved Catherine would not be there to receive its consequences.

117

Once out at sea they would sail for the pro tecting coasts of Sweden. Elizabeth migh threaten and demand their extradition as much a she pleased, her enemies at the Swedish cour would be only too eager to welcome the Gran Duchess as a refugee from the Empress's tyranny.

So Narychkin plotted treason and adultery obsessed with his longing for Catherine, unti every detail of the plan had been worked out.

The risk was tremendous and the penalty fo failure unthinkable, but if he had judged Cathe rine aright, she would not hesitate.

*   *   *

On the evening of the masque Catherine sat i her dressing-room, relaxing with closed eyes while one of her women brushed and combed he long, dark hair.

Elizabeth had, in fact, ordered her guests t wear the dress of the opposite sex, and the Gran Duchess's costume was already laid out on th bed. She could hear Peter cursing and exclaimin in the next room, and the thought of his appear ance in a low-cut hooped gown made her smil ruefully.

She would have been only too glad to plead sick ness and be excused from the night's enter tainment, but her position was too precarious t risk offending Elizabeth or even attracting her attention, and in this matter as in every other, Catherine followed her original precept for success—and obeyed.

Was it such a good formula after all, she wondered. Every word of Peter's crazy prophecy seemed to be coming true, as each day found her more alone and restricted, the Empress increasingly unfriendly.

Catherine frowned and opened her eyes; the train of thought was a familiar, tormenting one which gained her nothing and only served to increase her despair.

Thank God she had begun to read a little, for it beguiled the time and distracted her mind; novels were dangerous fare, she decided, for their themes of love and coquetry filled her with restless discontent. Instead she had ordered some of the works of philosophy that were creating such a stir in far-off France. She was curious to see these books, some of them already banned by a French king whose court was renowned as the most cultured in Europe.

In the midst of these reflections, Countess Roumiantzov hurried into the room. Seeing her evident alarm, Catherine abruptly ordered her waiting woman to cease her ministrations with the hairbrush and sat upright. One look assured her that the Roumiantzova, normally the most grace-ful and languid of women, had been running, for her face was flushed and her elaborate coiffeur had come tumbling down over her shoulders.

"The Empress!" said the Countess breathlessly. "She demands to see you at once. Put on a wrap and come with me. Hurry in Jesu's name, Her Majesty is beside herself with anger! Indeed 'tis years since I've seen her in such a rage," she added.

Catherine sprang up, calling for a robe; hur-riedly she drew on a long velvet gown, fastening it herself in her impatience.

A hundred possibilities raced through her head as she sped down the corridor to Elizabeth's suite, but the answer presented itself the moment she saw Peter, shambling in Brümmer's wake, taking the same path as her-self.

The storm over their marriage had broken at last.

*   *   *

The Empress received them in her dress-ing-room; for a moment Catherine looked for her in vain and then recognized the handsome, plump figure in male dress as Elizabeth.

She was already gowned for the masque, and

the costume showed off her slender legs and voluptuous form to advantage, hence her fondness for the custom that she had introduced.

Somewhere in the background Catherine saw another person, and with complete misgiving realized that the spare, soberly dressed man who regarded her with cold, questing eyes was Bestujev himself.

Elizabeth sat down suddenly and beckoned Catherine. Her face was crimson with rage and her beringed fingers clawed at the arm of her chair.

"Come here, Madame!" she ordered furiously.

Catherine approached and sank down in a curtsy at Elizabeth's feet.

"Explain yourself! Explain your conduct that gives scandal before the whole court. Nine months married and no sign of a child! Is it for this that I showered you with gifts, raised you from the gutters of Stettin to become my nephew's wife? What is this I hear whispered . . . this lie that you have never even bedded together!" Elizabeth glared at Peter, knowing full well the truth of her charge, and as always he quailed before her and looked away.

The Empress paused for breath, trembling with anger as she looked from one to the other.

There he stood, the sullen stupid oaf, pock-marked and hideous as Satan, lacking even the girl's quiet, stony courage. They had dared to defy her, to imperil her throne by their obstinacy and rob her of peace once more.

Catherine, whom she had welcomed like a daughter, had grown up to rival and flout her; those steady blue eyes could repel a man as easily as they could entice. By God, swore Elizabeth to herself, if she can do the former and deny me an heir, I'll give her naught but the bare walls of a cell to ogle! But nothing excused Peter, she thought savagely, and was glad because deep in her heart she hated him, and her dislike rejoiced in the excuse to punish. He knew his duty full well, he should have been man and Romanov enough to take his rights by force. Instead he flirted with one of her maids of honour, aping the virility that he did not possess. No sooner had she got rid of the Labuchkin than he had begun paying attentions to another.

Thanks to these two impudent creatures, both still in their teens, her magnificent marriage had become the laughing-stock of Europe, and her throne was still insecure.

If circumstances had allowed it, Elizabeth would gladly have put them both to death, in spite of her much boasted vow. Her father would have known how to deal with them! God's blood! she thought furiously, he would not have agreed to Bestujev's milk and water plan; if only her actions were not hampered by his damned politics. . . .

Elizabeth's expression deepened to one of truly frightening cruelty as her imagination reviewed the punishments she would have liked to inflict, and, seeing that look, Catherine abandoned caution and spoke up. Whatever happened, the Empress must know that the situation was Peter's doing alone.

"Your Majesty, I beg you to hear me. It is true that I am a wife in name only, but the humiliation of my state is not my fault I assure you!"

Elizabeth was about to interrupt her when the Chancellor interposed. "Let the Grand Duchess continue, Your Majesty," he suggested coldly. Fear had loosened many tongues, and he proceeded on the well-tried principle of giving the accused enough rope with which to hang themselves.

He was confident that in her own defence Catherine would ensure Peter's downfall as well as her own disgrace; also it was best that the blame should be shared.

Frederick of Prussia might seize upon any public injury to his subject's daughter as an excuse to renew the war which had just been concluded a few years before. And Russia was in no position to engage in war at that time; Bestujev preferred to do battle with his enemies upon the diplomatic field for the present.

He listened quietly to Catherine's frantic excuses and heard in them the ring of truth, while he waited his opportunity to remind Elizabeth of her grudge against Peter.

After the first stumbling sentences, Catherine burst into tears, and her distress betrayed Peter into the *lèse majesté* of a smile.

The Empress caught sight of his expression and promptly flung one of her gilt hairbrushes at his head. The missile clattered to the floor while the Grand Duke cowered back, and the Chancellor judged that the time had come to draw attention away from Catherine, whose disgrace was already accomplished, and focus his sovereign's rage upon her nephew.

"If I might suggest, Your Majesty, that you remove Demoiselle Carr from his Imperial Highness's vicinity, perhaps his eyes might be turned towards his wife instead. . . ."

It was a cunning reminder and one that struck Peter to the heart.

"'Tis a lie!" he cried as Elizabeth's eyes narrowed with sudden resolution, but the denial came too late. The Empress tugged violently at the bell rope and a lackey appeared in the doorway.

"Send for Demoiselle Carr, have her brought here immediately! And summon the guard!"

Catherine stepped back into the shadows; she was trembling and a fierce anxiety abruptly dried her tears. Only God knew for whom Elizabeth had ordered the guard; it might well be for her, and within the next hours she might go to swell the ghostly number of imperial wives who had disappeared into imprisonment and death. But Peter came towards the Empress, his disfigured face working convulsively as fear gained its usual mastery over his hatred of her.

Catherine had been the chief culprit until the Chancellor's ill-chosen remark; now it seemed that fearful punishment would befall him also, and he had no mind to share in whatever torments Elizabeth might devise for his wife.

"It is her fault," he shrieked. "She is to blame, not I! How can I live with her when I hate her so? She makes me shudder!"

The Empress sprang from her chair; for a moment Catherine thought that she would strike her nephew.

"Silence!" she shouted. "How dare you speak before I give you leave. Ah, here is another who thinks to defy my wishes," and she turned quickly as the doors opened, disclosing the figure of Demoiselle Carr, each plump arm in the grip of a

Russian guardsman.

The lady-in-waiting stood silently on the threshold, her eyes wide with terror; only the soldiers' support kept her from falling.

Elizabeth favoured her with a withering glare, mentally comparing her fat ungainly figure with the graceful, splendid Grand Duchess. What madness lay on Peter that he should prefer this creature's plainness to the other's beauty?

Whatever the reason, the Empress had no patience to enquire any further. One obstacle to her desire stood quaking and speechless before her, and mercy was not one of Elizabeth's failings.

She addressed the two soldiers who stood woodenly awaiting instructions.

"Arrest this woman!" she said harsly. "Take her to the Schüsselburg fortress!"

Upon hearing this sentence and that the dreaded prison was to be her destination, the unfortunate Carr began to struggle in her guard's grip, screaming for pity, and most ironically of all, for justice.

The sight of his favourite's distress roused an unexpected chivalry in Peter's breast and he flung himself down before Elizabeth and clasped her silken knees.

He had never lain with the unhappy Carr, nor

indeed with any woman, but his gnawing loneliness and incapacity had found solace and the pretence of manhood in her flattered companionship for a little while, and the savagery of Elizabeth's decree moved him to reckless unselfishness.

"Your Majesty, I beseech you . . ." he spluttered. "Have pity. She has done no wrong!"

The Empress jerked herself free of his hands and waved the soldiers away; immediately they withdrew, half carrying their hysterical, struggling prisoner, whose shrieks echoed faintly down the corridors and then died away. Like a woman in a dream Catherine looked about her; there was the huge luxurious dressing-room, its gilt fittings gleaming in the candle-light, the still dark figure of the Chancellor, a silent witness of the hideous scene, and the Empress dressed in her man's costume cursing Peter who knelt sobbing at her feet.

Elizabeth *was* mad. Only a lunatic would rave as she was doing and punish the hapless Carr with such savagery.

It only remained for the Empress to deal with her. Catherine looked across to where Bestujev stood, and for a brief moment their eyes met, the old shrewd courtier who had weathered so many storms to power, and the young foreigner he had determined to crush. So far he had failed, and during that momentary exchange the Chancellor

127

knew it.

She was not yet twenty and Elizabeth's wrath was an unnerving experience; she had wept and excused herself, but in his heart he was certain that Catherine was not afraid. Even the fate of Demoiselle Carr had not succeeded in quelling that relentless spirit.

Elizabeth's decision had not come a moment too soon. That decision was made plain to Peter and Catherine by the Empress herself.

Their households would be changed and responsible persons put in charge. A governor and governess had already been selected for their individual supervision and they would be absolutely under this new authority; M. and Mme Tchoglokov, a reliable pair whose strictness was only matched by their marital fidelity and fruitfulness.

All personal freedom of movement was at an end for them both.

The Empress's sentence upon them was little better than imprisonment; neither might go out alone, Catherine was not allowed to write or receive letters even from her family, Roumiantzova and the odious Brümmer had been dismissed and would be replaced the next day by these unknown Tchoglokovs who were nothing less than gaolers.

Peter and Catherine were to have no companions beyond these two guardians and no recreation outside their own suite in the palace.

*   *   *

Below in the great ballroom the Empress's masque was at its height, and Leo Narychkin encumbered by a heavy hooped skirt, searched frantically among the masked dancers for Catherine, while the carriage that was to have taken them to freedom waited outside a back entrance until day dawned.

But she did not come. The doors of Bestujev's cage had closed upon her and they were not to open for another eight years.

CHAPTER 6

In a room in the grand ducal suite in the Summer Palace, two women sat silently, their chairs drawn close to the fire; it was not a well-lit apartment and the elder occupant paused over the piece of cloth she was embroidering to draw a candelabra closer on the table at her side.

The movement shed more light upon her, while it cast her companion into deeper shadow, and the candle flames illumined her plain, sharp-featured face, cast in a perpetually disagreeable expression, and the clumsy shape of her body, distended once again in pregnancy.

It was seven years since the Empress had appointed her governess to the Grand Duchess, seven long years since the Chancellor Bestujev had given her his neatly written document instructing her how he required that charge to be carried out.

It was a task that appealed to her narrow, domineering nature, this taming of a woman, beautiful and gay as she had never been, and the faithful Mme Tchoglokov had obeyed it to the letter.

The object of her persecution sat in the opposite chair, her hands lying in sinful idleness in her lap.

The lovely girl in her teens who had stood in Elizabeth's bedroom and heard the sentence of this long martyrdom of spying and restriction passed upon her, was now twenty-three years old. She had grown to womanhood under the hostile, jealous eyes of Mme Tchoglokov; Peter's hated companionship and the lascivious furtive stare of the male Tchoglokov was the barren soil in which Catherine Alexeievna had bloomed to maturity.

The good Tchoglokovs were models of marital felicity, and the yearly fruitfulness of the unprepossessing, middle-aged guardian of her conduct filled Catherine with cynical disgust. On the subject of their two mentors, Peter and Catherine were in complete agreement, their hatred of the couple was only matched by the unbridgable dislike they felt for one another, and since he dared not rebel against M. Tchoglokov, it only remained for Peter to vent his misery upon his wife.

By day she must sit with her hands over her ears, while the Grand Duke scraped endlessly upon a fiddle, without tune or talent, and Mme Tchoglokov upbraided her for lack of interest in her husband's pursuits. This practice was suddenly abandoned when Peter installed a pack of hounds in the room adjoining hers, and there were times when Catherine thought to lose her sanity listening to the cries and yelps of the poor beasts as they tried to flee the lash their master wielded.

While the days stretched wearily ahead, each hour filled with empty tedious routine, the nights with Peter continued as before. In that lay the key to both their wretchedness. After seven years of marriage, Catherine's virginity was still intact. Not all the efforts and example of the Tchoglokovs had succeeded in forcing Peter to make love to his wife.

But in the midst of humiliation and unhappiness, Catherine had discovered an escape. A lackey had brought the antidote, wrapped in a parcel which had travelled some thousands of miles across Europe at the behest of the curious Grand Duchess, who was still at liberty when she despatched the order.

That was many years ago, and in the same room where she had explored the contents of the first package, Catherine sat waiting for the arrival of another.

When the door opened she did not look up, knowing that the watchful madame was already beckoning the caller into the room.

"What is your business?" she demanded.

"I would deliver this to Her Imperial Highness," replied the flunkey. Catherine raised her head.

"Give it to me," she ordered quietly. The

governess opened her mouth to protest at this boldness, but already Catherine's eager fingers had ripped the parcel open. It contained a quantity of books.

"What have you there, Madame?" demanded the Tchoglokov haughtily.

"Books," answered the Grand Duchess calmly.

The duenna breathed hard with anger; Catherine's attitude of icy composure never failed in its object of enraging her, and she rose with difficulty from the chair.

"I am aware of that. What kind of books are these? Kindly do not touch them further until I have examined them!"

Catherine handed her the volumes and watched her shake them as a terrier does a rat, eager for some forbidden message to fall from the leaves or the binding, until, her hopes disappointed, she peered stupidly at them under the candlelight.

"The works of Voltaire," she deciphered at length. "French, I presume?" The Grand Duchess nodded, aware that her companion was trying to hide her ignorance of the contents.

"What were those other books which came for you a little while ago?"

"The writings of Montesquieu," came the answer, which told the questioner precisely nothing.

Mme Tchoglokov abandoned her pretence.

"What is the subject of all these books, may I ask? Her Imperial Majesty must have a report of your expenses, and it seems you are amassing a library!"

Catherine eyed the pregnant woman with indifference.

"They are works of philosophy; I find that they improve the mind." The Tchoglokov sniffed indignantly and gathered up her embroidery.

"It would become you better, Highness, to study the Grand Duke and the state of your marriage, and leave such affectations alone! It is now time we retired," she added.

The Grand Duchess rose obediently, collected her precious volumes and walked past into the ante-room of her bed-chamber, the governess hurrying in her wake. At the same time Catherine caught sight of Peter stamping into his dressing-room, accompanied by his twin Tchoglokov.

There would be no time to read that night.

Within the covers of her slender library, Catherine the prisoner found such freedom as she had never dreamed existed. What had begun as a caprice, designed to lift her thoughts from the rut of sadness and unbearable ennui, had become a secret experience of extraordinary exhilaration.

Penned up in her gloomy apartments, month after month, year after year, Catherine's active mind explored the reasonings of the most brilliant and original brains of her century.

Within their pages she discovered theories which blew the accepted notions of her time away like so much dust.

Tyranny, they said, was the greatest evil which mankind could endure; the duty of the ruler was to protect and nurture his subjects. Mindful of her own oppressed state, Catherine agreed with all her heart.

Elizabeth, the great Empress, was only a despotic lunatic, invested with a power she was unfit to wield, and God, whom the tyrants and strumpets of the court professed to worship, and whose forgiveness they thought to buy with gold, the thinkers declared that He did not exist. His name was only Conscience, and man in his ignorance had made a Being out of an Instinct.

Reason was Voltaire's divinity, and under his influence Catherine set up the twin idols of Intellect and Humanity in place of the Christian deity. The final rejection of all things mystic was an easy one, but it remained Catherine's most closely guarded secret.

Whatever her personal convictions, the Grand Duchess observed the religious formula of the time with scrupulous care. Peter might fidget and mutter in church, careless of what offence he gave to the devout among his future subjects, but his wife, who lived under a permanent cloud of disfavour, appeared the very model of piety.

Catherine had long since recognized that there would be no divorce, or Elizabeth would have made an end of the situation within the past few years; the Empress would not live for ever, and thoughts of occupying that vacant throne possessed the Grand Duchess more and more.

She read and studied, deliberately training her neglected mind for the tremendous task ahead of her, and in the meantime she suffered Peter and the Tchoglokovs with what patience she could muster.

But the time was fast approaching when the gates of Bestujev's cage would open wide to Catherine, and the man who turned the key was none other than the Chancellor himself.

*   *   *

Elizabeth had a new favourite. At long last the devoted Rasumovsky who, some said, was secretly married to the Empress, had been dismissed, and the good-looking, ambitious Ivan Shuvalov took his place in the imperial bed.

It was an unfortunate exchange and the influence, political as well as amorous, that Ivan exerted over Elizabeth had begun to spell danger to the Chancellor.

The Empress was ailing in health, and her excesses with her new lover alternated between bouts of penance even more strenuous than before. Bestujev had not spent his life working for Russia to see it delivered into such hands as Peter's and possibly the Shuvalovs, if his Empress died.

First he must put an end to the feud between himself and the only person in line with the throne who seemed to care a straw for the country and, secondly, she must provide an heir.

With the plan already worked out in his mind, Bestujev went to see the Empress.

It was late afternoon and Elizabeth was still in bed when the Chancellor received his audience. The great bed-chamber was in some disorder, and he noticed a heap of slashed clothing lying on the floor. Of late the Empress often retired to her room so drunk that her clothes had to be cut off, and Bestujev suspected that Shuvalov had only just left as he came in.

Elizabeth looked at him through aching, blood-shot eyes, forcing her weary muddled brain to concentrate, still vaguely disappointed that her beloved Ivan's curiosity should have insisted on her giving the old man this interview, when she only wanted to sleep the day away in his arms.

"Your Majesty," he began dryly, "I have been

giving thought to a matter of great importance to yourself and to the realm. I speak of course of the Grand Duke and Duchess. . . ."

Elizabeth's lips narrowed ominously.

"They have been married for eight years, and there is still no heir," he added. The Empress raised herself in the bed and swore.

"God damn them both! Must you come here disturbing me to tell me that! The devils, impudent, disobedient devils. . . . Haven't I punished them enough, what more can I do? S'death, I do not even know for certain which of them is at fault any more. I thought it was Catherine, but now I am not sure."

Bestujev interrupted the flow of her words with a gesture.

"If Your Majesty will permit me, I believe that the Grand Duchess is the least to blame. . . ." Elizabeth looked at him with a flash of her old shrewdness.

"What change of heart is this, my friend? Who besought me night and day to penalize her? Who assured me that it was she who repulsed Peter and would betray him with others if I left her free to do so? What is the true purpose in your cunning brain? Come, speak out! My head aches and I am in no mood for diplomacy!"

The Chancellor smiled; this was the Empress he

loved and understood.

"I fear the Grand Duke to be impotent, and no amount of pleas or punishment can make a stallion out of a mule! He has never lain with his wife, nor with any other woman. These mistresses of which he boasts are nothing but a sham, Your Majesty. Russia awaits an heir from this marriage, and if Peter cannot father it, then we must provide someone who will!"

Elizabeth considered him in silence, battling with an upsurge of religious scruples which condemned in someone else the adultery that she committed so lightheartedly herself. Yet if a child was born, what a weight of anxiety would be lifted from her mind. Ten years of fear and disappointment would be wiped away, and no one need ever know that she had been involved in the deception.

"Whom had you in mind, Chancellor?"

"A man lately arrived in court, Your Majesty. A nobleman, healthy, and handsome enough to turn the Grand Duchess's head completely. And from his reputation an expert at seduction. . . . His great friend is Leo Narychkin, an intimate of the Grand Duchess in the past. The meeting should be easily contrived; a few words into the gentleman's ear, a promise or two, and the thing is done! His name is Serge Saltykov," he added.

Elizabeth had already remarked the good-looking newcomer. Indeed she had even considered that once or twice while Ivan was away and she felt lonely. . . . Now it seemed that Catherine was to have him.

She looked away and drew up the bedclothes to her chin.

"It is an interesting plan, my friend, and the outcome would be a blessing to myself and to my realm. But, of course, my conscience cannot approve. . . ."

Bestujev left her, smiling in perfect understanding of the arrangement. He could proceed with Catherine's seduction as quickly as he pleased, but the Empress must never be supposed to know.

Three days later a startled Catherine was informed by Mme Tchoglokov that the Empress was not as displeased with her as before, and wished the Grand Duchess to move about the court more freely. She also handed her a note written by Bestujev, in which he desired to present his compliments to his old enemy at a near date.

Catherine stood with the letter in her hand, reading and re-reading the contents, pondering the meaning of this sudden *volte-face* on the part of the man who had hounded her without mercy for so many years. Elizabeth's message was obviously inspired by him; could it be that her punishment was being lifted? The sight of Mme Tchoglokov trying to soften her hard features in an ingratiating smile made her certain that this was more than a mere surface gesture.

After nearly eight years of semi-seclusion, her gaolers had suddenly opened the prison door and were inviting her to step out as if nothing had happened. It was a miracle, but it might also be a trap.

The Grand Duchess smiled back at the detested governess, and declared herself delighted with the messages.

Mme Tchoglokov, still a little shaken and disappointed after her interview with Bestujev that very morning, suggested awkwardly that Her Imperial Highness might care to give a supper-party in her rooms one night . . . she had been so busy with her books, had seen so few people of late. The good woman shook her head with hypocritical admonishment as if the fault were Catherine's own, and the Grand Duchess heard her out with a look in her blue eyes that reminded Mme suddenly that she had not been altogether wise in persecuting the future Empress with such vigour.

Hastily she enquired whom Her Highness might wish to invite.

Catherine forgot her suspicions for a moment and an almost childish excitement took possession of her. Whom would she ask? What would she wear? Suddenly the prospect of a little gaiety drove all caution from her mind. The devil take the Tchoglokovs! The devil take their trap if it was one. She would make the most of the evening and let the outcome take care of itself.

"Ask Leo Narychkin," she said immediately. "And Countess Roumiantzov." The Countess had suffered in the general disgrace of Catherine and Peter, having lost her post and been persecuted for a time with the unreasonable malice peculiar to Elizabeth.

Catherine had heard of her misfortunes and promptly forgave the Countess her former harshness. Beside the Tchoglokovs, Roumiantzova appeared as gentle as a lamb.

The next two days were spent in preparations, supervised by Catherine herself, and even Peter was roused out of his sudden lethargy by her invitation and the hint that their lives might be easier from then on.

Roumiantzova accepted with delight, and Narychkin begged only that he might present a friend to the Grand Duke and Duchess; the young man had been pestering him for an introduction and he feared neither sleep nor peace would be allowed him unless the petition was granted. Catherine granted it with a light heart, and Mme Tchoglokov raised no objection.

As Catherine passed the day in pleasurable anticipation, Narychkin could scarcely wait for the hours to go by. In eight years he had not been close enough to exchange more than the most formal greeting, and the knowledge of her wretched circumstances had tortured him unbearably.

From the fatal night of Elizabeth's masque, Narychkin had lived his life in utter indifference to all women except the one caged up in her suites in the different palaces: the pale, proud Catherine, isolated like a leper.

Now her fortune had changed, and his passion for her flamed up as fiercely as ever at the prospect of their meeting. He had waited long enough, he thought recklessly, only let God give him the chance and he would cuckold Peter at the first opportunity!

It was a pity that his good friend Serge Saltykov should have begged him to get an extra invitation, he would so much sooner have had Catherine to himself, but there would be other times, and Serge was always so difficult to refuse. He was handsome and headstrong, and Narychkin liked him; if he had suddenly become smitten by Catherine, having, as he declared, seen her walking in the gardens, then Leo could not blame him.

That supper-party was everything, and more, than Catherine had imagined.

She dressed in the glowing red that suited her so well, and managed to coax Peter into some semblance of good humour. The Tchoglokovs she ignored; they had to be present, but they were not going to be allowed to spoil her evening.

Leo Narychkin was gayer, more likeable than ever, the Countess made delicious game of Peter who preened like a ridiculous peacock, and Leo's young friend was one of the handsomest men that she had even seen. Taller even than Narychkin, broad-shouldered and narrow-hipped as a wrestler, his straight features were of almost Grecian cast. It was a true patrician face, but the sensual mouth betrayed him and his hot dark eyes considered Catherine in a way that made her heart beat fast and foolishly.

Serge Saltykov. It was curious how his personality kept intruding through Roumiantzova's merry gossip, and Narychkin's sophisticated conversation. They played cards and he quickly seated himself beside her; she had a fleeting impression that Narychkin's good humour suffered a sudden check, but dismissed the idea as mere fancy.

After a while Catherine discovered to her

astonishment that a masculine knee was pressing hard against hers, so hard that it was no accident. For a moment she went rigid and her eyes sought his over the cards. She met a look that made her blood leap in her veins, and deep inside her some half-buried instinct stirred, forbidding her to move away, enjoying wildly the feel of a man's warmth and strength, the knowledge that she attracted him enough for him to risk insulting her.

It was foolish and undignified, but Catherine went on playing and did not stir.

When Serge Saltykov bowed his way out with the others, his knowledge of women told him that the task Bestujev had set him would not only be comparatively easy, but was worthy of being undertaken for its own sake.

*   *   *

True to her instructions, Mme Tchoglokov relaxed her former vigilance to such a degree that Peter and Catherine found themselves engulfed in a flood of entertainments, and by careful design Serge Saltykov was nearly always among those present. Yet his opportunities for speech with Catherine were limited; he never saw her alone and the affair must come to a conclusion before gossiping tongues had time to wag.

It was Peter who all unwittingly provided the solution. He decided to invite a party to his summer residence at Oranienbaum, where the grand ducal household repaired for a few weeks each year. Ordinarily such a request would have met with his guardian's instant refusal, but for some reason beyond Peter's comprehension, none other than Tchoglokov's formidable spouse expressed her approval of the idea, and suggested discreetly that Leo Narychkin and his protégé Saltykov might accompany them to the country.

The Grand Duke agreed with little interest; he was desirous of a certain lady's company on the vacation, and the presence of a few of Catherine's friends would make it easier for him to pursue his own furtive amorous experiments. For the moment Peter was too engrossed in his new-found freedom to trouble about his wife, so Catherine lived in comparative peace. The tide had turned for them; she knew that, and for the present the reason was not clear. Experience had taught her the dangers of supposing any action on the part of Elizabeth or her Chancellor to be motivated by pure good nature, but she suddenly did not want to question the change too closely.

Almost every day a messenger arrived with exquisite flowers, a book, or some other memento from Narychkin's friend, who seemed to have no thought of the risk he ran in paying court to the Grand Duchess. His letters Catherine had to burn, but she read them avidly, her heart racing at the expressions of love and ardour they contained.

Only now, since a man had leant against her at the card-table and kissed her hand at court with warm, deliberate lips, did Catherine's senses rise as from a long sleep, and their clamour drained her cheeks of colour and painted tell-tale shadows under her eyes.

As for Saltykov, the game moved far too slowly. His contact with Catherine at court functions and informal parties only presented a growing challenge and whetted his quickening desire.

As the weeks went by, and the prospect of the time at Oranienbaum tantalized him more and more, Saltykov's original concept of the affair began to fade. Bestujev, with his costly bribes of honour and position, took second place to a growing sentiment towards the unsuspecting woman whose virtue he had promised to destroy.

An opportunist, vain, self-seeking and immoral, Saltykov possessed that essential of the successful lover, the ability to persuade himself and the object of his desires that his whole heart was involved as well as his senses. Charm was his profession and even Peter's erratic nature fell victim to it. Saltykov found himself an ever welcome visitor with the husband he planned to betray. Everything conspired with Bestujev and his plan, not least the fact that for the first time in her life, Catherine Alexeievna had fallen in love.

Catherine the future empress fought and lost against Catherine the woman. Her wardrobe was re-stocked and the inscrutable Elizabeth raised no objection at the expense. It seemed that fortune truly smiled on the Grand Duchess at last; her enemies had relented and a man who loved her and was not afraid to say so had come into her life.

*   *   *

That summer Peter and his little court journeyed to Oranienbaum for a stay of some weeks. Narychkin and Saltykov travelled with them, and among the company was a certain Mme Grooth, a charming widow of exceptional amatory talent whose reputation had intrigued Peter for some time.

Of them all Catherine was the gayest; her happiness shone out irrepressibly in every word and deed. She was no longer alone; Peter, the Tchoglokovs did not matter any more when she had only to look up to see Saltykov watching her, waiting the opportunity to whisper his admiration into her ear.

The weather was fine and brilliant with

sunshine during those first weeks; the old palace echoed with laughter, Mme Tchoglokov retired diplomatically to bed with some convenient illness, and Catherine's heart sang as joyously as the birds in the gardens of Oranienbaum.

One man alone among them was not so merry. Leo Narychkin, with the insight of his own love for Catherine, realized in an agony of jealousy that her smiles and glances were directed at the protégé he had introduced. He knew Serge and his reputation well, but in his eagerness he had never visualized him as a rival.

Now, to Saltykov's mounting rage, Narychkin managed to chaperone them so effectively that their stay was almost at an end before Serge got his chance to be alone with Catherine.

The whole party went riding one fresh morning, led by Peter and the widow Grooth; Catherine looked radiant in her riding habit, her face framed by a feathered tricorne hat. As they galloped out across the parklands the Grand Duchess urged her mount ever faster, lost in the exhilaration of speed and the thudding hoof-beats. She was a superb horse-woman, far better than any of those who rode with her, except Saltykov, and together they began to outstrip the rest of the party.

Catherine looked over her shoulder at Serge and laughed aloud; one quick glance behind showed him that a rise in the ground hid them from view, and without a word he leant across and caught the bridle of Catherine's horse.

Before she had time to protest he was urging both mounts off the path and into a wood. She drew rein and turned to him in surprise.

"Serge, why did you do that? Why did you . . .' Her words were drowned by the thundering progress of the others as they galloped straight on up the route which she and Saltykov had left. Without a word he dismounted and took the reins out of her hands.

"Forgive he," he said breathlessly. "I had to do this, I had to speak to you . . . let me help you down." He lifted her from the horse and set her on the ground, still holding her under the arms.

For a moment they looked at each other and Catherine's heart began to beat violently. Every warning instinct cried out to her to wrench herself free and gallop back to the others before it was too late.

Her dalliance with this man, his hands holding her, sliding round her waist, drawing her close, it was treason and death. . . .

"Catherine, I adore you," he said. "I have loved you since my first sight of you. For all these weeks I have been unable to sleep for thinking of you. . . ." The words came out in a flood of passion as Saltykov pressed her to him and felt her first trembling response.

Catherine made a last desperate effort to control her feelings and turned her head, avoiding his seeking kisses.

"Serge, Serge, don't, I beg you! Only think what this means. . . . Oh, God, don't torment me, I love you so and yet I dare not show it! Please . . ."

He cut short her protest with a determined forceful movement, and for an instant she stood rigid, the fire of that first kiss burning from her lips right through her body. Then something broke inside her; the frustrations of years of nightly humiliation and neglect surged up in a tidal wave of emotion.

All the womanhood, so cruelly crushed by circumstances and ambition, took possession of her, and the cool rationalist Catherine flung her arms round Saltykov's neck and her desperate inexperienced kisses mingled with her tears.

When at length she looked up at him Serge the seducer was shaken with a passion as strong as her own. "God's death!" he muttered. "What ails that husband of yours? Catherine, you cannot deny me now! You love me, and I cannot live without you, my adored one. Promise me that you will make me happy, promise me, Ekaterina, my darling. . . ."

She drew back from him a little and her lips trembled wretchedly. "I cannot, Serge, my beloved. For myself I care nothing. I would give my life to be an hour in your arms, but I love you too much to give yours, and that would be the penalty. . . ." This sudden unselfishness was not what he had expected, but her love for him gave Catherine strength and purpose. Gently but firmly she freed herself from his embrace.

"Do not dismiss me, for the love of God!" he begged. "It must be possible that I should have your love; give me your promise you will not refuse me. . . ."

"Serge, it will be you and only you, that I swear," she answered. "But not at the price of your life."

Slowly they turned the horses and began riding back to Oranienbaum.

Within the month the grand ducal court had returned to Petersburg, and a very uneasy Mme Tchoglokov had to report to Bestujev that so far Catherine's virtue had stood the test.

Inwardly Bestujev acknowledged that he had underestimated Catherine once again. That indomitable will of hers had resisted temptation, not out of virtue, he felt sure, but from policy. The possibility that she might be thinking of Saltykov's safety did not occur to him.

Unless he took some drastic action, his plan would go awry, and already he felt his position with the Empress to be weakening. But the day Catherine was delivered of a child, Elizabeth would be under a debt of gratitude to her Chancellor that no favourite would be able to wipe out.

Bestujev made his decision.

"Ask the Grand Duchess to grant me an audience this evening," he said, dismissing Mme Tchoglokov. The woman had made a better jailer than a confidante, and he made a mental note to dismiss her from her post. Also it might be as well if she retired from court once the affair with Saltykov had begun. The Chancellor placed small reliance upon female discretion.

*   *   *

Catherine sent word that she would receive him after supper. Peter retired to his own apartments in a sullen fury at his enemy's intrusion, and only the waiting-woman Vladyslava was present to show the most powerful man in Russia into the Grand Duchess's boudoir.

Catherine, regardless of etiquette, rose instantly and gave him her hand to kiss. The old statesman bent over it politely and then accepted the seat she offered him. Vladyslava poured wine for them and then vanished discreetly.

Bestujev observed her as he sipped his wine. The past was unfortunate, but he judged her clever enough to recognize the value of his friendship and to forget old wrongs.

The Grand Duchess smiled across at him and put down her wine cup.

"This is a great honour, Excellency," she said.

Bestujev bowed. "The honour and the pleasure is mine, Madame," he countered. "I have but one regret . . . that my visit was not made some years ago. Much misunderstanding could have been saved."

He glanced shrewdly at the Grand Duchess, but her expression told him nothing.

"Firstly I wish to ask, Madame, that you will count my humble self among your friends; seek my advice if anything should trouble you . . . and be sure that my protection will not fail you."

"Thank you, Excellency. Those are words I never thought to hear, but they have made me happy indeed. I never wished to be your enemy, and yet it seemed I could do nothing right. However, I have had eight years in which to remedy my faults," she added slyly, and only the glint of mockery in her eyes showed the remark to be without malice.

Bestujev accepted the rebuke with a wry smile, and then judged the time ripe for frankness.

"Forgive me, Madame, if I remind you of the reason for my apparent harshness and for Her Majesty's disappointment in you. Oh, I know the Grand Duke to be far from ideal as a husband, but none the less the crown will one day pass to him. His health is poor; it is vital to the peace of Russia that he should have an heir."

Catherine looked him straight in the face.

"As I told you and the Empress one night a long time ago, the lack of a child is not my fault!"

"I know that, Madame, and the time has come when your duty to Russia must outweigh your married scruples," he said gently. "There are two men, I believe, who are very much in love with you?" Despite herself Catherine blushed; she knew of one at least. . . .

"Saltykov is a handsome fellow, I have heard tell he worships you, or perhaps it is Narychkin you prefer. . . ."

At last the Grand Duchess saw the two-fold purpose behind Bestujev's visit; the peace he offered her after their long feud was a conditional one, and the price he asked was the fulfilment of her heart's desire . . . but he spoke of Leo. He was surely mistaken? Leo was a dear friend, but as a lover . . .

"No, Excellency, I assure you Narychkin means nothing to me," she said quickly. Bestujev rose

155

and kissed her hand.

"Then it is Serge that pleases you; I commend your taste. As a proof of my friendship I will send him to you this evening. As a proof of yours, give Russia an heir!"

With that promise he was gone.

The Grand Duchess ran to the bell-rope and pulled it vigorously. Vladyslava. . . . Where was she? She must make a toilette, the most important of her life. This night she must be worthy of her lover.

Catherine hurried into her robing room and chose a loose gown of red velvet hung with lace, while the impassive waiting-woman let down her hair. When she left, Catherine paced the room in a fever of happiness, remembering her cold, distasteful vigil on her wedding night, contrasting it with her present state of ardent impatience.

This was what it meant to wait for a lover, this terrible tumult of tenderness and desire, the faint tinge of fear common to all women who have yet to know the ardours of the final embrace.

She turned quickly as her door opened and closed softly. Saltykov stood there, his arms wide, his handsome face aflame with the longing reflected on her own.

Without a word she ran to him and his embrace crushed the breath out of her body; in a curious haze she felt herself lifted into his arms and knew that he was taking her to that inner room which had been the grave of her marriage with Peter Feodorovitch.

*   *   *

In the spring of 1754 Bestujev went in person to Elizabeth and informed her officially that the Grand Duchess Catherine was pregnant at last.

CHAPTER 7

In her bedroom in the Winter Palace at St. Petersburg, the Grand Duke stood looking down at his wife. He stood in the forefront of a pressing crowd of courtiers grouped about the mattress on the floor, placed according to custom beside the state four-poster bed; the Empress Elizabeth was kneeling at his side, and he could hear her intoning prayers under her breath.

The atmosphere was stifling and Peter unbuttoned his uniform coat for greater comfort. His back ached with standing, and he longed for his comfortable bed, but so long as the Empress continued her vigil, so must he.

How much longer, he wondered savagely, would that gasping, writhing creature on the mattress keep them all waiting before she gave birth? He raised his eyes from the contemplation of Catherine's sufferings, and looked round at the other watchers with cynical amusement.

How many of them, he wondered, had been duped into believing that the woman whose birth pangs they were witnessing bore anything but a bastard in her womb.

Saltykov's child was rending its adulterous

mother in two; soon now the spectacle would be over, and the waiting crowds of Petersburg would hurry home to toast the birth of an heir to their "beloved Grand Duke and Duchess. . . ."

Peter's grim amusement deepened; the utter falsity of the situation appealed to his warped sense of humour. He had kept them all dangling for eight years by adhering to the policy formed on his wedding day—never to lay a hand on his bride except to knock some sense into her with his fists.

He glanced down at Elizabeth, noting her closed eyes and the desperate look of concentration as she prayed, and his ugly face twisted in an open grin.

This was one night the imperial strumpet would spend out of Ivan Shuvalov's embrace.

Peter had found a communicating door between one of his antechambers and the Empress's bedroom. Several small holes had been bored in that door, and an enquiring eye saw scenes of his aunt's middle-aged passion that caused him convulsions of laughter. He had even invited one or two of his most trusted friends to avail themselves of this privilege.

His Aunt Elizabeth was getting plump and her once lovely face was lined and rouged till it resembled a withered, painted apple. She had frequent fits of violent colic and her tempers were

159

more hysterical and less effective.

Rumour said that she saw Ivan's image, chained and blinking like a blind man from his twenty years in captive darkness, and that she screamed for wine to stupefy her senses and banish the spectre of her guilt. In every room in her apartments there was always a quantity of wine.

Looking down at the Empress, Peter hoped with all his heart that she would not live long. The moment she died, he knew what he would do.

He would become Emperor for just long enough to declare war on the foes of his idol Frederick the Great, and he felt that never would worthless Russian blood be spilled to better cause; he would murder and imprison his enemies, and the first person on whom his wrath would fall would be that woman on the mattress.

Then he would retire to Holstein and leave Russia to her fate. Catherine gave a sharp cry and the midwife hurried close to her.

The Empress opened her eyes and started up; Peter leaned forward. . . .

She had made him suffer, and perversely he hated her because she had betrayed him with another man, because he knew that other to be handsome as he was hideous, strong and tall as he was thin and weakling. Now she was giving birth to the child of that betrayal, and he must call it his before the world for as long as Elizabeth Petrovna lived.

At twelve o'clock on that morning of September, 1754, the Grand Duchess was delivered of a baby boy. The midwife and the doctors exclaimed over him, kissed Elizabeth's hands and placed the infant in her arms.

The Empress held the tiny, crying bundle close, and a flood of fierce affection for it, mingled with a passion of relief, swept through her.

The dream of ten years ago was realized at last, her childless arms were filled, her throne had an heir; God in His mercy had heard her prayers, and only the wicked obstinacy and ingratitude of her nephew and his wife had made it necessary to achieve these things by adultery and deceit.

The need for self-justification roused a cold rage within Elizabeth's breast; Bestujev's opinion of Peter had since been proved disastrously wrong, for the widow Grooth had made a man of the twenty-four-year-old Grand Duke at last, as the Empress knew beyond possible doubt, and Catherine had enjoyed her adultery with Saltykov unnecessarily. What was worse, she had made the Empress a party to the crime; and for that Elizabeth would never forgive her.

As for Bestujev, he had added one more portion of guilt to her tormented conscience, and the fruition of his cherished plan was in fact to be the downfall of his ministry.

With a single, frowning glance at the exhausted Catherine, the Empress swept out of the room, the new-born baby in her arms.

One by one the courtiers followed her; Peter shambled out to receive congratulations and then fall into bed; the midwife and the doctors hurried after Elizabeth and her wailing burden. The whole great room emptied in the space of a few minutes, leaving the mattress and its occupant alone.

Catherine lay back exhausted; two tears of pain and weakness coursed down her sunken cheeks, the black hair was soaked and matted to her head with sweat, and a burning thirst tormented her.

For a while she lay very still, dimly conscious that the nightmare of pain she had endured so long seemed to have ended, and that her tongue was swelling in her mouth for want of water.

At last she turned her head, very slowly for it felt heavy as lead, and her eyes scanned the empty room. There must be someone there, in a part of the chamber that she couldn't see, perhaps, but some servant at least, who could give her a drink of water. . . .

With a great effort she called out, but there was no reply, no movement. They had all gone. The child was born and they had all left her as if she had died once her purpose was fulfilled; Catherine began to sob with thirst. A fearful abyss of loneliness and fear opened up before her as the hours went by and no living soul entered that room.

The sound of cannon shook the windows, as the fortress guns of St. Peter and Paul fired a salute to the royal baby.

A hot wave of fever enveloped her, shot with sudden pain, and the thought came to her that this was Elizabeth's answer to her affair with Saltykov.

She was being left deliberately alone to die.

Towards evening one of the court ladies looked casually in through the chamber door and reported that the Grand Duchess was unconscious.

Two hours later the midwife left Elizabeth and went to her patient. While the court and the city celebrated with feasts and bonfires, while prayers for the baby Grand Duke were offered in churches all over Petersburg, the mother lay on her mattress, senseless and racked with fever.

From the depths of her heart the Empress hoped that Catherine would die; her beauty, her cleverness and the scandal of her adultery would all be conveniently buried in an elaborate tomb, while the tiny creature to whom she had given life would belong to Elizabeth alone. . . . Peter got hilariously drunk on the strength of the news and the court shrugged indifferently and went on amusing itself.

Only the people of Russia heard that the Grand Duchess was likely to die, and in their thousands the people mourned. They remembered her wedding day; and her smiling beauty had become almost a legend. The great silent masses of the people kept the image of the sick mother in their hearts, and they went in confident supplication to that other Mother who had also borne a Son.

*　　*　　*

One month later Catherine was sitting up in bed. She was out of danger physically, but her spirits were weighed down with depression, and for once her abundant energy seemed to have drained completely away. Vladyslava waited on her, and her ministry was kind and efficient.

The Grand Duchess had charm; even in her feeblest moments she had managed to thank Vladyslava courteously and to apologize for the trouble she was giving. The waiting-woman's Russian heart warmed to her mistress under such unaccustomed treatment, and pitied the melancholy plight of a mother who had never been permitted to gaze on her own child since the day of its birth.

The Empress had taken full possession of the baby; it was wet-nursed and kept in her apartments; Elizabeth, herself the thwarted mother, refused to let the infant out of her sight, and after a while Catherine ceased to ask for her son; she only turned her face to the wall and wept.

Now she no longer cared. It was not her child, her arms had never held it, her fingers had never stroked its head; she knew it only as discomfort and suffering that was mercifully difficult to remember, and slowly, inexorably, the maternal instinct died in Catherine as she lay alone in her great bed.

She had no son, no husband, for now Peter had vacated her apartments altogether, but there was one who cared for her, one who had held her close, who had kissed her lips till they ached and pulled the pins out of her hair like a mischievous boy.

She had not seen him and he had sent her no word.

In her loyalty Catherine applauded his discretion, until the empty hours and lengthening days of silence bred a fear for his safety in her mind.

What if Elizabeth had harmed him, now that he, too, had served his purpose? Catherine knew well enough that the Empress had been aware of Bestujev's arrangement, and her terror for Saltykov compelled her to confide in someone.

Vladyslava, faithful, silent Vladyslava, who had shown him to her bedroom that night so many months ago. . . . She could be trusted.

"Find him," she begged. "I will give you money to send messengers to his home if he is not at court, only let me know that he is well, Vladyslava, bring me one word, one letter from him!"

The waiting-woman patted her mistress's thin hand and promised speedy news, while the sight of Catherine's anxious eyes, fixed on her in an expression of desperate pleading, caused her to curse the heartlessness of men.

When Vladyslava returned that evening, Catherine sat up eagerly.

"What news, is he in Petersburg? Have you seen him?"

Her waiting-woman came towards the bed and sat down on the edge of it without speaking. A spasm of fright clutched at Catherine's heart and she went pale.

"Have you a letter from him?" she whispered.

Vladyslava cleared her throat and her dark eyes met her mistress's gaze squarely.

"Forgive the bearer of bad news, Highness. M. Saltykov is not at court; he is not even in Russia by now. The Empress sent him on a mission to Sweden, just after your son was born. . . ."

"No! *No!* I don't believe it!"

The Grand Duchess's voice rose in a shriek; she seized the older woman by the shoulders and tried to shake her.

"He wouldn't go like that! He wouldn't leave without a word to me . . . he could have sent one word. Oh, God. why do you tell me this! Where did you hear this lie?"

Vladyslava freed herself and gathered the hysterical, shaking Catherine into her arms.

"M. Narychkin told me, Madame. Think no more of him and do not cry like that, my little one, poor little one. He is gone and all your tears will not make a lion out of a jackal. No man is worth such grief. Perchance he will send word from Sweden."

So the good Vladyslava lied and comforted, forbearing to tell the unhappy Catherine that her lover had departed laden with honours from Bestujev, without a thought in his handsome head for the woman he had seduced. His task was over, and he was only grateful that it had been such an agreeable one.

In the long night hours when sleep refused to come, Catherine Alexeievna lay and thought of Serge Saltykov.

At first she wept, silently in hopeless loneliness and disappointment, mixed with traitorous longing. But self-deception had never been one of

167

Catherine's failings. The change in Mme Tchoglokov's attitude, the behaviour of Serge on that first night, his fearless pursuit of her at Oranienbaum and then Bestujev's intervention, it all added up to a single, loathsome conclusion. Her love affair was pre-arranged from the beginning.

For one thing only she was thankful. At least Elizabeth kept the child out of her sight. It had been christened Paul, with all the pomp so dear to the Empress's heart; the ceremony was one to which the baby's mother was not even invited, and for this insult, too, Catherine was grateful.

The months dragged by, and the Grand Duchess kept to her room, sick in body and in mind, watched over by Vladyslava, who reported to Elizabeth that Peter's wife was fretting herself into a decline.

The Empress shrugged and dismissed her; let Catherine pine and keep to her rooms. She might have youth and beauty, those two gifts which were deserting the Czarina with such fearful speed, but Elizabeth had sent her lover away and taken possession of her child. Elizabeth had won after all. . . .

* * *

One afternoon Vladyslava entered Catherine's room to see her mistress seated as usual by the

168

window, staring blankly out into the garden, her face supported by her hand in an attitude of utter listlessness. She might have been a statue; even as the waiting-woman's loose slippers pattered over the polished floor, the Grand Duchess did not look up.

"Your Highness, a gentleman wishes me to give you this."

Catherine turned indifferently and stared at the little gilded box Vladyslava held out to her. She took it slowly and examined the delicate workmanship; it was a beautiful box and her fingers opened the lid with a hint of curiosity.

Some mechanism inside it whirred faintly and then a thin tune tinkled out of the bottom of the casket; inside a folded piece of paper lay boldly on a bed of crimson velvet.

Catherine smoothed it out and her eyes widened at the few lines of writing, crabbed and distorted in disguise.

"With the gift, the sender dares to offer his advice. It is time for the mother of the future Czar to show herself. Only the head can mend the heart."

There was no signature.

Catherine closed the box and turned to

Vladyslava.

"Who gave you that?" she demanded. Vladyslava did not know his name, but she gave a clear description of a Foreign Office clerk well known to the Grand Duchess.

So the box and the note came from Bestujev. It was so typical of him, the man of iron, to guess why she ailed and to add that single caustic line of reproof and advice.

"Only the head can mend the heart. . . ."

In other words she was a weakling woman and a fool, pining in solitude while he, Saltykov, amused himself in Sweden. One love affair and all her resolution fell to pieces. . . . In a sudden burst of rage Catherine flung the musical box across the room and it shattered against the wall, its delicate mechanism scattering over the floor.

Vladyslava stepped quickly back; she expected tears and prayed for them that they might ease the weight of sadness which oppressed her mistress. But they did not come. For some moments Catherine stood looking out of the window, her hands tearing the note into shreds, while a voice inside her repeated the words of it over and over again.

The mother of the future Czar!

It was true, she was the mother of Paul Petrovitch, no matter how Elizabeth might try to make the world forget. And it was time she listened to her head and sacrificed her heart with all its weakness. She had sacrificed it when she married Peter. And for what?

Catherine knew the answer as Bestujev knew it. For the crown of Russia.

In a passion of relief she thanked him for reminding her. This last blow to her pride had crushed her long enough; the time for tears and sentiment was over.

Catherine turned round from the window and looked at the waiting-woman.

"How long have I been in Russia, Vladyslava?" Her voice was deceptively even.

"Almost twelve years, Highness. I saw you come to Moscow with your mother."

"Twelve years," repeated Catherine quietly.

Twelve years of misery and injustice at the hands of that same Elizabeth Petrovna who had kissed the shy Augusta and welcomed her so warmly. So full of promises of favour and friendship . . . it might almost have been yesterday that she had worshipped and imitated the beautiful Empress who protected her against Johanna's jealousy.

As she sat watching Vladyslava light the candles in her room, her thoughts scanned back across her life in Russia, piecing together the strange perverse pattern of events that had made her husband and the Empress into enemies, and turned Bestujev the implacable into a friend.

For twelve years she had been patient and loyal, counting on virtue to bring its own reward, arguing that the crown she coveted would pass to her by right as Peter's consort, bearing a burden of persecution and unhappiness that would have crushed most women to the ground.

Well, it had not crushed her; marriage to a drunken idiot, impotent until his twenty-fourth year, snubs, loneliness and nerve-racking supervision, all these trials she had borne with a determination fed by the hope of better times ahead.

Now she had given them an heir, child of her adultery with a paid seducer, and Elizabeth judged her uses at an end. She was to be left to break her heart and sink into obscurity from which she could never hope to rise again.

Catherine smiled grimly to herself. She had been hurt to the limit of endurance since her son was born. But the time for bearing wrongs was over; it had gained her nothing, and Bestujev, himself now fallen from grace, so rumour said, counselled a decisive move.

He was right, and she knew it. Catherine Alexeievna, the obedient young woman whom no one feared, was dead and buried in the silence of that room, while Vladyslava sewed in a corner and the candles burned lower in their silver sockets.

Supper was brought as usual, and for the first time in many months, the Grand Duchess ate well and drank draughts of the full-bodied Russian wine. She needed physical as well as spiritual strength, for the battle ahead of her would be a trial of endurance and resolve.

"Vladyslava, to-morrow I want to see my dress-maker. And send my hairdresser and jeweller to me. I shall need a new wardrobe."

"Yes, Highness, it shall be done."

Suddenly the Grand Duchess appeared to her waiting-woman almost a stranger; that square jaw, the hard-set mouth and the icicle coldness in her blue eyes robbed Catherine of her beauty in a moment; she did not even seem young, and despite herself Vladyslava shrank back.

If this was what the Empress and Serge Salty-kov had done to the Grand Duchess, then she pitied them the results of their own harshness. This woman whose sufferings she had witnessed all these months had suddenly flung her despair to the winds; whatever the thoughts and feelings that possessed her, she gave no sign beyond the wild de-struction of Bestujev's box, but sat calmly at the supper-table, giving orders.

"There is a deal to be done, Vladyslava," Catherine continued, "and I would trust you with

173

a message. Present my compliments to the Chancellor, tell him the contents of a box sent to me by a friend have cheered my spirits greatly.

"And tell him that on my husband's birthday, one month hence, I hope to see him. I have chosen that day for my return to public life."

CHAPTER 8

IN a room at the British Embassy in Petersburg, the British Ambassador, Sir Charles Hanbury-Williams, sat at his writing-desk, chewing the feathered top of his quill pen.

He had a despatch to write that evening, and far from being the routine document he had sent home regularly since his arrival in Russia a few months past, there was now something of importance to record. Sir Charles was physically tired, he had journeyed back from Oranienbaum that evening, but his shrewd brain was excited and alert.

He had set out the tedious details of his activities and recounted the current political gossip going the rounds of the capital; admitted, too, that he had failed to interest the Empress in an alliance with England at the expense of France, and he knew that this fact would not please his superiors. In his own defence he had added that Elizabeth was obviously unbalanced and frequently drunk, and it was difficult to secure her attention about anything.

As for her nephew and heir, Sir Charles wrote contemptuously that his mental powers and conversational level would have disgraced a child of twelve years old. . . .

"But this day I was received by the Grand Duchess Catherine," he wrote. "She is a most remarkable woman; her personal beauty is only matched by her extraordinary intelligence and the charm which she displayed towards me might have deceived a less interested observer into overlooking a personality at once determined and ambitious.

"Her conversation at dinner showed her to be the most cultured and knowledgeable woman I have met in Russia so far. I reflected that she would one day be Empress Consort; as Elizabeth Petrovna is in very poor health that day may come sooner than expected, and I very much doubt whether the imbecile Grand Duke will retain his power for long with such a wife at his side.

"It seems she has been much persecuted in the past, and I cannot conceive of any action more foolish than to make an enemy of her. . . . It will certainly be in England's interests to secure her as a friend."

Sir Charles completed his despatch, sanded and sealed it carefully, and decided to see if his secretary had returned before he went to bed.

Stanislaus Poniatowsky was more friend and protégé than anything else, and the Ambassador regarded his civilized society as a boon; it was a relief to speak with an intelligent man of the world, after the hours he was forced to keep in the company of people he described as heathenish and quite incomprehensible by Western standards.

As he approached Poniatowsky's door, he saw a light shining from underneath it and without bothering to knock, Sir Charles opened it, and went in. The Count was sitting on his bed, still dressed, and he smiled at the sight of the older man.

"Good evening, Sir Charles, I thought you had retired." Williams sat down heavily in a chair and stretched his legs.

"No, my dear Stanis, I've been penning damned despatches most of the night. I'm devilish tired too, but for once the day was worth the fatigue! How was the Countess's card party?"

"Expensive but instructive. I lost quite a sum of money, but the talk was vastly interesting."

"Humph! What was it?"

Poniatowsky lay back on the bed and clasped his arms behind his head. Looking at him, Sir Charles reflected that he was a handsome fellow, a trifle sensitive-featured for English taste, his appearance was usually described by ladies as "sad and romantic", a description which fitted the young Polish nobleman exactly.

Fortunately he possessed other qualities besides social charm; he had sharp ears and a long memory, both attributes which the card players had forgotten that evening when they chattered so freely.

"The talk was mostly of the Grand Duke and Duchess," he said. "It seems that the delightful Peter has a new mistress to whom he is more than ordinarily attached. A Mlle Elizabeth Vorontzov; she was at Oranienbaum to-day."

Sir Charles snorted in disbelief. "God's death, I remember her well enough and I don't believe it! She's pock-marked all over, a hideous creature with table manners that nearly turned my stomach! I wondered what the devil such a woman was doing at the Grand Duchess's board. D'ye tell me that Peter would look at an ugly wench like that when he has legal rights to a wife like Catherine?"

Poniatowsky nodded. "It must be true; he has strange taste in bedfellows. The Princess of Courland was a hunchback, remember. Now he declares he's lost his heart to the Vorontzova, and most of Petersburg thinks he actually has some affection for her. At any rate, it's whispered that he wants to divorce his wife. . . ."

"Does he indeed? Then the man is certainly mad!" declared Sir Charles. "You spoke to her,

Stanis. What did you think of the lady? And don't tell me that you didn't notice her especially, for I saw the eyes starting out of your head during dinner!"

Poniatowsky laughed, but despite himself he coloured as he answered the question.

"I'll be truthful, my friend. I thought her one of the most beautiful and fascinating women I've ever seen in my life. If you must know, I've thought of precious little else all day! Gossip declared that her son Paul is a bastard, born of a love affair with some Russian, and that she and Peter have never bedded together in all these years. It may be hearsay, of course, who can tell, but she seems a woman who has been much alone."

Sir Charles looked at him keenly. "For a man of fashion, who's had his choice of many lovely ladies in several capitals of the world, and refused them all, you appear to be quite partisan to the lady. I dare say you would care to relieve her solitude, eh?"

His young secretary's mouth pursed in a disappointed line.

"I'm afraid I should have little chance. It's rumoured that a certain Leo Narychkin, who has been a close friend for years, is about to be rewarded for his devotion. It is a year since the little Grand Duke was born, and that's a long time for a woman of her beauty and warmth to sleep alone. God knows, he's fortunate!"

Sir Charles got up and stood by the bed. He had never seen the other so disturbed before.

"Are you in love with her, my boy?" Poniatowsky looked up at him and then turned his head away on the pillow.

"I don't know, Sir Charles! How can I tell, I've only seen her once, only spoken a half-dozen words to her. Women have never really stirred me you know that. How many men are there of my age, twenty-three, who have never been in bed with a wench? Well, I tell you this one looked and smiled at me this afternoon and I've never had a moment's respite since."

Sir Charles bent and patted his shoulder.
"Truth to tell, Stanis, I've not had much peace myself, so you're not alone in that. But don't despair, boy; she seemed mighty gracious to you, and this Narychkin is not in her bedroom yet by your account."

With that the Ambassador went to his own rooms, and before he fell asleep it occurred to him how suitable it would be if the future Empress of Russia should take one of his own staff as a lover.

*   *   *

180

That night, while Charles Hanbury-Williams snored peacefully at one end of the house, Stanislaus Poniatowsky turned restlessly upon his bed till dawn. The image of Catherine Alexeievna had taken possession of his mind and refused to be dismissed.

In the palace at Oranienbaum Catherine also lay awake. It had been an exhausting day and a test of her powers as hostess; the Empress had remained at Peterhof with baby Paul, and the despised Grand Duchess had stepped forward to receive the court and all the foreign dignitaries in Elizabeth's place.

Now she lay in her large cold bed, reviewing the incidents as a general marshals his regiments for a battle.

The English Ambassador had been extremely friendly; Catherine had studied the political situation well enough to guess the reason for his cordiality, but it pleased her immensely to realize that he considered her important enough to seek out. Her resolve to assert her position was growing stronger every day, and Elizabeth, her time divided between Ivan Shuvalov and Catherine's baby son, was making the path extremely easy.

Bestujev, still clinging precariously to the nominal post of Chancellor, was ever at her back as guide and mentor; his day with the Empress

was done and he knew it. Elizabeth's sun wa
gradually sinking beneath the seas of ill-health
and the old statesman had securely attached him
self to the orbit which must inevitably rise.

In one short year Catherine the recluse, th
forgotten Grand Duchess, had recovered almos
every foot of advantage she had lost as a youn
bride all those years ago. She had been a foreigne
then, still faltering in the Russian tongue, hal
educated and obsessed with the desire to please
believing she need make no enemies.

Well, time had taught her differently; the lesso
had been a harsh one but at least it had bee
learnt.

Only now could she hope to have influence
when the Empress was ageing and the thron
coming nearer and nearer to Peter every day.

The court sensed that change was not far off
and the men who had snubbed and sneered a
Peter a few years ago were crowding round him i
attempts to win his favour, while the wome
preened themselves like courtesans whenever h
appeared. Never had Catherine seen such a
example of human opportunism and falseness
They all hated Peter, but within a year or two h
might be Czar. And his wife would be Czarina.

There were many who remembered that, an
they flocked to pay court to her as well; aware tha

the sycophants divided their time between fawning upon her and the Grand Duke's current mistress, Catherine received them with grim amusement in her heart.

Yet in spite of all her plans and vows to live for ambition alone, nothing could banish the fact that Catherine needed love. Her beautiful healthy body cried out for it, and her heart ached for affection and companionship.

Celibacy might have been wiser, but she admitted freely that for her it was a torment and a hindrance. She needed a lover, and most of all she needed to be loved; who else but Leo Narychkin could she choose? Weeks ago Catherine had made up her mind to offer herself to him, yet for some reason she delayed the final move.

She was truly fond of Leo, but familiarity had robbed him of romance. Why even that Polish secretary of the English Ambassador had roused her interest as Narychkin never could. He had a gentle face, she remembered, the face of a dreamer and an intellectual, refined but sensual in a poetic way.

Suddenly Catherine chided herself for a fool, wasting the night hours thinking about a stranger who had been one of hundreds at Oranienbaum that day.

To-morrow night, she determined, would find Leo at her side, and that would be the end of her imaginings.

But for Leo the day passed and the evening followed without event; there was no sign from Catherine that his long siege to her heart would be rewarded.

If he noticed that the English Ambassador had sent his secretary over from Petersburg to pay a call upon her, the incident held no significance for him.

*   *   *

For the next few weeks Poniatowsky found excuses for visiting Catherine regularly, and Sir Charles encouraged the friendship. By this time Stanislaus was obsessed with passion for the Grand Duchess, and he made no secret of the fact to his friend and protector.

"Every day I love her more," he declared wretchedly, "and before God there are times when I think that she is not indifferent to me! But what can I do, Sir Charles? I dare not speak of it; even if she took me as her lover how long would it be before the affair was discovered and I ended my days in some hole in Siberia . . . if I was not assassinated?"

"Damned nonsense, my dear boy," declared the Ambassador. "What are you quibbling about? There's little risk in having an affair with her, tell you—have you less courage than Narychkin? She's a young woman of some influence, no one will interfere too much with her, I'll swear. The next time you're alone with her, speak your mind, Stanis, tell her you're like to die of love for her, no woman can resist that, and if she gives you the key to her door, snatch it and don't come back to me till morning!"

But it was not till the court returned to Petersburg that Poniatowsky declared himself to Catherine.

They were seated in the gardens, in that very same arbour where Countess Roumiantzov had delivered her lecture to the young bride-to-be nearly fourteen years before.

Now the unhappy bewildered girl had grown into a lovely, passionate young woman, who had lured her hesitant lover to this secluded spot with the express purpose of bringing the situation to a head. Vladyslava had absented herself discreetly and they were quite alone.

He did love her; Catherine knew it well, for he betrayed himself in a hundred different ways, and she herself had fallen victim to that handsome charm he had evinced at their first meeting.

She who had kept the unhappy Narychkin dangling, only to disappoint his hopes altogether in favour of the Pole, found herself unable to endure the suspense of this strange, hesitant courtship any longer.

But it was he who broke the silence.

"I am grateful for this opportunity to have a few words with you in private, Madame; I was afraid that I should have to leave Petersburg without unburdening myself to you except by letter."

Catherine swung round on him.

"Leave Petersburg! But why, is Sir Charles sending you away?" Poniatowsky looked down avoiding her glance as he answered.

"Only at my request, and very unwillingly at that. But it is quite impossible for me to stay here any longer."

The next moment he felt Catherine's hand close over his, her fingers slipping into his palm.

"I thought that you were happy here," she said quietly, aware that her heart was beating hard with fear lest he should really leave her. Stanislaus sighed and for the first time met her eye.

"I will speak plainly to you, Catherine. I am the unhappiest man in Russia because I am so near to the woman I love and yet so far from her. Other men may see you day after day, talk to you, look at you, and be content with only that; but if I cannot possess you then I must go far away, where you will not be in my sight to drive me almost mad with longing!"

There was no doubt of his sincerity. His handsome face was blanched and drawn with wretchedness, he seemed on the point of tears.

Catherine was no longer the awkward young virgin who had submitted so helplessly to Saltykov, she knew her own attractions and desperation made her bold.

"If you doubt my feelings, dear Stanislaus, then here is your answer," and she put her arms round his neck and her lips to his mouth.

For some moments there was silence in the arbour, and any passing tattler would have been able to tell all Petersburg that the Grand Duchess and Count Poniatowsky were locked in each other's embrace, kissing shamelessly in the middle of the afternoon.

When at last he released her, Catherine put her head down on his shoulder and smiled with content.

"Are you still leaving Petersburg, Stanislaus my love?" she whispered.

"You know I can never leave you now. But only one thing will satisfy me, my beloved. . . . Yet you have a husband who would delight to find you out in some fault, and the Empress's way with us both would be short and terrible."

He bent and kissed her again, smothering the words of protest that she was about to utter, and

Catherine clung to him.

Always Elizabeth and Peter stood in the way of her happiness. Fear of their vengeance was holding Stanislaus back, and it was strong enough to dismiss him altogether; the thought of losing him turned her unaccountably sick, and the prospect of the last twelve months of loneliness filled her with wild determination.

Not three years ago authority had chosen the destroyer of her virtue and delivered her to him without a qualm. Perhaps the time had come to remind the Empress of that early and convenient lapse. Saltykov had been rewarded for his service to the crown; so far Catherine had received nothing, and now she was going to Elizabeth to ask. . . .

"We shall have our hapiness, my Stanis. I promise you nothing shall keep us apart. And what is more, you'll come to me with the Empress's blessing before many days are done!"

But it was three weeks before Elizabeth Petrovna granted her an interview, and then for the first time in twelve years Catherine found herself in the Empress's private rooms.

While waiting in the antechamber, the Grand Duchess remembered the last occasion when she had entered that inner room with Peter and marvelled at the courage she had since achieved to come of her own free will to beard the imperial lioness in her den.

It was a curious feeling, this lack of fear for Elizabeth, and its absence revealed the change that had taken place in her over the years. A few formal words in public, brief encounters at state ceremonies, these were her only contacts with the Empress until now, and yet the prospect of a private interview did not deter her in the least.

Catherine Alexeievna passed into the Czarina's bedchamber with a serene expression on her lovely face and the intention to blackmail in her heart.

The Empress was lying in bed, and she looked childishly small and frail propped up on a pile of satin cushions in the middle of the huge canopied and gilded structure.

Some two weeks had passed since her ladies had carried her to that same bed writhing in a convulsive fit, and the doctors had bled her weakened frame according to the custom of the time, until they could pronounce the poisons drawn from her veins.

This seizure was not the first she had experienced, and Catherine gasped inwardly at the sight of her in a wrapper and night-cap. Stripped of her gorgeous jewels, her dresses and her paint, Elizabeth was revealed as an old woman, tired and sick almost to death.

Her eyes followed the younger woman coldly as she curtsied and seated herself beside the mountainous bed; they grudged her bitterly the health and beauty that radiated from her in that room heavy with the scent of illness and decay.

Mixed with her envy, the Empress experienced a sudden wave of panic. What if Catherine had come to ask for her child? There was no other reason for the audience that Elizabeth's tired brain could envisage, and her puffy hands clutched at the bedcovers in alarm.

Little Paul Petrovitch was all she had to live for; lying there, ailing and hideous, she dared not permit Ivan Shuvalov to see his mistress in such a sorry state, but the child was brought to her for hours each day; it lay cradled in her tired arms and smiled the sweet, knowing smile of babies in response to her endearments.

Whatever this self-possessed creature desired of her, it had better not be the custody of her son!

"It was good of Your Majesty to see me. I hope you are recovered now. . . ."

Elizabeth waved her formalities aside.

"Do not be false with me, Catherine. You have displeased me for too long and pretty courtesies will not avail you. Why have you sought me after all these years? What have you to say to me?"

The Grand Duchess leant forward in her chair;

if the Empress had a mind for frankness, so had she.

"First I would beg your forgiveness for whatever I have done to cause such a breach in your affection for me. In fact, I have lived so long under Your Majesty's displeasure that I have quite forgotten what it is to hear a kind word from you. And not knowing the reason, I have been unable to mend my offending ways."

They were humble words, but Catherine's tone was not conciliatory. Her instinct told her that weakness now would lose her everything; only boldness might turn the scales in her favour with that travesty of a woman in the bed.

"I have given you the heir you wanted, and I come now to beg my reward; for some respite from the loneliness that is my married portion."

Elizabeth raised herself up on the pillows and her haggard eyes were dark with alarm. It *was* the child that Catherine sought.

"If you speak of your son," she began hoarsely, and the Grand Duchess perceived her agitation and rightly guessed its cause.

Inwardly she was thankful that the Empress's barbarous conduct at her lying-in had utterly destroyed all her maternal love. A request for the solace of her own child's company would have been savagely refused.

"No, Your Majesty," she answered calmly. "I come about another matter; though my son's welfare is dear to me, I know that he receives from you the love and care that I could never hope to give him. I only ask your protection from the slanders that threaten a friendship which has become a great comfort to me in the continued unfaithfulness of my husband."

In her relief, Elizabeth scarcely heard the last part of the sentence. There would be no need to banish the mother in order to retain the child, and the Empress's fevered brain had been contemplating measures of outrageous severity had Catherine dared to ask for Paul.

She spoke of friendship, of comfort in Peter's unfaithfulness. Mentally Elizabeth could imagine nothing that would please a wife more than the absence of a husband like her nephew; but always people played the hypocrite with her, and Catherine whom she had once loved was no exception.

"What friendship would you have, Madame, that scandal could threaten if it were quite a fitting one?"

The question came at Catherine with something of Elizabeth's old caustic harshness.

But the answer was ready on her tongue and she spoke it bravely.

"I give my word, there is no cause for scandal in

my friendship for this person, any more than there was reason in the lies spread by evil tongues about M. Saltykov and myself. . . . Indeed it has even gone abroad that the Grand Duke is not the father of my son! Such tales are dangerous, Your Majesty. I promise to scotch that rumour vigorously if it should be within my power; so will you not give me your word that I may enjoy a new companionship without fear for the other person or myself?"

For a moment Elizabeth gasped with amazement at the audacity of the creature who sat there so calmly and threatened to expose the fact that the Empress's precious heir was a bastard unless she was given a free hand to begin a fresh amour!

Two years ago Elizabeth Petrovna would have known how to deal with such a situation, and the Grand Duchess would have sobbed out her contrition on the rack before that very night was out; but wine, over-indulgence with Ivan Shuvalov and bouts of rigorous penance had drained that once formidable constitution to a shell; the cruelty and despotism were still there, but the will to enforce them had weakened.

It required effort to become really angry as of old; Elizabeth saw a vista of complications opening up before her, and quite suddenly she collapsed.

Watching her, Catherine saw the colour leave her face and the rage die out of her eyes as they closed wearily.

"You have my permission," she muttered. "But for friendship alone, remember. One breath of scandal, and you'll be answerable to me! I'll not tolerate immorality, Madame. I've had it in mind to take that nephew of mine in hand for some time. Later, when I am well, I shall attend to him."

And to you, Catherine Alexeievna, she thought; if I catch you out in one false step, I'll give you reason to regret your impudence this day. . . .

Catherine took her cold hand and kissed it.

"My humble thanks to Your Majesty," she said.

*   *   *

That evening most of the court attended a play, including Peter, who sat publicly fondling Elizabeth Vorontzov and getting drunk as usual. Unfortunately the Grand Duchess was unable to be present; she was keeping to her room with a headache, and Sir Charles Hanbury-Williams repeated the story with a perfectly straight face to all who remarked upon her absence.

In the warm, candle-lit privacy of her bedroom Catherine Alexeievna lay in Poniatowsky's arms, his sleeping head on her breast, and there was no sound in that room while the candles burnt themselves out and the fire finally died in the grate.

She slept at last, her lips smiling with the contentment of a woman who has shared and witnessed the first fever of passion in a man who has lost himself in love.

Stanislaus Poniatowsky was no Saltykov; this time it was really he who loved her.

The next months of Catherine's life were the happiest that she had ever known; Poniatowsky was a lover whose adoration warmed and heartened her in secret, while for the first time she thrust her fingers into the tangle of political intrigue and began to grasp at the threads of power.

She saw herself at last through the infatuated eyes of Stanislaus, and listened while he told her again and again that she and not Peter ought to sit upon the Russian throne. So he urged upon her what Catherine already knew; she must gain influence and profit by the change of fortune that had laid Elizabeth low with ill-health and brought Bestujev's friendship to her aid.

One pressing need of hers was money, money for presents and bribes and for the settlement of her own debts.

It was Sir Charles Hanbury-Williams who came forward, smiling and courteous, with large sums from the exchequer of England, which he begged the Grand Duchess to accept. In return he only asked her friendship for his country, and Catherine pledged it.

In the arms of the gentle Pole she discovered the element of security in love; the tranquil knowledge that his love for her was the most genuine and disinterested emotion any woman can expect, and that the fire of physical passion could never burn out the depth of his feeling for her, no matter how fiercely it consumed them both. Nothing would ever efface her image from his heart, and there were moments when Catherine felt strangely sad because she knew herself to be far less the slave of love than he.

While English gold flowed into the Grand Duchess's empty pockets, a second stream found its way into the coffers of another needy subject of the Empress, Chancellor Bestujev.

He, too, was grateful for it, and his ear inclined to Catherine's partisanship for England against France. Frederick of Prussia was about to attack their Gallic ally, and that would encumber Russia with a treaty war. His plans for the future could find other uses for Russian arms and money; as Elizabeth suffered yet another seizure and her hated nephew began boasting of his intentions on succeeding her, Bestujev decided that the future might soon become the present.

Neither he nor Catherine nor the English Ambassador wanted to see France aided at that moment, and they proceeded to hinder the event as much as they dared.

With Elizabeth lying ill, they had only the Shuvalov faction to watch, and the new Vice-Chancellor Vorontzov, uncle to Peter's ugly mistress, could be side-tracked into less important channels.

Catherine had her lover, a large bank account and growing political power; Peter's existence was almost forgotten.

But it was he, egged on by the ambitions of Elizabeth Vorontzov and by years of mounting hate and fear of his wife, who watched through informers' eyes and listened with their ears, until he decided that the time had come when he could destroy her.

On the 8th of January, 1758, the blow fell.

Bestujev left a sick-bed to appear at the Conference Hall in answer to a summons from the Empress.

When he set foot there, he was arrested.

CHAPTER 9

"HAVE you ever seen a penitent's cell in one of my aunt's nunneries, Elizabeth, my love?"

The Vorontzova shook her head and grimaced across the supper-table at the Grand Duke. "Never, thank God. I've heard of the places and that's enough for my curiosity! Why do you ask me?"

"Because if all goes as I have arranged, that is where my dear wife should be before another day is past!"

Peter sat back in his chair and grinned at his mistress; his sallow face glowed with excitement and his grimy hands shook as they picked at the food on his plate. Ever since the court had been electrified by Bestujev's arrest on a charge of treason, the Grand Duke had been a man transformed; his habitual sullenness had given place to an air of mocking geniality and suppressed triumph; suddenly no one was safe from the clumsy malice of his tongue, and the Vorontzova had found him so domineering that she had wisely asked no questions until he chose to vouchsafe an explanation. Now he had told her, and Elizabeth Vorontzov made no secret of her delight at the news.

"Highness, it cannot be true! Should we be rid of her then?" Peter nodded grimly.

"By God we would! I tell you, Elizabeth, if my aunt listens to me and to Ivan Shuvalov, Catherine will go where she'll no longer hinder our plans. And you know what my plans are. . . . I mean to divorce her; I've always meant to, since the day I married her. Once I have no wife, then I can think of taking another!"

The Vorontzova flushed and held out her hand to him across the table; he had so often spoken thus, drunken threats and longings which she had prayed so fervently might be fulfilled. If only Catherine were dead or imprisoned, Peter would marry her.

"When I left her two hours ago, she was in a very nervous mood," she said. "Not outwardly, Highness; you know her, she shows nothing of what occupies her thoughts. She was deadly pale, I noticed, but always with that same smile graven on her mouth. I believe she'd smile at her own execution," she added, and shivered.

"When I am Czar," Peter remarked slowly, "if the convent hasn't killed her, then we'll arrange the opportunity for her to prove your statement."

The Vorontzova roared with laughter at her lover's subtle humour.

199

"I should like that! If you knew how often she has slighted me, Peter. If you love me, promise me that I shall be revenged! Swear that you will show no mercy."

"Don't trouble yourself, my dove," the Grand Duke sniggered. "We'll both have our vengeance; leave the manner of it to my aunt. Oh, I cannot wait to see it; to hear her, the liar and whore that she is, account for the letters she wrote to General Apraxin on the Prussian front! To deny that that spying old Englishman Williams gave her money, that she corrupted the Imperial Chancellor himself until he was taking bribes and aiding her intrigues! Ha, I tell you not even the devil himself, whose daughter she is, can help her to escape the consequences."

He drained his beer mug and flung it into the corner, where it smashed to pieces; beside himself with hate he sprang up from the table and began pacing the room, while Elizabeth Vorontzov watched him, fascinated yet afraid.

"I have waited so many years for this moment! God knows what I have endured since I set foot in this accursed country; the loss of my freedom, exile from Holstein, and that woman for my wife! Pah! The thought of her sickened me and her nature made it like living with the devil!

"But I've seen a great many things. From the

moment I saw her, God knows how many years ago, I didn't trust her! I hated her smooth ways and that damned, deceitful smile! I tell you, she's not human, not like other women; her face is always a mask and behind it there is every evil except fear! She prays and grovels in church, but I swear that too is sham. She worships no God; I've seen those books she reads. My aunt would have the writers of such things torn limb from limb, but their mind is the true mind of my wife, the pious Catherine!"

Elizabeth Vorontzov crossed herself hurriedly.

"Pray God, she goes to that convent cell you spoke of; truly she frightens me. . . ."

Peter stared moodily in front of him, and unconsciously he pulled his cravat loose with a nervous gesture.

"She has always frightened me," he mumbled. "My aunt is a tyrant and a slut . . . don't hush me, damn you! I'll call her what I please! She's cruel and mad; I never thought to find a greater devil clothed in female form. But there is something terrible about my wife. . . She gets no pleasure out of cruelty, not as most people do. No one believes her capable of evil, because she faints at public floggings, and spends hours feeding the birds at Oranienbaum. . . . No one knows her as I do, Elizabeth, not even you, who hate her so. But this time she has gone too far. . . . By morning we'll be rid of her."

Suddenly he crossed to the table and dragged his mistress to her feet. His ugly face was flushed and twisted with excitement, his hands trembled as they closed round her waist. The Vorontzova responded instantly to his advance; this was to be their night of triumph, and already she saw herself mounting the throne at his side. She, the thick-set, pock-marked failure of the family, had found favour with the man who would hold all Russia at his mercy once the Empress died.

Some hours later, Peter Feodorovitch left her embraces for the long-awaited audience with his imperial aunt.

It was three o'clock in the morning, and at the same moment his wife was being escorted to Elizabeth's apartments to stand her trial.

*   *   *

Outwardly Catherine was very calm. She had been waiting in her rooms fully dressed for this summons; waiting alone, for her women had excused themselves one by one, and her sharp ears had heard the shuffle of a sentry's feet as he took up his position outside her door.

Never in all her life had she been in such mortal danger; the rumour of her downfall had spread through the court like a high wind, and overnight she found herself deserted. They had all counted the Empress in her grave too soon; even the experienced Bestujev, who had spent a lifetime in intrigue, had abandoned his old mistress prematurely.

Elizabeth had lain in her sick-bed and affected not to notice the interference of Catherine and her friends; then she had risen like a tigress and struck, first at her Chancellor, who had been flung into prison, then at the English Ambassador, who at that very moment was sailing back to England, recalled at the Empress's command.

Only Catherine and Poniatowsky remained untouched, surrounded by an ominous quiet that frightened the Grand Duchess more and more. She was the chief target of the anti-English faction, disliked by Ivan Shuvalov, hated by the Vorontzova and by Peter; she knew beyond doubt that they delayed only to compile a formidable case against her and, worst of all, none realized more clearly than she what evidence existed to support their accusations.

Blinded by love for Stanislaus, urged on by Williams and Bestujev, she had committed her views on the war, the Empress and the succession to paper countless times. Until that night those letters had hung over her head like the executioner's sword. If they were found, then no defence was possible.

But as she followed in the wake of Elizabeth's page, conscious that the sentry who guarded her rooms had left his post and fallen in behind her, Catherine Alexeievna repeated two phrases over and over under her breath:

"Have courage. I have burnt everything."

One of the lackeys had dropped a screw of paper into her lap while she sat at supper, trying to eat, and those few words scrawled in a well-known hand had sent her sinking spirits high. From his dungeon Bestujev had contrived to get that message to her, knowing that her own turn had come, and it answered one persistent, torturing question that had burnt into her brain in the last days.

They had no real proof of treason. She had taken money, yes, but not even Elizabeth could kill her for that; and there were letters to General Apraxin, but they were coded and read harmlessly enough. What other charges would be brought against her, what proof laid before Elizabeth?

The page stood back at the portals of Elizabeth's suite and watched the Grand Duchess walk past him firmly, dry-eyed and composed despite her pallor. No one would have guessed that her heart was thudding in her breast with terror as the great gilded doors of the imperial bedchamber were swung open and the dim, forbidding figure of the Empress regarded her silently from within.

Elizabeth Petrovna had but lately recovered from her last illness, but she was fully dressed. The room was shadowy, for the Empress declared that too much light hurt her eyes, and the scene was illumined by only two candelabra.

Their glow dealt kindly with Elizabeth, softening the harsh lines of sickness and the hollows graven in her painted face; she looked almost young and for a moment it seemed to Catherine that she curtsied before a ghost, a phantom of the Empress who had received her so affectionately nearly twenty years before. Behind her stood Ivan Shuvalov, his handsome face in shadow, one hand resting on the back of his royal mistress's chair. The Grand Duchess knew that she might expect no mercy from him, and her eyes lingered for an instant upon the other smaller figure who leant against the Empress's gilt dressing-table.

So Peter was to be among her judges. Catherine knew then that she had underestimated the forces to be aligned against her; his hatred had always been an asset to her enemies, but she had not expected to find it expressed openly; his presence in that room betokened only one thing.

The conclusion was in no doubt; her fate had

already been decided and Peter was there to witness the sentence. One lightning glance at the faces of Elizabeth and her favourite, hard, expressionless masks in the flickering candle-light, gave her a sudden inspiration.

They wore a pretence of impartiality, but Peter's ugly mouth was curved in a spiteful, triumphant grin.

She knelt at their feet in the rôle of wrongdoer, hoping for mercy in spite of her crimes, and they waited with the practised cruelty of inquisitors for the victim to begin to plead for it.

Catherine continued to kneel, but she raised her head and stared at the Empress with fearless eyes.

"I come to Your Majesty with a request," she said suddenly. For a moment the musccles of Elizabeth's face twitched in surprise; the tone and phrasing of Catherine's first words were not what she had expected.

"You request, you dare to speak of a request . . . ?" The Empress hesitated.

"I crave Your Majesty's forgiveness and beg that you will not think me ungrateful or hasty in what I am about to ask. On my knees, I beg you to have pity on my unhappy state and to send me home."

Ivan Shuvalov made an almost imperceptible movement and the Empress stiffened.

"You ask me to send you back to Germany? Can I believe my ears? What devilish impudence is this, or are you unaware why I have sent for you?"

Catherine shook her head slowly.

"I only know that once again I am in your disfavour, and God above is witness that I have done nothing to deserve it! I find a sentry at my door, my rooms deserted, and rumours of my disgrace in every corner of the palace. I have neither slept nor eaten, and once Your Majesty has told me what my fault is supposed to be, then I pray you to return me to my family or I shall surely die of sadness and ill-treatment!"

It was the most insolent, astounding statement that had ever been delivered to Elizabeth in her life, and for a moment bewilderment and rage robbed her of speech. The accused was becoming the accuser; this woman, whose guilt had been drummed day and night into her tired ears by Shuvalov and Peter, knelt there with the air of a victim demanding restitution.

She was surely either mad or innocent.

"You ask what faults are charged against you?"

With relief the Empress heard her lover's voice taking up the interrogation.

"With Her Majesty's permission, I will acquaint you with them. . . ." He bent down and picked up a packet of papers which had been hidden in Elizabeth's gold wash-basin.

"These letters were found among the private correspondence of General Apraxin, who commands our forces on the Prussian front. Do you deny that you wrote them?"

Catherine glanced at them and held out her hand with an imperious gesture. "Until I have examined them myself, I cannot say whether they are mine or not!"

Despite himself Shuvalov reddened with anger. Would nothing daunt this insolent creature, who spoke to him as if he were little better than a lackey.

After a short scrutiny, Catherine returned the packet to him and addressed the Empress.

"Those are my letters, but surely Your Majesty is not displeased with the sentiments expressed in them?" Formal exhortations to bring glory to Russia and his sovereign by routing the Prussians were all that could be read into those epistles, except by one who knew the code message her words concealed.

Elizabeth scowled. "You know it is forbidden to write letters upon any matter of policy in peace or war! How dared you disobey by penning your damned scribblings to my General!"

Catherine bowed her head and bit her lip in contrition. "I was indeed wrong, but enthusiasm led me into error. . . . I beg you to forgive me."

Shuvalov threw the letters on to the Empress's dressing-table, and cut in quickly before the growing sense of anti-climax had time to dawn on Elizabeth.

"Do you deny that you intrigued with the former Chancellor Bestujev against the Empress? His guilt has been proved, and he was your close friend and confidante. Admit that you knew of his attempts to delay the despatch of imperial troops to Prussia! Admit that he is devoted to you and obeys you rather than his Czarina!"

Oh, no, my clever Shuvalov! Catherine thought to herself. I am not such a fool as to send Bestujev to the scaffold for you, and be convicted of complicity out of my own mouth at the same time. . . .

"The Chancellor was my sternest critic and indeed my enemy for many years. He merely relaxed his attitude towards me of late, that is all. I know nothing of any treason or disobedience to Her Majesty, and had I done so I should have revealed it at once!"

"Bestujev, too, is obstinate," remarked Elizabeth grimly. "As he persists in lying, I shall have him tortured. Then we will see what he will say; perhaps it would be as well if you were present, Madame, to remind him of the truth. . . ."

Only the throbbing of a small vein in her neck

209

betrayed the sickness and horror that enveloped the Grand Duchess at this awful threat. Torture was Elizabeth's favourite method of extracting information which she wished to hear; witnessing it had become quite a court pastime.

God help Bestujev; God pity his withered body and frail bones.

"By all means torture him, but if he says I knew of any treason towards Your Majesty, much less committed it, then I swear to you that he will be lying to put an end to his pain!"

Elizabeth stared down at her through narrowed, doubting eyes, and Catherine returned her look, fairly and without a hint of the fear she really felt.

"You speak honest words," the Empress muttered. "And you show the fortitude of innocence. . . ."

"Or the cunning of the Devil!"

It was Peter who had spoken, unable to hold his tongue a moment longer, while his victim gave every sign of wriggling out of the trap he had set for her.

"Be silent, curse you! Who told you to speak!" shouted the Empress suddenly, and Ivan Shuvalov laid a restraining hand on her shoulder. Trust that spiteful imbecile to interrupt at the wrong moment and irritate Elizabeth. . . . But the damage was done; Peter's precarious nervous balance fell to pieces under the strain of watching Catherine parry her questioners so skilfully and, without waiting any longer, he launched into his own personal attack upon her.

He advanced round Elizabeth's chair and pointed accusingly at his wife; his features were contorted with hate and his shrill voice echoed through the huge room.

"She lies!" he yelled. "She is guilty to her soul of every charge. Put her to the torture, never mind Bestujev! Tear the truth out of her, let her wriggle on the rack instead of in bed with her Pole!"

"I have warned you, Peter, hold your tongue," panted Elizabeth, striving for self-control. What a little monster he was, this nephew who would one day inherit her throne, shouting and twitching like a maniac.

"She kneels there, the hypocrite and harlot, deceiving you and acting the innocent! She begs to go home does she? Then I beg a favour too. She has a complaint to make has she? Well I have one to lay before you! My wife is an adulteress! She soils my marriage bed with a filthy Polish creature named Poniatowsky; he has been sleeping with her for nearly two years, coming up the servants' stairs to her room every night.

"The whole court knows of it, and I demand

that she be divorced and punished! She is a strumpet who makes no secret of her shame and my dishonour. And Poniatowsky is not the first—there was a certain Serge Saltykov . . .''

Elizabeth sprang from her chair and turned on him like a tigress.

''Not another word! Damn your lying soul to all eternity! What slanders would you cast in the name of spite? . . .''

Serge Saltykov, father of little Paul. Peter had been about to repudiate the child and name it bastard!

The Empress's breast heaved with fury and alarm, and all her deep-buried hatred of her nephew boiled up and overflowed. He accused Catherine of infidelity, he, the pock-marked, ill-shaped oaf. . . .

''I repudiate her,'' he shouted. ''She is no wife to me; let her be divorced and shut her up where she can do no harm!''

Catherine watched him fascinated, while hope and thanksgiving rose in her heart. What protecting star had put it into his mouth to mention Serge, thus touching the Empress on her most vulnerable spot?

The more he screamed and demanded, the angrier his aunt became, and with one of those intuitive flashes that had saved her from so many dangers, Catherine Alexeievna caught at Elizabeth's silken skirt for protection.

"So you would divorce Catherine, eh?" snarled Elizabeth, supporting herself on the edge of the dressing-table.

"And who would you put in her place? That pit-faced slut Vorontzova, who couldn't sit gracefully in a cowshed, much less on my mother's throne? Ah, you cunning, impudent dog, I know you, I read your black heart! This is the wife I chose for you, and your wife she remains until I decide otherwise. Chancellor Vorontzov! Come here!"

There was a rustling movement and the figure of Elizabeth Vorontzov's uncle stepped from behind the tall painted screen where he had been taking notes of the interview.

"Tell your niece that she can abandon her hopes of becoming Grand Duchess for as long as I live at any rate! Now go!"

The new Chancellor bowed in silence and left the room.

Peter watched him leave, and as the doors closed behind him, he stared down at Catherine, knowing in mingled rage and fear that once again the victory was hers.

His most cherished opportunity had come to nothing, his wife knelt there, clinging to the Empress's skirts while Elizabeth glared balefully at him, the husband and accuser.

Ivan Shuvalov met his wild glance and looked away hurriedly; Peter had torn down the last shreds of the net which they had drawn so carefully about Catherine and brought Elizabeth's wrath upon himself; the favourite cursed him mentally and edged away from him.

The failure had best lie his head where it belonged, and he, Shuvalov, must set about righting himself with the Grand Duchess.

The Empress stared from one to the other, and suddenly her plump fist descended with a crash among the glass and toilet articles on the table.

"Get out, both of you! Leave me!"

Catherine watched them go, Ivan Shuvalov, the ambitious would-be diplomat who had just learned the hard lesson of a man who discovers that he knows far less about his mistress than he thought, and the Grand Duke, his large head sunk in despair, shambling back to face the disappointed Vorontzova.

As soon as they were alone, she raised Elizabeth's hand to her lips and kissed it; at the same time, deciding that the time for self-control was past, she burst into a flood of tears.

The Empress sat down wearily, her swollen leg ached and her head throbbed as it always did when she lost her temper or became excited. She leant back and said nothing while Catherine wept helplessly at her feet.

What had become of the charges that had been levelled against her only an hour or more previously? Those terrible words, treason and adultery, had been cried out in impeachment; had they been answered? Somehow Elizabeth believed they had, how else could Catherine kneel there crying with relief? She was innocent, and the Empress was suddenly aware that she had never really wished her to be otherwise.

The shadow of death was on Elizabeth Petrovna, a thousand ghostly voices cried for justice, her countless lovers paraded before her conscience's eye, reminding her of the terrible sins of the flesh she had committed. Ivan, whose crown she had taken, still lived on in his prison, a breathing monument to her cruelty, a menace to the safety of the little Grand Duke Paul and the throne she intended him to occupy one day.

The time for petty jealousies and vanities was past; Catherine's youth and beauty had suddenly ceased to matter. The Empress no longer resented them, and the misunderstandings and wrongs of former years faded and died while the minutes ticked by and only the sound of the younger woman's sobs disturbed the silence in the room.

"Look at me, Catherine Alexeievna."

The Grand Duchess raised her head, wiping the tears away with her fingers:

"I look at you, Little Mother Elizabeth."

"Have you been true to me and to your country? Answer without fear or deceit: there is only time for truth between us now."

"I have been true; I swear it. I vow on my son's head that I have never been false to you, Elizabeth Petrovna, even in thought! As for Russia, for my country . . ." Catherine's face glowed with genuine feeling; "I would give my life to protect its interests!"

The Empress nodded. "I believe you, Catherine. I shall not ask you about this Poniatowsky; I warned you that there must be no scandal, and since there is a scandal he must go! Get up, child, and draw that stool near. I have been severe with you perhaps. . . ."

The Grand Duchess dismissed her life with the Tchoglokovs, her pathetic first love, the theft of her child, with a quick gesture of denial.

"But I am an old woman and my body aches and sickens for rest. I see Death before me and, because of the love I bore you when you came here as a girl, I would warn you. Look to yourself, Catherine, for when I am dead, Peter Feodorovitch will kill you. And I fear for the child Paul. It will go hard with both of you when my protection is no more."

The Empress's carmined lips tightened and she looked past Catherine into the shadows of the big draughty room, her eyes searching unhappily into the future, gazing on the vast rolling lands of Holy Russia and the nameless millions of her subjects.

They were her children and she must deliver them into the hands of Peter, who spoke of the German King Frederick as his lord and master, and whose drunken boasts that he would make a vassalage of her country had come all too frequently to the Empress's ears.

Every drop of Elizabeth's Russian blood cried out in protest of her father's crown being placed upon the head of such a man, and as her eyes settled once more on Catherine's face a fierce unhappy resolve was born in her.

Years ago at the Troitsky Convent she had spared the little Princess Augusta in the hope that she would bear a child, and the faint echo of her own secret thought returned to her. "If Peter has a son, then perhaps he need never succeed to the throne at all. . . ." Well, he had a son, the boy she had brought up and worshipped as her own, and why should not the diadem of Peter the Great encircle his brow instead of passing to the man whom the world politely acknowledged to be his father?

This clever, sharp-witted young woman who had displayed such admirable courage and resource that very night . . . . who better to destroy Peter and protect the little Grand Duke Paul than the estranged wife who knew her husband's succession to mean her own death?

So Elizabeth Petrovna's mind worked with shrewd and deadly cunning as she stared in silence at Catherine and found words with which to aid her plan.

Suddenly she leant forward and the candle-light bathed her face in a merciless glow, stripping away the painted facade of youth from her mouth and eyes, exposing the harsh patches of rouge on her sunken cheeks. The Empress reminded the watching Grand Duchess of a terrible animated skull, the bones clothed in flaccid, dying flesh, a glittering Death, grotesquely plump and bedizened like a frightened harlot.

"I fear to think of my country given into Peter's hands. I fear his madness for my enemy Frederick and the harm that he will do my people when the power of the Czars devolves upon him. . . .

"You, Catherine Alexeievna, you can give peace to my last days! Grow strong while there is yet time; form friends of influence while I still live to protect them and you!

"And not such men as Poniatowsky, for all his

pretty looks. You need men of different mettle. One man, if you will, who can stand at your elbow as Bestujev stood at mine in the days of my youth. Before he became corrupted and tried to act against me. I shall send him to Siberia for that! No, you shall not have Bestujev, you must find your own champion. But I should die with an easy mind if I believed that Russia would pass to my little Paul, with you as Regent!"

Despite herself, Catherine started to hear her most secret thoughts spoken aloud.

"We cannot usurp the throne, Your Majesty!"

Elizabeth laughed harshly.

"I shall name your son Czar in my will, when the time comes. Then it will be in your hands what you do. If I did not love my country and cherish my people, I would not deliver my sister's son into your mercy, Catherine, for if I'm any judge of woman, I think that you will show him little!"

"It is he who speaks of prisons and death, not I, Your Majesty!"

"Yes, he threatens, but by God you will act! Go now, Catherine Alexeievna, before I repent me of my treachery to my own blood. Go, and hold your tongue about what I have said to you. Those who covet a crown must have strong necks to bear its weight. Mine is already weakened to the point of death. Farewell!"

As the Grand Duchess walked quietly back to her own apartments, back through the same deserted corridors that she had trodden earlier that night, the squad of soldiers who had been kept in weary vigil to arrest her dispersed yawning to their quarters, and the closed carriage which had waited in a back courtyard of the palace, ready to carry the royal prisoner to some living grave, clattered empty away into the early dawn.

With his shaven head cradled on Elizabeth Vorontzov's huge breasts, the Grand Duke Peter wept and cursed himself into an uneasy sleep.

Catherine his wife had returned to her rooms a free woman and all his hopes and plans had come to naught again.

*   *   *

Catherine said farewell to Poniatowsky within a few short weeks. The scandal had subsided a little, and after endless waiting and precautions the lovers met for the last time before his return to Poland.

The separation and anxiety had been a nightmare to the Count. Loving Catherine as he did, he yet lacked the initiative and daring that had impelled another man to plan elopement when he knew her to be in danger. So he remained in his house in the capital until at last her messenger assured him that they might meet in safety.

In that same bedroom where he had known his first night of supreme happiness in her arms, Poniatowsky spent his last hours with her.

Elizabeth had spoken truly; with the insight of her long experience she had damned Catherine's lover in one brief descriptive phrase. What use had he been to her that night, what protection in her hour of mortal danger?

Time was short, and her search for the champion Elizabeth had counselled must begin. Bestujev, languishing in Siberia, now relied upon her triumph for release; his support was gone and replacement must be made.

Where in all Russia would she find a man strong enough to shake Peter Feodorovitch off his throne and place her on it, ostensibly deputizing for her son? Only force would avail in the end, and Catherine, bidding farewell to Poniatowsky on that grey morning, with the first streaks of daylight patterning the room, thought of the search ahead of her and despaired.

Where would she find such a man?

But in the end it was he who found her.

*   *   *

Many years earlier, in the days of Peter the Great, soldiers of the Strelitz Regiment had dared to mutiny. The insurrection failed and the ringleaders were lined up on a public scaffold one freezing winter's morning to pay the penalty for their crime. The headsman did his work under the eyes of the Czar, whose love of bloodshed went to such lengths that he had been known to take a hand with the axe himself on occasions.

It came to the turn of a gigantic Russian to kneel for execution, one Orlov, known throughout his regiment as a man without fear or respect for God or man. His booted foot disposed of the severed head of a comrade which happened to lie in his path, and the observation that he must make room for himself came clearly to the ears of his Czar.

Better even than horrors, Peter the Great loved bravery and the mutinous soldier was pardoned on the spot; he was transferred to the Guards, the *élite* regiments of the Russian army, and eventually became an officer and was ennobled.

So on a scaffold the fortunes of the Orlov family were founded, and it was at the Grand Ducal Palace at Oranienbaum that the grandson of the first Orlov and the daughter of the pious, humble Christian of Anhalt Zerbst met for the first time.

* * *

"I tell you Gregory, you must be mad! For

God's sake remember that the scandal over that damned Kurakin woman has scarcely died down."

The speaker lay at full length on a couch, his huge frame clad in military uniform covered the whole structure, and the side of his face, which was turned towards another figure outlined against the window, was fine-featured and singularly handsome. The other side, mercifully pressed against the cushion under his blonde head, was scarred from brow to chin by an old sabre cut.

Alexis Orlov, one of the three grandsons of the Strelitz ranker, was trying to instil caution into the head of his elder brother, who stood with his back to him, staring moodily out of the window on to the fair, green vista of the gardens at Oranienbaum.

Caution and Alexis were strange bed-fellows, and he inwardly despaired of dissuading his beloved brother from a course of action which he would most probably have pursued himself, had that accursed sabre scar not marred his chances.

"Wait until you have seen her yourself before you deliver any more of your damned lectures!" Gregory Orlov turned and faced his brother. He was startlingly handsome, fair and light-eyed and possessed of a magnificent physique. "As for the Kurakin, I got out of that, didn't I?"

"I could never understand why you didn't just

seduce the woman instead of risking your neck by kidnapping her under the nose of your Colonel. And you escaped the consequences of abducting his mistress because the Prussians were considerate enough to kill him for you at Königsberg!" returned Alexis shortly.

He laughed and seated himself at the head of the couch.

"She wouldn't be seduced, my dear Alex, and how was I to know that she'd sicken me within a week? Enough of that any way! Since I came here I've had no room in my head for memories of the fair Kurakin or any other woman. By to-morrow night you will have the evidence of your own eyes to convince you that our half-witted Grand Duke is married to the most fascinating creature in Russia!"

Alexis rolled over on the couch and closed his eyes.

"And he has an ugly, pock-marked mistress! But that doesn't mean he would lend his Grand Duchess to warm your sheets, my friend! Have affairs with every woman in Oranienbaum; you never have any difficulty; but for God's sake be wary before you begin pursuing this one. I can think of better ways to lose my head than over a wench, however high-born!"

Gregory swore and stamped out of the room.

He had been presented to her for the first time at a ball, and had never seen a more beautiful figure than the Grand Duchess in her crimson and gold brocade dress as she had proceeded down the lines of courtiers waiting to be received by her.

He had bowed low and kissed her hand like the rest, while his looks expressed admiration and desire with the boldness which had proved the downfall of so much female virtue in the past.

For a single moment her eyes, blue and vivid as his own, had met that impudent hunter's glance, and he knew beyond doubt that his message had been understood.

Since then he had seen her almost every day, at court, out riding, and walking with her ladies in the garden. She had conversed with him, graciously and without apparent guile, while the atmosphere of unspoken tension grew between them.

He wanted this woman; her tall, voluptuous body tormented him with angry longing, and the haughty, calculated wariness of her manners towards him filled him with a savage masculine desire to crush it out of her in the one situation where her sex and weakness could find no refuge in their different status.

Also he hated his Grand Duke and future Emperor.

To Gregory Orlov as to many others, Peter Feodorovitch was a German whose years in Russia had never succeeded in teaching him the language properly, whose habits and dress were insultingly foreign, and whose puny physique and drunken eccentricities were contemptible and strange to a people familiar with the bloody caprices of the Great Czar Peter and his daughter Elizabeth.

As a man, the Grand Duke's choice of mistress filled Gregory Orlov with angry scorn; he had a beautiful wife, and the pick of numerous pretty women if he liked variety, but the embraces of Elizabeth Vorontzov betokened a depravity beyond the healthy, vitual lusts of the handsome Gregory.

While Orlov fumed and sweated, Catherine Alexeievna was torn with doubts. The image of the blond Lieutenant of Guards burning into her brain, his hot blue eyes following her out of the shadows, the insistent voice of her own heart which declared that men of his kind were rare and valuable, urged her to make a move.

But yet she hesitated. Here was no powerful diplomat such as her necessity demanded, and there would not be room for two lovers in her life. She ought to wait, counselled her head, enquire about him and decide whether a few weeks of summer madness would be worth the risk.

He was superbly handsome, powerful as a bull,

deep-chested and broad-shouldered; he towered above her and touched her with impudent design, and at the thought of him she trembled and grew strangely weak.

No man had ever mastered Catherine, and though, womanlike, she loved the domineering male in theory, her independence shrank from him in the flesh. She had heard a great deal about Gregory Orlov and his brothers. The exploit with the lovely Countess Kurakin had caused a tremendous scandal, and the man capable of such brutal recklessness was not one to be trifled with or underestimated. If she relented and yielded to the undoubted fascination she felt for him, her freedom might be difficult to regain. All these considerations tormented her and fought against the growing inclination to be as other women and surrender.

Other men had loved her. Saltykov, Poniatowsky, Narychkin, whose careless manner concealed a burning passion which had never been assuaged. But none of them were men like Orlov; money would never buy him, gentleness was a quality entirely lacking in his nature, unsatisfied devotion to a woman would have roused only his contempt and disbelief.

Every look, every smile that lit his handsome arrogant face, mocked her for evading the inevitable, and careless of Peter's spiteful glares in her direction, careless of watchful eyes and growing gossip, Gregory contrived to be for ever at her side.

One evening the Grand Duke gave a masque: Catherine's excuse of a headache was violently disregarded and she was ordered to appear.

The Empress was in Peterhof, clinging obstinately to life and surrounding herself with the old court. In her absence Peter had planned an ominous revenge for Catherine's victory that night in Petersburg.

While Elizabeth lived the situation could not be altered, but few would mistake his intentions of future change after the night's entertainment. . . .

Catherine dressed with deliberate magnificence, sensing that her husband intended to place his mistress in the centre of the stage and it behoved her to attract attention.

Vladyslava fastened a gown of deep black velvet over a wide hoop; it was edged with ermine and revealed a brocade petticoat, stiff and shimmering with silver embroidery. A heavy necklace of rubies glittered round her throat and sparkled from her ears and wrists. Her black hair was piled high and a black mask edged with diamonds covered half her face.

The waiting-woman looked after her mistress

and shook her head. The gods had bestowed on her too many gifts: beauty, courage and brain. It would not be life as Vladyslava's long experience had proved it, if the possessor of them was not made to suffer in return.

*　　*　　*

The ballroom at Oranienbaum was small compared to the vast state-rooms at Moscow and Petersburg, but on that night it resembled Elizabeth's glory of setting in miniature. The chandeliers blazed with candles dripping scented wax, liveried servants lined the walls and the Grand Duke's personal orchestra played from a dais at the end of the room. The apartment was filled with masked figures, glitteringly dressed, and among them the Grand Duchess in her black gown stood out as if in mourning. Peter was already drunk and his eyes were bloodshot behind the satin mask; he, too, watched that unmistakable figure, conspicuous in its funereal magnificence, and he cursed her repeatedly.

The Vorontzova was grotesque in cloth of gold, her ungainly person blazing with precious stones all clustered together without style or taste. She had never looked more the mistress and Catherine more the future Empress, which was not what the Grand Duke had intended at all.

229

Orlov had not troubled to disguise himself; the full dress of the Guards' artillery and a plain mask comprised his costume and he leant against a long table drinking wine and watching the Grand Duchess.

There was something in the air; he sensed it in Peter's furtive, vindictive manner and the uneasy glances of his repulsive bed-fellow. Catherine was aware of it also; some strong undercurrent was present among that light-hearted company, and the rumours of a "surprise" during the evening did nothing to relieve her curiosity. She was sure of one thing; if Peter had had a hand in its inception, then the elements of the unpleasant and macabre were certain to be strong.

For some three hours they danced and drank, and Catherine looked on impassively while Peter led out a gavotte with Elizabeth Vorontzov. He had a mistress, and she had only to make one sign towards the man standing a few feet away with his eyes fixed on her and she could have a lover. . . .

Then at a sign from the Grand Duke the floor was cleared and chattering groups of courtiers assembled round the walls. This seemed to be the moment chosen by Peter for the highlight of his entertainment.

Catherine seated herself and opened her black

lace fan. She knew the nature of Peter Feodoro-vitch too well to view this secrecy and preparation without misgivings of some kind.

The first part of the entertainment proved to be a concert; the Grand Duke had discovered a singer whose voice pleased his ear, and Catherine, whose musical appreciation had been ruined for ever by those early ear-splitting recitals on the violin which had been her husband's favourite pastime under the Tchoglokov régime, sat listening to the performance in utter boredom. It seemed as if the lady's songs would never end, while the royal music lover sat there applauding vigorously.

But end they did, and Catherine watched with sudden interest while the lackeys prepared a stage, complete with items from the palace furniture, in the middle of the floor.

This then was Peter's surprise, a mummer show, and she leant forward quickly as the players came into the room, made their bows before her husband and herself and took their places on the improvised stage.

Peter's orchestra played softly in the back-ground, while the mummers enacted a domestic scene the nature of which caused Catherine's heart to beat with unaccustomed speed.

A husband and wife mimed their parts before the company, and the gilded crowns upon their heads proclaimed them to be no ordinary pair. It was gracefully done; indeed the actress taking the queen's role expressed the nature of the imaginary character in a way which left small doubt as to the personage's morals and demeanour.

Presently the lady's lover appeared upon the scene and, upon dismissal by the outraged husband, was swiftly replaced by another.

The room was suddenly very quiet, and Catherine's fan closed with a tiny snap.

With a swift pattering of feet, a troupe of mummer soldiers came running; they crowded the stage and laid stern hands upon the adulterous, protesting queen, while something like a murmur of horrified comment whispered through the assembled court. The orchestra had ceased playing and Catherine was aware of two things: Peter was leaning forward in his chair and not even the mask concealed the hate which contorted his features, and Gregory Orlov had moved close behind her.

In absolute silence the Grand Ducal Court watched the miming of Catherine's rumoured love affairs and the punishment which Peter had devised for them, until the mummer company came back, bowing before Peter, and knelt in homage with arms outstretched.

After a second's pause the Grand Duke rose to

his feet, caught Elizabeth Vorontzov by the hand and walked with her towards the stage. Every drop of colour drained from Catherine's face as he took the sham mummer's crown and placed it on his mistress's head.

Still there was silence until Peter himself turned towards the Vorontzova and began to clap. Then thunders of polite applause broke out, and the Grand Duke paused before his wife and glared down at her defiantly.

"I hope, Madame, that you enjoyed the play. I wrote it myself!"

Catherine looked up at him and her voice was harsh with anger.

"I congratulate you, Sir! But the authorship of a morality play befits you strangely—I consider your entertainment in false and questionable taste!" Dignity in such a situation would be merely weakness, and sufferance of that insult and all it implied to her was impossible.

Without another word she rose, swept her husband a frigid curtsy and walked swiftly down the room. The lackeys sprang forward and opened the doors for her, and before they swung to behind her, Catherine heard a buzz of voices rising in the ball-room.

Let them comment! Let Peter fume at her behaviour! Let him arrest her now! As she mounted the staircase to her own apartments she discovered suddenly that she was crying. Her limbs were trembling and she leant against the portals of her own door for support, shaken by a storm of nervous terror. . . .

"I think you dropped your fan, Madame."

Catherine swung round and found him standing right behind her, noiseless as a cat, her black fan in his hand.

"Thank you . . . Count Orlov," she whispered and, in a last attempt at composure, nodded and turned to open the door and go in. But his arm shot out and his fingers found the handle first, so that Catherine stood imprisoned between his body and the door which he held shut.

For a moment Gregory Orlov looked down at her pale face, the tears streaming down her cheeks under the mask, and saw that her mouth trembled. Despite her height, she was small compared to him, a woman who had left that ballroom in a truly imperial rage only to weep with the weakness of her sex when out of sight, a woman humiliated and threatened in a way that made Orlov long to tear his Grand Duke limb from limb.

The victory was his and he knew it. She was alone and helpless and the strength which emanated from him was breaking her down; the corridor was deserted, it was the small hours, and in the laxness of Oranienbaum there was not a lackey in sight.

He gave her no time to cry out, even though he knew in his heart that she would not have done so.

His arms went round her in an embrace of crushing force and he bent her head back at the same moment, kissing her mouth, tasting the salt tang of her recent tears.

The frustrated passion of his long pursuit welled up in a furious tide streaked with tenderness and rage; in a haze he became aware that her hands had ceased to beat against him in a futile protest. They had entwined about his neck, and his great fingers sank into her shoulders as he felt her response.

For one brief moment Catherine almost fainted while a fire of longing enveloped her whole body and her consciousness wavered under the fierce strength of his embrace and the painful pressure of his kisses.

Then quickly he flung the door open and half lifted her inside. The room was in darkness except for a fire burning in the grate, and Vladyslava lay asleep in another room, waiting for her mistress's bell.

Orlov tore the mask from his eyes and ripped Catherine's away.

"Do you come to me of your own free will? Do

you accept my protection from this day onward?"

With shaking hands Catherine tried to loose the ruby necklace which had been pressed into her skin in that wild encounter in the corridor; for a moment she could find no words for the tumult of emotions which possessed her. Accept his protection, live however briefly in the arms of a man who had stormed and taken her with the ruthless abandon of a marauding Cossack. . . .

"God help you, if you love me!" she panted. "After what you saw to-night—have you no fear?"

Orlov laughed and caught her in his arms; with a swift movement he tore the necklace from her throat. "I love you, Catherine; and believe me, I have no fear!"

The night hours ticked away and Vladyslava snored peacefully on her mattress in the disrobing room, undisturbed by the Grand Duchess's bell.

The grandson of the common soldier who had earned death for mutiny, and the daughter of the modest provincial German Prince of Anhalt lay in each other's arms, until it seemed to Catherine as if Orlov gave her death, and that they drowned in their own passion, only to rise above the seas as by a miracle, bruised, shattered, breathless, but alive.

CHAPTER 10

DURING the long hot afternoons at Oranienbaum, while Peter and the rest of the household slept or played cards in the high-shaded rooms, Catherine slipped out of her apartments and kept a daily rendezvous with her lover.

In the seclusion of the old Summer Pavilion, situated in the centre of a large lake and screened by trees and wilderness, Orlov waited for her, watching for the small boat to cross from the mainland, rowed by a taciturn boatman who accepted the roubles his pretty passenger gave him and asked no questions even as he answered none.

The pavilion was in disrepair, and had long ceased to be frequented by any who stayed at Oranienbaum; there was no safer place in the whole palace, and Catherine had managed to secure some furniture and a low couch for an inner room.

There Gregory received his mistress, and when the storm of their love-making had at length subsided, he would lie beside her on the ottoman, her dark head on his chest, and play absently with long strands of fine black hair, wondering what magic lay in her embraces that with each passing day and hour he loved and wanted her the more.

Love was an emotion new to his experience; physical passion was as natural and essential to him as the air he breathed, but women never roused in him the instincts of protection and concern. Once the mistress of the moment had left his arms, Orlov turned carelessly to other pleasurable pursuits, whether they were bounded by the card-table or the battlefield.

But this woman was not one to be so dismissed.

Away from her or at her side, she obsessed his thoughts even as she dominated his desires. Catherine alone could satisfy him, and one fact only permitted his arrogant spirit to bear this servitude with patience. She was bound with bonds as fierce as those which shackled him. He had allowed no reservations, and the proud Grand Duchess, with her superior mind and cultural veneer, had been forced into abject surrender from which there was no possible return.

Gregory had mastered her and she loved him hopelessly. She loved him because he was coarse-tongued and honest, because he was brutal and masculine and in the grip of his own passions treated her with savage disrespect, because in his barbarian soul she knew he loved her in a primitive, uncomprehending way, and because in all his reckless life he had never known fear.

He was cruel and driven by ambition, pitiless towards the weakling or the coward, ruthless and quick-witted.

There were times when Catherine almost hated him for the way in which he read her thoughts, sensing the secret hopes of the succession which sometimes whispered across the surface of her mind when they were alone together. He knew her better than she knew herself and stripped the illusions of courtesy and charm from her character with laughter and contempt.

With him she practised no diplomacy; he spoke her thoughts aloud and there was little difference between them when he voiced his own.

"I love you for four reasons, my Catrina," he said one day. Catherine turned her head towards him and smiled.

"Tell them to me."

"Because you are beautiful, because you love like a Siberian tigress in spite of all your book-learning, because you are brave, and because you are going to be Empress of Russia!"

"I think my husband plans it otherwise! Will I be all these things to you when I'm in prison? Or will you make love to Elizabeth Vorontzov instead?"

Orlov pulled her down to him and kissed her. After a moment he pushed her aside and sat up.

"To the devil with your husband and his plans! I tell you 'tis time we made a few plottings on our own account. Act now, and I'll wager a year's pay that that crazy German cockerel will end in his own dungeon while you take his throne. Then you can do what you like with the Vorontzova!" he added.

Catherine shook her head.

"You are too impetuous, Gregory. The Empress is still living, and there is always her promise that she will name my son as her successor. I believe that she will keep her word, and when her wishes are made public it will be time enough to show our hand.

"Since I have you, nothing in heaven or hell can daunt me. Only give me time to strengthen my own forces within the court itself, find me an ally among the ministers, and prepare the way by stealth. When the moment comes, then you shall have all the action that that Tartar's heart of yours desires!"

Orlov got up and walked to the long window, where the rays of the setting sun streamed in and bathed his wrestler's body in a flood of warm golden light.

"You are a clever woman, mistress of my soul," he remarked after a moment. "And I admire your cleverness. But all knowledge does not come from books and ball-room intrigues; you speak of friends with influence, of building a strong faction of your own. . . ."

He turned round suddenly and stared at her.

"What greater strength could you have than the army?" he said softly. "What revolution, including the little affair which placed our glorious Empress on the throne, has ever taken place without the Guards?"

Catherine frowned, mentally conceding him the point, remembering that all the ministerial protection of Russia had failed to save Ivan from Elizabeth and her handful of soldiers.

"That is the truth. Yet how am I to enlist the army in my favour? I am not even Russian."

"Pah! Leave that to me; I'll sing your praises in the barrack rooms and messes until every little soldier in the regiment knows your fame! My brothers will take care of the army. Once win over the Guards, my Catherine, and the crown of Russia is as good as placed upon your head!"

"Yes, the army and the people. I need them both, Gregory, and from my heart I believe that they need me! I know too well what Peter Feodorovitch intends for them. . . ."

She rose and went to him, putting her arms around his neck, standing on tiptoe to reach his face.

"In a few days we leave for Petersburg, beloved, and our freedom with each other will be much reduced. But we will not be idle. We will work hard, you and I, that the day may come when Peter will have no power to separate us. Promise me, Gregory Gregorovitch, that you will make no move, that you will guard yourself and me for still a little while?"

Orlov held her close and his great arms trembled.

"Even in Petersburg, I shall find a way to see you every day. And to-night I will see my brothers and speak to them of the things we have decided."

*   *   *

In his own rooms in the palace, the Grand Duke sat playing cards and drinking quantities of beer. The windows were tight shut, and a blue haze of pipe tobacco hung heavily in the airless chamber. Elizabeth Vorontzov sat at her lover's elbow, her attention wandering from the play; she was hot and rather drunk and the prospect of their return to the capital depressed her.

Stiff, etiquette-ridden Petersburg, with all its attendant drawbacks of waiting on the Grand Duchess and moving under the Empress's jaundiced eye, had yet another disconcerting aspect.

Her young and lovely sister, whose wealthy

marriage had thrust the Vorontzova into the background until Peter's choice had fallen on her, was coming to court; and if there was one other woman whom she hated more than the Grand Duchess it was the fiery intellectual, Princess Dashkov.

Peter was merry that day; his reedy laughter echoed through the room and his limbs twitched with nervous energy. All was well with Peter's world that afternoon; the thought of assuming Elizabeth's crushing burden of responsibility and power, the unmanly qualms that Catherine's presence contrived to inspire in him, fear, indecision and sickness were distant and forgotten. The day and the hour were happy for him and utterly free from the morbid cares which normally beset him. But faint and indistinct as yet, the shadows had begun to gather about the head of Peter Feodorovitch.

*   *   *

It was Leo Narychkin who introduced the eighteen-year-old Princess Dashkov to the Grand Duchess.

The Dashkova was not a woman whom he could admire, despite her rare culture and intelligence. She was the sister of Elizabeth Vorontzov, and Narychkin instinctively withheld his trust on that account, and her dark, intense good looks did not appeal to him.

Yet when Princess Dashkov, gazing up at him with bright, intent brown eyes, asked for an introduction to the Grand Duchess whose charm and beauty were greater even than rumour painted them, Narychkin repressed the desire to despatch the lady to her sister with her request, and himself mentioned the new-comer to Catherine.

As always she greeted him with a smile and her expression told of a genuine affection that in its very innocence struck Narychkin to the heart. And while she spoke, he sensed immediately the change in her.

Never, even in Saltykov's day, had such an air of confidence and happiness radiated from her. The assurance she possessed came neither from her status nor the knowledge of her beauty. She moved and talked and laughed with the glowing poise of a woman supremely satisfied in love, and it seemed to him as if her liaison with Orlov shrieked its presence aloud to every man or woman who had eyes to see.

Of course she would receive the princess, and her full lips twisted mischievously; as a source of common interest there was always the charming Mlle Vorontzov to discuss. . . .

But the subject of Peter's mistress never arose

between them at that first meeting; to her astonishment Catherine found herself conversing with someone whose knowledge and precocity made an excellent foil to her own talents.

The young princess, slightly built and a head shorter than the Grand Duchess, had the air of a studious schoolgirl as she stood looking up at the older woman, her brown eyes wide and serious, her remarks accompanied by quick, nervously impatient gestures, while the imperial court stood by and watched them in cynical amazement.

The sister of her enemy and rival hung on Catherine's every word, and her reluctance to end the interview was both genuine and flattering.

The friendship and distinterested admiration of a woman was something new in Catherine's chequered experience of the vagaries of human nature, and the irony of the situation made her smile.

On the one hand Peter's grotesque bed-fellow, ugly and gross-mannered as the lowest strumpet who roamed the city's streets and alleys after dark; on the other, this serious vital girl, her youthful mind burdened with learning even as Catherine's own had been during the tyranny of Mme Tchoglokov, her innocent virtue charged with the idealism and fanatic principles of one whom time had yet to disillusion.

And her heroine was Catherine; the Grand Duchess, beautiful, gracious, gifted with a tongue as scintillating as her mind and garbed in the tragic robes of an ill-treated wife, became the model of fine womanhood, the symbol of that tolerance and feminine superiority at which the Princess Dashkov aimed herself.

So in the weeks and months that followed, every instinct of her passionate, partisan nature fastened upon Catherine as an object for the pent-up love and hero-worship which had searched in vain for a satisfactory outlet. The Princess Dashkov, with all the ardour of her years and temperament, settled down at Petersburg to the championing of a cause.

And the cause was Catherine Alexeievna, abominably treated by a half-wit husband, whose disloyalty to his country was only equalled by his cruelty to his wife.

The Dashkova was a mere girl, but she was a passionate nationalist and no one denied that despite her pedantry and stainless reputation, she was clever and observant. She was also reckless, in the cold-blooded way of martyrs and great gamblers, and it was not very long before Catherine discovered that her plan with Orlov had also occurred to the calculating Katrina Dashkov, and that even as Gregory left her arms in the early morning to continue his work of sounding the army in her favour, so the charming companion of her leisure hours occupied her time in careful probings among Elizabeth's ministers.

At first the Grand Duchess attempted to dissuade her, fearful that in her youth and enthusiasm the girl might draw suspicion upon herself and her protectress, but the princess shook her small dark head and smiled.

"Believe me, Highness, I know how to guard my tongue! I would it were torn out at the roots before it caused you harm by even a single word."

The two were seated in Catherine's boudoir, talking and sipping hot chocolate, and the Grand Duchess regarded the speaker quietly over the rim of her porcelain cup.

"If my husband had his way you would be sister to the Czarina; would that mean nothing to you? Why would you prefer my cause to that of your own flesh and blood?"

The Dashkova set down her cup hurriedly.

"Elizabeth may be of my blood, our mother was the same but as to the fatherhood, God knows! As a sister she means nothing to me; she is an ignorant slut with a mind as graceless as her body. I hate her because she has made you suffer and added to your humiliations. I love and admire you, my dearest Madame, as the most wonderful

247

woman I have ever met, but your patience terrifies me. The Empress is sick again; what if she dies and Peter becomes Czar? What will befall you?"

Catherine smiled and stroked the princess's arm, for she was trembling with agitation.

"Your friendship has touched me deeply, my little Katrina, and I am aware of your wisdom, but for the moment I can do nothing. Peter threatens, he has done little else since the day of our wedding, and I must know well whom I can trust before I dare to think of action."

"I will find out those on whom you can rely, Highness. Everyone talks to me. They think me young and innocent, but they know how I adhere to you and many will hint to me what they dare not suggest to you. In fact there is one person whom I suspect to be a staunch a friend to you as he is enemy to the Grand Duke. . . ."

"And who is that?" Catherine questioned, suddenly alert.

"Your son's tutor, Count Nikita Panin!"

Panin, fat as Bestujev was thin and dry, unctuous and power-loving, in favour with the Empress and reputed to be ambitious for his charge—was he really well-disposed towards her? There might be truth in the princess's words, and Catherine recognized that the friendship of one so close to Elizabeth and with a finger in several ministerial posts would be invaluable. It would be well to seek him out.

Late that afternoon the Dashkova took her leave, and Catherine pondered with quiet amusement whether the entrance of a lover into the princess's life might not cool her devotion towards her friend.

How horrified the girl would be, still entrenched in mental virginity, if she were to discover that her idol often wore a fichu because her arms and breasts were marked by the impetuous brutality of Gregory Orlov, that the fair Catherine, garbed in vestal purity by her sycophant's jealous imagination, spent hours of passionate love-making, wild and abandoned as a Tartar woman of the steppes, in the fierce arms of the most notorious gallant in Russia.

Orlov came to her as often as he dared and, sitting together in her firelit chamber with Vladyslava keeping faithful vigil outside the door, he told his mistress of the progress of their plans. Grudgingly he admitted her caution to be well founded; the army murmured against the war, the lack of food and money, and the general corruption in high circles which was costing many soldiers' lives, but their loyalty to the Empress was as strong as ever.

Whatever the disasters that befell their arms,

the pious Elizabeth, Little Mother of her people, still held their hearts with the legend of her vanished beauty. Rumours had reached the war front that she lay sick and near to death, and though many voices had been raised in curses against the thought of her nephew's assumption of imperial authority, yet no serious move to counteract the possibility was made.

The regiments at Petersburg had as little love for Peter as their comrades who were that moment fighting his beloved Frederick, but no revolt was really contemplated. They hated the Grand Duke and suspected his loyalty, but they knew of no one who could take his place.

That was where the Orlovs could provide a remedy.

Had nobody heard of Peter's wife . . . and son? The Grand Duchess was proclaimed the most ardent patriot next to Elizabeth herself, a woman whose beauty was only equalled by her brain and courage.

Alexis and his brothers, sensible of the glory such a boast reflected upon them, let it be widely known that the persecuted Catherine had fled to the arms of a Russian officer of the Guards for consolation in her misery and protection for her person.

Gregory, with money supplied to him from

Catherine's purse, toasted her health in rivers of wine, and before long his position as her lover was a matter of personal pride throughout the army.

And through the mouth of Alexis Orlov a picture of the Grand Duke began to take ominous shape in the minds of his listeners. Peter was an imbecile, a drunken treacherous foreigner who threatened to deliver the whole country into German hands as soon as power was his. He wanted to ban the Church, the Orlovs declared with blasphemous oaths, and their listeners crossed themselves with superstitious horror. The whole army would be trained and uniformed in imitation of the hated Prussians, and at this threat there were many who sprang to their feet with drawn swords.

Catherine, the atheist disciple of Montesquieu and Voltaire, was painted as the guardian of orthodox religion, the generous-hearted, hot-blooded patroness of soldiers, whose only longing was to drown the German King and his forces in a sea of their own blood.

Of Paul Petrovitch a good deal less was said. He was the prop upon which the legitimists could hang the crown if they wished; but the true focus point for discontent became his mother, the Grand Duchess.

While Gregory and his brothers formed the core

of revolt within the military, Princess Dashkov's observations about Nikita Panin bore rewarding fruit.

The ailing Elizabeth received a humble request from Catherine that she might see her little son, and the Empress was too sick and low-spirited to refuse.

The Grand Duchess could expect a visit from the boy and his tutor the following afternoon.

Catherine dresssed carefully for that interview, and her rôle was one of maternal dignity and solicitude. No hint of the flamboyance which had enslaved Gregory in the hours of their intimacy must mar the impression she wished to make upon the worthy Panin.

The Count was a man in middle years, and over-indulgence at table had clothed his face and body in a cocoon of fat. Like many obese people, he moved lightly with almost cat-like grace, and his sharp, small green eyes appraised his hostess with inward admiration.

She looked charming in her white wrapper, youthful yet serious, and at first glance one might find the tales of her promiscuity difficult to believe.

But Panin was not concerned with Catherine's virtue and his nature rendered him safe from her sensuous appeal. From previous formal contact with her, he had formed a particular opinion of her character and talents, and a great deal depended upon whether this private interview would strengthen or dispel the illusions which he cherished concerning her.

He stood back and waited while Catherine went forward to embrace her son.

The little Grand Duke Paul regarded his mother with suspicious eyes; this tall handsome woman was to all intents and purposes a stranger to him, though her name was among those automatically included in his nightly prayers.

She was his mother but he did not know her; she had never held him on her knee or carried him in her arms, her lips had never bestowed one kiss upon him and, as she advanced towards him, he shrank from her.

Where was his adored "mother Elizabeth", she who had nursed and cared for him since birth? For a moment he stiffened as his mother put her arms around him and touched his small cheek with her mouth; mercifully the embrace was short, and Catherine straightened up, one hand placed on his head in a gesture of maternal affection which she was far from feeling.

Her glimpses of the child had been rare and her memory of him vague; now in the privacy of her own drawing-room she looked at him, and a spasm of superstitious horror enveloped her.

With her eyes on the boy, Catherine wondered what hideous irony of fate had bestowed fair hair upon Saltykov's son; the child of lovers whose colouring was dark as night was blond-headed and milky-skinned, his pale blue eyes were prominent and his small, weakling body and truculent expression bore a stamp of impossible familiarity.

Paul Petrovitch resembled neither of his parents.

Some frightful trick of fate had fashioned him in the image of the Grand Duke Peter. Only Catherine's iron self-control kept her hand on his head and forced a smile to her stiff lips. Angrily she shook off the superstition that had overwhelmed her, and the thought raced through her mind that the boy was some changeling, a bastard of Peter's whom Elizabeth had substituted for her son—any explanation rather than the fact that it was possible for Peter Feodorovitch to be reproduced in the person of a child he had never fathered.

Count Panin watched her closely and, aware of his scrutiny, the Grand Duchess turned to him and bade him sit down; then her strong fingers caught the child's hand and drew him to a sofa.

The little Grand Duke climbed up on to the brocade seat and sat stiffly, regarding his buckled shoes and wishing that his mother would release him. Decidedly, he did not like her.

Catherine smiled at the Count in her most charming manner.

"My son is indeed a credit to your care, my dear Count Panin," she said. "It is a great comfort to me to know that he is in your charge while the Empress is ill."

"I am most grateful to you, Highness. I find him an admirable child; obedient, intelligent and good natured. Well fitted for his future destiny," the tutor answered, and his little eyes glinted at the Grand Duchess.

If he had indeed made an overt gesture by that remark, Catherine intended to probe his meaning further. She looked down at the boy, whose small hand was still clasped unwillingly in hers, and sighed audibly.

"There are times, Count, when my Paul's destiny seems unhappily obscure. Dearly as I love him, I fear that my husband is somewhat lacking in paternal feeling. . . ."

Panin eased himself back in the fragile gilt chair and crossed one plump leg over the other. He had been right in his supposition after all; Catherine and he had one idea in common. He knew of Elizabeth's plans for Paul; she had told him of them herself, and he approved with all his heart.

The more his shrewd eyes saw of the Grand Duke, the less he wished to see him mount the throne as Czar.

Now he must sound the feelings of the indomitable mother of the little Czarevitch, the smiling, gracious Catherine who had played a sinister waiting game for all these years.

She must be Regent; the Empress had so named her, and Nikita Panin could think of no man better fitted to assist her ministry during Paul's minority than himself.

"It is unfortunate that the Grand Duke has such little liking for his son. It is a great grief to Her Imperial Majesty; she fears for his safety when her nephew becomes Czar. . . ."

Catherine released the boy and turned right round to face the speaker. The pretence was wearing thin between them, and she decided upon a bold move.

"As a mother, Count, my love for my child transcends even my duty to my husband; I would that neither he nor Russia should fall under the absolute dominion of the Grand Duke!"

Panin lowered his eyes, wondering whether to speak of Elizabeth's intentions then or hold his hand until another day; it was almost certain that Catherine knew of them, and if she did, then she would doubtless mention the matter herself.

"There are many, Madame, whose esteem of yourself and loyalty to your son incline them to a similar view. . . ."

Catherine rose to end the interview and the boy jumped down and ran to his tutor, eager to escape. Panin raised Catherine's hand to his lips and bowed as deeply as his bulk would allow.

"I hope that Your Highness will honour me with a further audience; we might discuss the most suitable subjects for the education of the future Czar."

The Grand Duchess's smile did not quite extend to her eyes, but her response was perfect.

"By all means; attend upon me as soon as you wish, my dear Count. And perhaps you would accord me a little favour?" The tutor nodded blandly, his instincts sharp with suspicion.

"I must not correspond with prisoners, you understand. But if you should send a message to the former Chancellor Bestujev, remind him that Catherine Alexeievna will always be his friend. . . ."

As the Count led his charge back to the suite adjoining Elizabeth's, he remarked to himself that the Grand Duchess evidently did not forget her friends when disaster overtook them. She had not forgotten Bestujev in his disgrace, and those words were a clear promise that she would secure his release at the first opportunity.

If Elizabeth Petrovna's will was enforced, as Panin and others intended it should be when the hour arrived, then the old Chancellor would return to Petersburg. It behoved Panin to become quite indispensable to the future Regent in the meantime.

*   *   *

Alone in her room, Catherine walked to the window and stood staring absently out on to the view of trees and lawns, meticulously laid out and threaded by narrow ribbons of pathway, flanked by the broad shining waters of the Neva; down below small figures moved like toys, court ladies taking an afternoon walk; a platoon of uniformed guards marched under her window and disappeared into the palace; all about her the life of Petersburg went on, heedless of the growing drama which was unfolding day by day in its midst.

Whatever the Empress's will, she had never meant to keep to it for more than a few short months. Let Elizabeth depose her nephew in favour of the boy Paul; let Catherine assume the mantle of temporary authority which she could declare had been thrust upon her as a duty; let Nikita Panin believe her willing and eager for this compromise; once Peter was gone without the tumult of revolution, Orlov and she would know how to deal with her small son and his faction.

But the Dashkova had been mistaken about Panin; he was no friend to Catherine, but the emissary of a third party which had grown up secretly at court; the patriots who wished to see Paul Petrovitch ascend the throne. They needed the Grand Duchess for the completion of their scheme, and she in turn needed them for the furtherance of hers.

She and Orlov would welcome Panin and his unprepossessing little charge into their conspiracy, and Catherine smiled grimly at the thought.

Catherine looked down through the window. This city, dominated by its vast palace, the teeming populace which had won her heart and wrung it with pity for the poverty and the burden of slavery which oppressed it, all the vast dusty plains of Russia, parched with heat in summer, frozen and limitless in their mantles of winter snow, the savagery and barbarism, the humility and magnificence of Holy Russia, one day it would all be hers.

Hers by right of conquest and by the right of love; for she loved it as Peter Feodorovitch hated and feared it. They had become her people, mixed of race and strange of custom, antithesis of the bleak, ordered Germans who had left her young imagination uninspired.

The dying Empress, enslaved by her own distorted passions and unhealthy fears of hell and punishment, the Grand Duke, his feeble brain tottering under the weight of suspicions and excesses which his mistress had not the sense to discourage, smooth-tongued Panin, with his straining paunch and cunning eyes—she, Catherine, was a match for them all. . . .

Suddenly the colourful pattern of the gardens beneath her window became blurred. She caught at the wall to steady herself as the whole scene shifted and began to recede; the ground seemed to melt under her shaking legs, perspiration broke out over her face and a wave of sickness preceded the blackness which enveloped her as she fell.

*   *   *

Vladyslava found her lying unconscious on the floor by the window, and the waiting-woman revived her where she lay.

Catherine came to her senses slowly, and for a moment her eyes followed the other woman in her ministrations with a curiously frightened look. Cushions had been piled under her head and her dress had been opened to facilitate her breathing.

Vladyslava smiled at her and held a cup of water to her lips. Catherine frowned, fighting off nausea, trying with all her strength to deny the horrible suspicion which was fast taking possession of her. Vladyslava destroyed her last illusion when she spoke.

"Forgive me for not putting you to bed, Highness, but when I found that you had fainted I thought it wiser not to call for help. You will be well enough in a moment. 'Twas sickness, was it not?" Her mistress nodded.

"Then it is as I thought. Better for you that none should know just yet and go tattling round the court. Come now, Madame, raise yourself and lie upon your bed. I remember that it was like this with you before, when you carried the little Grand Duke Paul. . . ."

Catherine lay on the big canopied bed and wept with helpless fury.

This then was nature's price for the passionate ecstasy which Gregory had given her within the darkness of these same brocaded curtains and upon the softness of this mattress.

On the eve of the most decisive period in her life, she was pregnant.

*   *   *

For the first few months the Grand Duchess became something of a recluse; she pleaded poor health openly and spent hours lying on her couch or driving slowly in her carriage. The gossips would have soon remarked upon her pallor and listlessness, and the cause would have been guessed immediately, but Catherine forestalled them. She declared herself ill and the declaration was accepted without interest.

Vladyslava alone witnessed the convulsions of sickness which racked her and observed the signs of advancing pregnancy in her body. Her ladies never saw her undressed and her thickening contours were perfectly concealed by the swaying hoops and voluminous skirts which fashion had made a godsend to the presevation of feminine secrets such as hers.

The Grand Duke rejoiced at the decline in his wife's health; the Dashkova, kept in judicious ignorance of the truth, mourned and redoubled her attentions to her friend; and Panin took advantage of the period to have many discreet conversations with the Grand Duchess. His vision of himself as chief minister during the Regency grew clearer with every visit, and before long he was able to present Catherine with a list of court nobles and officials who would support her son's claim against Peter.

The Grand Duchess thanked him warmly and added the names to those already compiled by Princess Dashkov.

The princess was proving an invaluable ally; she had made many friends among the serious-minded and her infatuation for the Grand Duchess began to spread to her intimates. Catherine's explanation of Panin's plan had caused her to stamp with rage.

Why waste time with a six-year-old boy when the true ruler of Russia, ordained by God and born for the task, was at hand in the person of his mother?

But the Dashkova was a child of the great world; at eighteen she was well schooled in intrigue and her shrewd scholar's mind had been trained to dissemble as well as to reason; she saw and agreed with her beloved friend's attitude towards Count Panin and, with a ruthlessness almost the equal of Catherine's own, prepared to use him before the time came to enlighten him as to the end for which he had really been working.

There were mornings when the Grand Duchess took her drive alone and, once out of sight of the palace, her coachman would turn off in the direction of a solitary house some versts from the centre of Petersburg and slow his horses until they ambled gently.

He was a good servant and devoted to his mistress; Catherine had once discovered him listening outside her door some years before and, departing from her usual courtesy, had furiously boxed his ears. This truly regal gesture had won her a follower for life, and when the door of the house opened and a handsome giant in Guards uniform sprang into the carriage, the Grand Duchess's coachman neither looked to left nor right, but whipped up his horses and drove until his mistress gave the order to return.

These meetings with her lover were an indispensable part of Catherine's life, while she carried his child. The old nightmare of Saltykov and desertion haunted her and made Orlov's presence a luxury which she refused to do without.

Those many mornings Catherine flung herself into his arms and submitted desperately to his embraces, conscious that his treatment of her was angry and ungentle.

Often he hurt her and cursed savagely at the child she bore, and Catherine's heart leapt with perverse joy. Orlov wanted her; no glimmer of paternal feeling stirred in him. The babe whose claim on his affection she had dreaded so jealously, was to him a damnable trick played upon them by a malignant Fate.

Again and again he urged her to rid herself of the burden. "Come, Catherine, make an end of it! 'Tis impossible for you to have a brat at this time; God's blood, if this is discovered, Peter

Feodorovitch will have you walled up alive for adultery! I tell you it is madness. . . ."

Catherine, her head resting against his shoulder, would smile in firm refusal. "I know all these things, my love, and I am no more pleased than you. But the risk of discovery is not so great. The sickness is gone and I show no signs that careful dressing does not perfectly conceal. Peter shall never hear so much as a cry when the time comes; I have made all arrangements. Also I cherish my life; what you suggest would like as not mean death, and I'll not die even for the joy of being beautiful again for you!

"Wait, Gregory, have patience. Only a few short months and I shall be light of our child, shapely and pleasing to you again, and ready to act when the time comes."

So she promised and placated while the closed carriage sped on its unobtrusive way until it paused once more by the house where Orlov parted from her. But the time was to come sooner than she or anyone else had anticipated.

On the 25th of December, 1761 (January 5th, 1762, by the English calendar), Elizabeth Petrovna died.

CHAPTER II

THE ante-rooms of the Czarina's suite were crowded; Elizabeth's subjects had gathered silently in accordance with the custom of their time to await the death of the sovereign and the proclamation of her successor. Catherine stood in the chamber immediately adjoining the Empress's bedroom.

A silver crucifix was clasped in her hands and her eyes were closed as if in prayer; many among the great nobles and ministers who thronged that stuffy room were kneeling, and there were some who wept.

The Grand Duchess stood stiffly, her back against the gilded wall, watching the door to Elizabeth's bedroom through half-closed eyes.

Within were four people; the Empress, stretched upon the death-bed she had fought so long, the favourite Ivan Shuvalov, whose hour of power was done, her Chancellor Vorontzov, and the priest who had come hurrying from the Imperial Chapel to comfort his royal mistress on her journey into the unknown.

The Grand Duke Peter Feodorovitch was also in that inner ante-room, and he stood insolently with his arms folded, glancing around him with an air of defiant good humour.

This was among the happiest days of his life, in that it marked the death of the woman who had domineered and overshadowed his existence for more than twenty years. His aunt was dying, surrounded by her superstitions and idolatries, none of which could save her from the dread, common fate of man; and Peter, whose whole memory of her was tainted sour by fear and hate, remembered his aunt's own terror of eternity and, careless of who saw him, stood and smiled.

Catherine Alexeievna saw his expression and bent her head over the cross she held. He grinned, while his aunt's subjects wept or kept vigil in silence, no matter what wrongs they owed Elizabeth; could any man have worked more steadily towards his own destruction?

A destruction that should be accomplished within the hour of Elizabeth's death. Nikita Panin stood quite near, holding the little Grand Duke Paul by the hand, his fat face expressionless, though she knew that he too watched that closed door.

He waited, as she did, for the end to come, for the Chancellor to produce the casket in which he knew the Empress's will to be kept, and for the words which would make an

Emperor of his fidgeting charge:

"Our beloved great nephew Paul Petrovitch, by the grace of the most High God, shall upon the hour and day of our death, succeed and reign in our stead, to the exclusion of all others who might make claim to our estate and Kingdom. His Imperial Highness the Grand Duke Peter being of unsound mind and unable to fulfil the burdens of our realm, is hereby disinherited, to our great grief. . . ."

Panin knew those words by heart; he had seen them, penned in the Empress's own hand and placed in the jewelled casket which had belonged to Peter the Great. Catherine knew them also, for he had repeated them to her, and she had heard the further sentences in which Elizabeth decreed her Regent.

The Grand Duchess risked a quick glance at Peter and then looked down as he met her eye. He favoured her with a scowl of hatred, and the threat in his expression did not escape her. Already he was savouring the prospect of his long-delayed revenge, imagining her helpless, unaware in his crazy triumph that his Imperial Aunt had deprived him of the Crown. Catherine closed her eyes and sighed inwardly.

How long, in God's name, before that mumbling prelate came to the door and the sickening suspense was at an end.

What would Peter do when that will was read? What would be the effect upon those waiting crowds, not only the great ones born in the shadow of the throne, who filled the outer rooms and passages, but that other concourse, humble and nameless, whom she had seen from her window, gathered outside the walls and gates, kneeling in the bitter, driving snow.

Suddenly her heart leapt in her breast and, despite her show of piety and self-control, the traitorous colour flamed in her cheeks. The handle of the door was turning, and at the sound every head was raised.

Slowly the great double doors swung open and the jewelled vestments of the Orthodox priest gleamed softly in the light of the candles which burnt in their crystal chandeliers.

He advanced a few steps into the ante-room, and Catherine could see the figure of the Chancellor, Elizabeth Vorontzov's uncle, moving behind him.

"Her Imperial Majesty, Elizabeth Petrovna, Empress and Autocrat of all the Russias, died upon the stroke of two o'clock. May the Most High God have mercy. . . ."

It was come. Catherine breathed hard and looked at Panin. Her hands gripped the crucifix until the image of the dying Saviour was imprinted upon her palms. Twenty years of patience, of suffering and humiliation, of ultimate intrigue and treason were about to bear fruit.

Peter, smiling and moving forward before the priest's announcement was even delivered, would be eliminated from the throne and her son and Saltykov's would seem to mount it. For the moment. . . .

The thought flashed through her mind that she would send Peter to the Schüsselburg, that massive tomb of stone from which few prisoners escaped. The prelate had ended his speech and Peter elbowed his way to the royal bedroom as the priest stood back to let him pass.

The heir to the throne must pay his last respects before his accession was proclaimed. The Grand Duchess blinked away spurious tears and followed him, the blood in her veins racing with excitement, her brain, clear and calculating to the end, bidding her remember her condition and be calm.

Elizabeth lay in the centre of her state bed and the embroidered curtains were looped back that her body should be visible to all. Her face was very pale and the delicate features a little sunken, but in death something of her vanished beauty had returned; the crimsoned mouth was firm, the painted eyelids shut, her hands, still white and glittering with the rings that nothing would induce her to remove, were clasped over her still breast, and the priest lifted one of them reverently for Peter Feodorovitch to kiss.

The Grand Duke stood by the side of the huge bed and made no move. She was dead; his enemy and persecutress, symbol of all that he detested in this alien, horrible land that she had called on him to rule. If there was indeed a hell as fierce as her guilty conscience had envisaged, then Peter consigned her to it with all his heart.

Outside the church bells had begun to toll in the curious discordant Russian fashion, and the sound came to them, muffled by the heavy, falling snow. Elizabeth Petrovna was dead. Now let her successor be proclaimed.

Catherine's eyes were fixed on the Chancellor, and Panin, leading the child Paul to do homage to the late Empress, also watched him closely. With measured tread Vorontzov advanced into the centre of the room, and it suddenly occurred to Catherine that his hands held no casket such as her son's tutor had described.

In the shadows around the state bed a man knelt weeping. It was Ivan Shuvalov. Weeping for his dead mistress and the eclipse of his power.

Suddenly the Chancellor stopped; his right hand went to his heart and his voice rang out

271

through that still room, echoing into the ante-chambers until it seemed that the walls of the palace reverberated with his words.

"Peter the Third, Emperor and Autocrat of all the Russias! Long live the Czar!"

Back came the cry, rolling in a deep, toneless murmur of submission. "Long live the Czar!"

For a single, desperate moment Catherine Alex-eievna looked at Count Panin, and saw in his face a bewilderment and horror equal to her own. The plan had miscarried; Elizabeth had revoked her promise, there was no will. Then slowly the Count followed the Grand Duchess's eyes and his hand clasping that of the boy Paul began to tremble.

On an inlaid chest Catherine saw a small casket encrusted with jewels. It was open.

Then her gaze rested for a terrible moment upon the face of the Chancellor, uncle to the Grand Duke's mistress.

On the mosaic floor, near the grate which held a roaring fire, there remained a few damning wisps of blackened ash.

*   *   *

"This means revolution!" The Princess Dash-kov was seated on a stool at Catherine's feet, and the two women were alone in the newly occupied Czarina's apartments in the palace.

Catherine leant back in her chair and her square jaw jutted out; it occurred even to the violently prejudiced Dashkov that her adored friend's expression made her less than beautiful. For a moment the mask had slipped and Catherine looked every day of her thirty-two years; the chiselled features were granite hard and spoilt by the aggressive angle of that jaw, her full soft lips were set in a determined line and she stared coldly over the princess's head, looking with bleak eyes at some vision of her own.

This means revolution. Orlov had spoken those same words only a few hours before, his great fist descending upon her inlaid dressing-table with a force that set the golden toilet articles scattering. The ruse had failed; Elizabeth Vorontzov's kinsman had seen and destroyed the will which placed the Consort's crown for ever beyond the reach of his niece, and the oath of allegiance had been taken by Peter III in the Cathedral within a few hours of the Empress's death.

Not one voice had been raised in protest. The court, the army and the people had bent their necks to the new yoke with the characteristic fatalism of their race. The despised Grand Duke, once the object of universal scorn, had suddenly become the lord of all the Russias, the mightiest ruler in the world, and all men's lives were in the

273

hollow of his idiot hand.

The new Empress had stood among the crowd as an ordinary spectator, and no mention of her name or her son's had been made to those taking the oath.

"I cannot understand it," the Princess said, gazing unhappily into Catherine's face. "I was so sure that some demonstration would arise . . . only one word, one voice was needed for your friends to have begun the cry: long live the Empress Catherine! Oh, I almost shouted it myself when I stood there in the Cathedral, listening to that old hypocrite preaching his sermon, comparing the advent of this little monster to the coming of the Christ!"

Catherine smiled and shook her head. "I fear it will not be Peter's fault if I do not go to my heavenly salvation before the day appointed by old age!"

The Dashkova's small face flushed with love and admiration. Only a woman as brave and wonderful as Catherine could have found it in her heart to make a joke of the danger she was in.

But in fact, Catherine's show of humour covered a fury of disappointment and uncertainty. There she sat, comforted by this girl of barely nineteen years, her plans confounded, her greatest enemy riding on the crest of power, carrying in her body the child of an adultery which would demand her life as forfeit if it were discovered.

Orlov had been right; she should have rid herself of the child she carried. Now it was too late; she must wait until nature delivered her from the thrall of physical weakness, wait and hope that Peter's friends might advise patience before testing his new-won power by imprisoning his wife too hurriedly.

Orlov and the Dashkova had set the pattern for the future with their words. There was no course left to her but revolution . . . . if Peter did not strike first.

*　　*　　*

The year 1762 opened with a Czar upon the throne of Russia for the first time for many years. Peter the Third assumed the mantle of autocracy which had been worn by a succession of women and had rested for a brief period on the shoulders of the tragic child Ivan.

He accorded his new position the respect with which he treated all things Russian, and spent the first days of his accession in an orgy of drunkennes and hysterical debauch. He was ruler at last; all men's lives and property were his to dispose of as he wished; the limitless expanse of a kingdom so vast that it comprised almost a continent within its borders had come under his domain; wealth and power without measure had devolved upon him; and Peter Feodorovitch took refuge in the comforting oblivion of wine.

For twenty years the spectre of the Russian Crown had tormented and oppressed him; the magnitude and responsibility which was Elizabeth Petrovna's legacy had filled him with rebellious terror, even as the immensity of her power had threatened to overwhelm his weaker personality when he should be called upon to wield it. His vision of vengeance and freedom had never quite dispelled his fears, and the new Czar regarded his kingdom and subjects as if he had been suddenly thrust into a cage of wild beasts and left to tame them.

His aunt, whose corpse lay in state on a huge bier in the palace, had used her authority to persecute and punish him, to banish his friends and honour his enemies. Peter emerged from his dissipations with the fixed intention of imitating her actions in reverse.

Almost his first thought, once the long, colourful ceremony of swearing allegiance to him was ended, had been to send soldiers to arrest his wife, and only the habit of unwilling obedience had caused him to listen to the exhortations of Chancellor Vorontzov.

"I beg Your Majesty to wait. To arrest the Empress now would be a sacrilege so soon after the death of your Imperial Aunt; only restrain your justice for a few more months; wait until you have truly gathered power over the people. The Empress is helpless, Majesty, and her repudiation will be a simple thing. It has been done a hundred times by other Czars, but not within the hour of their inheriting the throne. Such an affair would make her a martyr and brand you a tyrant! Within a few months you will be as firmly settled at the head of the State as if you had ruled it a dozen years, and the arrest or death of Catherine Alexeievna can be accomplished overnight."

His words were persuasive, and at last even his niece's slow intelligence acknowledged the wisdom of his advice. Let Catherine wait, suffering the torments of suspense, and the thousand last humiliations which Elizabeth Vorontzov and her royal lover would be able to inflict upon her in the meantime.

Yet despite all the efforts of his advisers, Peter had begun his reign by affronting those traditions most dear to his people's heart; careless of the Chancellor's entreaties, he received his ministers and reviewed his troops dressed in splendid Prussian uniform, glittering with German decorations.

By contrast, the Czarina spoke Russian fault-lessly, her habits, dress and bearing entirely belied the German blood which ran in her veins, and none took greater care than she to disguise her foreign origin.

The child she carried stirred with life; within a few short weeks it would be born, and the burden of incapacity would be lifted from her. No one but Gregory and Vladyslava knew her secret, and the impatient Princess Dashkov urged her day and night to give the word for which a growing number of conspirators were waiting.

Among them, still in his post of tutor to the little Czarevitch, remained Count Nikita Panin.

The good Count had lost a little weight in recent weeks, his rounded cheeks were pale and his little eyes blinked warily. Without the Empress's will to legalize his plans, Panin was inclined to hesitate; his abundant flesh crawled a little at the thought of an unsuccessful rising and the conse-quences for him as a chief conspirator.

Quite soon after Elizabeth's death, the Count made his way to Catherine's rooms, his visit excused by the Czarevitch Paul, who dragged unwillingly at his heels.

It was his first interview with the Czarina since Elizabeth's death, and his intention was to with-draw from the plot he had himself proposed to her during the summer of the previous year.

Catherine received him seated in a high-backed gilt chair. Her black velvet gown accentuated her pallor but her blue eyes were hard and glittering. She guessed only too well the reason for this visit; clever, unscrupulous Panin was going to step down from a cause he judged to be already lost, and with him would depart a host of useful sympathisers. But, for all his shrewdness, he had made the mistake of many; even his acknowledgment of her talents and ambition had under-estimated Catherine Alexeievna.

The first thing the Count noticed was that the Czarina was not alone; a man stood by the window, his immense height silhouetted against the sunlit panes, his back towards the room and its occupants. It seemed to Panin as he bowed over Catherine's hand that the outline of that figure was familiar. . . .

Smiling, he presented the little Paul to his mother and waited while Catherine embraced her son with indifferent haste. If Panin was going to play the innocent, then she must shatter that pretence as only she knew how.

"His Imperial Highness is well, Your Majesty," commenced the tutor. "I have only good reports of progress and behaviour. . . ." Catherine held up her hand for silence and regarded him with a hard, unsmiling stare.

"I shall hear your praises of my son another time, Count Panin. Send the boy into the next room where Vladyslava will amuse him. I have other matters to discuss with you." The bland expression on Panin's face became a trifle strained but he could not disobey. Once the door had closed behind the Czarevitch, Catherine turned towards the man whose identity was puzzling the good Count.

"Gregory! Come here; I would present a friend of mine!" Orlov, whose stance had never altered, left his post by the window and walked over to the Czarina's chair; he stood behind it and looked long and searchingly at Panin.

"Count Orlov, this is my son's tutor, Count Nikita Panin. A fellow conspirator," Catherine added distinctly, and the minister winced. The two men bowed and Panin began to sweat under the other's unblinking scrutiny. He knew Count Orlov by reputation as well as by sight, and his attitude in that room left no doubt as to his relationship with the Czarina. How long had that been going on under the noses of them all?

Catherine watched Panin with hard eyes. So he had come to wriggle out of his own plot, had he? Well, doubtless after she had done, he would have changed his mind!

She came at once to the point.

"Since her late Majesty's will has been destroyed, I think it as well that we should review the situation. Doubtless that was your reason for coming to see me."

The minister shuffled and tugged uncomfortably at his cravat. Damn the woman, she knew very well why he had come!

"A most unfortunate occurrence, Madame. Quite disastrous to our plans," he stammered.

"Unfortunate, as you say, Count, and criminal as a deed. But I would not describe it as disastrous. You yourself informed me of Elizabeth Petrovna's wishes and, whatever the actions of a traitor, it is our duty to see that her last desires are carried out."

While she spoke, it occured to Panin that neither she nor the fearsome Orlov intended to let him withdraw; he wished with all his heart that the silent Lieutenant of Guards would cease staring at him with those cold, pitiless blue eyes.

How alike they both were, the barbarian soldier and the beautiful cultured Czarina, hard-eyed and implacable in the pursuit of their design. Well fitted for one another; and for the first time Nikita Panin glimpsed the true nature of the woman he had thought to use for his own ends. A tigress of ambition lurked behind that false exterior; as he looked at her he saw the fruition of Bestujev's early judgment, the mask of dignity and charm no longer quite concealed the passionate sensuality which could bind such a man as Gregory Orlov. Lover and mistress they appeared without a doubt and, despite himself, Panin felt his resolution weakening. His fat hands fluttering nervously; he made a last attempt.

"In principle Your Majesty is right, of course. But to carry honour to such lengths—to endanger your life and the life of your son—I would beg you to consider; might it not be better to forget our plan? Elizabeth Petrovna is dead, there is no proof she ever left a will. When the Czar is crowned it will be difficult to persuade anyone that the throne does not belong to him."

"The Czar is not crowned yet, Count Panin. And he has named no date for his coronation. You speak of danger in this enterprise. . . . Well, I think you cannot be ignorant of what everyone in Russia knows; that my husband intends to repudiate and murder me! I have no doubt my son would also share that fate. We have little to lose, my friend, that Peter the Third has not already declared forfeit in his heart. We are all in this affair together and I fear that you will be one of those who stand or fall with me!"

The Count went very pale and his face shone

with perspiration. Catherine regarded him without mercy, once she had made this threat.

"I think the Count understands the wisdom of your words, Madame," remarked Orlov abruptly. "I think the Count would prefer your protection and my friendship in the days to come. The lack of them could cost him his head," he added flatly.

Panin had been a statesman for too long not to know when he was beaten. If anyone could wrest the throne from Peter without a legal right to it, it was this woman and her lover.

He bowed low over her white hand.

"Your Majesty can count on my loyalty and support. Believe me, I have no love for tyrants!"

"Nor I, my dear Count. I knew I could rely upon you; and I promise you that in the hour of my success I shall know how to reward my friends!" For some reason, Panin believed this assurance to be as genuine as the threats which had preceded it. She would reward him, if the *coup d'état* succeeded, just as she would implicate him without hope of extrication if he withdrew or betrayed the plot.

He left the royal apartments, wiping his face with an embroidered handkerchief, dragging the protesting Czarevitch by the hand. He was considerably shaken by the ordeal, and not until some hours later did he realize that the Czarina had never mentioned her son's succession to the throne. . . .

*　　*　　*

As the months went by and the great yearly migration of the court to the Summer Palace took place as usual, an air of growing tension and uneasiness spread over the capital.

Peter the Third was escaping the restraint of his Chancellor and the wily Volkov who had become his secretary; they poured advice into his ear and Peter, whose whole life had been spent in bending unwillingly to the dictates of others, decided that he did not need to listen. He was getting used to power, to the odd sensation of giving an order, however ridiculous, and seeing it instantly obeyed. The ever present sense of his own inadequacy took a perverted turn and urged him to test the strength of the chain which tethered his subjects in obedience.

To the horror of Vorontrov, he began to interfere with the Church. He hated the dogma, pretensions and elaborate ritual of Orthodoxy. Also Elizabeth Petrovna had been devoted to the Church.

The thunderstruck Archbishop Arssenij received a demand from the Czar that all ecclesiastical lands should become the property of the

State. Further messages revealed that the new Emperor intended to have his priests shorn of their beards and dressed in the simple cassocks of Lutheran clergy, and that he proposed to build a Protestant chapel in the palace itself.

Not even Catherine had dared hope for such an act of lunacy; the whole organization of clerical power rose in violent opposition and all over Russia the name of Peter was vilified and denounced by priests who saw in him a menace to their sacred rights.

While the Czarina went regularly to church, the Czar declared himself a patron of heresy, and it was one of the ironical jests of Fate that the might of Orthodoxy should range itself on the side of the atheist Catherine.

Outside the Russian border the world waited, watching Peter Feodorovitch proceeding obstinately along the path of his own destruction, wondering when the Czarina would break her silence and make a move. It was not the first time that a madman had sat upon the throne of the ancient Muscovy Czars, but few of them would have been lunatic enough to leave a wife like Catherine at liberty for so long.

The hope of Vorontzov that he could make a popular ruler out of Peter was fast vanishing; no man's word could turn the Emperor from the course of alienating the loyalest of his subjects, and it came to the Chancellor's mind that the arrest of Catherine in the beginning could hardly have caused more scandal than Peter's violation of every known law of Church and State.

In conference with Volkov, the Chancellor decided that the two focal points of discontent were Catherine Alexeievna and the legendary prisoner Ivan, now grown to manhood in his dungeon. Revolution might be proclaimed at any moment in the name of either one, and the only way of securing Peter on the throne was to eliminate any possible successor. In time Ivan Ivanovitch could be accorded the merciful release of silent death. But it would be as well to deal with Catherine first.

*　　*　　*

"Gentlemen, I tell you it is a damned insult to the army! I swear I'll run my sword through the first cursed Prussian who shows his nose in the palace!"

Alexis Orlov drew the weapon out of its scabbard as he spoke, and the shining blade flashed in the smoky, torchlit barrack-room. The long, bare chamber was filled with men, some sitting round the table which ran down the centre of the room, others leaning against the wall, all of them with glasses in their hands. Their body servants moved

286

among them carefully, refilling empty cups, and there was silence while Alexis spoke.

A little further down, Gregory sat drinking and watching his brother; Alexis was the orator, and he presented a fine picture in his handsome uniform, sword in hand, and that hideous scar on his face throbbing with emotion. It occurred to Gregory that his brother was most probably in love with Catherine himself. . . .

Alexis glared round him, and there were many faces among the assembled officers whose expressions matched his own.

"The night our Empress dies, the Czar sends to make peace with the Prussian King. On *Frederick's* terms, by God! Like a defeated nation forced to sue for mercy, we abandon the war after five years, when victory was in sight! So the Czar signs an armistice with our enemies—but does he give the country peace? No, my friends, he prepares for war against Denmark! And for what? To restore some cursed piece of Holstein that the Danes have taken! I say the whole of Russia means less to him than this cesspit in Germany that gave him birth!"

There was a shout of agreement at these words and Alexis raised his sword to still the tumult.

"We swore allegiance to him, you and I and all his people. Every little soldier in the army would lay down his life for him because he is the Czar. He is our father, our protector, and we of the Guards are his dutiful sons! But that is not enough for him! Our Emperor does not want us; the glory of Russian arms is nothing to him. *We*, the personal troops of the sovereign, are not to act as bodyguards to Peter the Third! Our Czar goes and sends for a regiment of Holsteiners instead!"

This time there was no silencing the roar of anger that greeted the announcement.

There were officers of the famous Ismailov Regiment and some from the Preobrazhenskies present in that barrackroom, men whose valour and nobility had received a mortal insult when their Emperor had summoned a force composed of their late enemies to fulfil the duties regarded by the Imperial Guards as a sacred right and privilege.

Alexis Orlov, his Russian blood aflame with hatred and resentment, knew well the sore spots of pride which his denunciation had opened afresh. The wine was flowing and tempers were rising; by to-morrow they would have calmed down, but the seed he planted in their hearts was destined to bear fruit.

"Thank God we have a patriotic Empress!" he roared, and his brother Gregory took up the cry.

"God save Catherine!" And from every throat

the salutation was repeated. "God save Catherine! God save Catherine!"

In the midst of the uproar that ensued, Alexis saw a soldier approach his brother and whisper a few words in his ear. Gregory's expression changed and he took a crumpled piece of paper which the other gave him and read it anxiously. The messenger departed with a few kopecks in his pocket and Gregory Orlov edged his way out of the excited throng of officers, his handsome face clouded and frowning. He pushed his way through to his brother, and Alexis knew that whatever had been written on that note, the contents had disturbed him considerably.

Gregory drew him quietly aside. "What is it?" Alexis asked him.

Orlov held the screw of paper in the flame of a smoking wall sconce, and it flared up instantly. Before replying, he trod the ashes under foot.

"That was a message from Vladyslava," he muttered. "It said, 'the tree is bearing fruit'. That means she is in labour! God's blood! If the Czar gets word of this he'll have her murdered where she lies! I cannot go to her, I cannot even be near in case aught should go wrong."

Gregory looked at his brother.

"If anything happens to her I swear before God I'll kill Peter Feodorovitch with my own hands."

Alexis glanced around him; in the general babble of excited comment which his oration had aroused, they were unnoticed by the rest.

"Nothing will go amiss; I'll wager my life she will have taken all precautions. Calm yourself, Gregory, or you'll be noticed. I'll make my way to the palace; I've a little mistress there who is excuse enough for my presence, and if there is any trouble, word'll reach you on the instant! Do you stay here now and see that the wine flows freely. If all goes well to-night, we're going to need our brother officers!"

Clapping his brother on the shoulder, Alexis Orlov pushed his way to the door and was gone. He paused only once as he walked through the darkness towards the Summer Palace, and that was to loosen his sword in its scabbard.

Leo Narychkin was making his way towards the Czar's apartments in answer to a summons which had just been delivered to him by one of Peter's pages.

The order to appear before his Emperor filled Narychkin with suspicion and distaste; this cultivation of his company was an ill-natured caprice on the part of Elizabeth Vorontzov, who delighted to see the Czarina's oldest friend forced to play the jester for her benefit. Several nights a week the unwilling Leo had been ordered to recite, or use his gift of mimicry, for the royal amusement, while uncomfortably aware that Peter sat at the head of the long dining-table, his elbows on the board, his bulbous eyes watching Catherine's staunchest supporter with an expression in which there was no laughter. Narychkin should pay for his loyalty to her with his head, and that was the message which Leo read in the face of his Emperor during those evening gatherings.

When or where the order to arrest him would be given Narychkin did not know, and the suspense added a spice of cruelty which appealed to Peter. Only one thing was certain, that the ending of the Vorontzova's little jest had long since been decided, and it might be sprung at any moment. Perhaps on that very evening, while his tormentors sat at table. . . .

Leo walked down the long palace corridors with a casual, unhurried step, mounting the carpeted stairway which led to the Emperor's suite. Since Fate seemed to have delivered his beloved Catherine into the hands of her hated husband, it mattered little what the future held for him.

Such thoughts as these were in his mind as he approached the carpeted gallery preceding Peter's rooms; it was a quiet part of the palace, occupied only by sentries standing motionless guard at intervals along the route to the Czar's suite, and for all his inward melancholy, Narychkin was startled to hear the sound of someone running.

Turning, he saw a man approaching from behind, his coat-tails flying as he ran towards Narychkin. The other stopped abruptly and caught at Leo's satin sleeve; he was panting and shaking with excitement.

"Is His Majesty in his rooms? Tell me, you are of the Household! Where is he? I must find him!"

Suddenly every instinct in Narychkin's long experience flashed a warning. He gripped the man by the arm and held him, and his tone was one of haughty anger.

"Damn your insolence! How dare you address me with familiarity. What business would you have with the Czar?"

The man was dressed in the palace livery. Narychkin judged him to be one among the thousands of servants living within the imperial walls, but he answered with a disrespect that would have cost an ordinary lackey the skin off his back.

"I pray you, sir, direct me to the Czar. There is not a moment to be lost. He'll have my head, and yours also if you detain me! I have news for him which will not wait! In God's name, can I find him here?"

Narychkin gripped the other firmly; the man was no lackey, his words and manner belied the uniform he wore. And what information had he for Peter, that the delaying of it even for a moment might cost men's lives?

"What is this news of which you speak! Tell it to me and I'll inform the Czar. The Emperor does not speak with servants."

"I am no servant," came the answer, "I am Chancellor Vorontzov's man, and the Czar will listen to me. . . . Only release me and I will find him without your assistance since you refuse to give it!"

Leo Narychkin was a tall man and strong, despite his slim proportions. His hands gripped the Chancellor's spy about the coat collar and his fingers were but an inch from his throat. He shook him gently and his eyes were black and merciless. "I am a curious man. Tell me what news you have for the Emperor; then I shall release you and tell you where to find him. Tell me, or I'll choke you for your insolence . . . lackey!"

The spy swallowed, and his face was livid with fear and helplessness.

"As you persist . . . . I go to tell His Majesty that the Czarina Catherine is giving birth to a child in her apartments at this very hour! Do you still hinder me. . . ?"

Narychkin's heart almost stopped beating.

Catherine was having a child! At that moment

in her rooms, she lay in labour. God in heaven! This man, this miserable spy, had found her secret out, and sped to Peter with the news! Without a thought for the consequences to himself, Narychkin drew his little court sword to silence the betrayer where he stood, but the spy, seeing the evidence of his own doom, made a desperate lunge at his captor and struck him in the face. For a second the blow dazed Narychkin and his victim tore himself free, even as the sword blade passed within inches of his evading body, only to strike the wall and shatter into pieces.

The next moment Vorontzov's spy had taken to his heels and was running like the wind down the gallery; he was already within sight of the next sentry and Narychkin quickly abandoned all hope of catching him. The man was gone, gone on his way to the Czar, bearing the message that would have Catherine Alexeievna and her illegitimate child slain on the mattress where they lay.

There was one faint hope, so slender that he sickened with dread for her even as he turned and began to run in the direction of her suite. She must be warned. He must reach her first and give the word that Peter knew and would be coming to surprise her secret—coming with soldiers and witnesses to prove her adultery and guilt. Doubtless among them would be found men ready to kill the

Empress when their master gave the sign. Unless he could get to her in time.

CHAPTER 12

PETER FEODOROVITCH was at table when he heard the news.

The Chancellor's spy knelt before him, gasping for breath, stuttering his message in a voice loud enough for everyone seated round the board to hear. When he had done there was a moment of deathly silence; not even Elizabeth Vorontzov dared speak while the full import of the informer's words sank into the brain of her royal lover.

Peter rose slowly to his feet, his sallow face had flushed a deep crimson and his eyes seemed about to start from his head; a horrible flood-tide of hatred rose in him, and mingled with it was a triumph so intense that it robbed him of speech.

The Chancellor watched him fascinated. If he had been capable of feeling for Catherine, then her probable fate at the hands of this madman might have aroused some spark of pity; as it was, he merely congratulated himself upon the wisdom of placing a spy so close to the Czarina, but wondered uneasily whether Peter might not emulate his illustrious aunt and have a seizure from excitement.

Suddenly the Czar threw back his head and

laughed aloud; it was a shrill, demoniac sound, mirthless and inhuman.

"If this is truth, I'll kill the she-devil!" he shouted. "No more of your cautionings, Chancellor! The penalty for whores is death!"

He drew his jewelled court sword, and the thin bright blade flashed in the candle-light; the movement of his arm upset the golden wine goblet placed on the table before him and the dark red liquid spread in a slow stain over the embroidered cloth.

The spy still knelt at the feet of his Czar, wondering whether he might tell of the courtier who had tried to intercept and kill him before he could deliver his message. The noble had been in the Czarina's pay; he too should be dealt with. . . .

The Emperor would reward him with rivers of gold for his services that night.

"Sire," he began. "On my way to you I was hindered, one of your household tried to kill me."

But his words went unheard; Peter was not listening, neither were those who surrounded him. The spy had spoken the death knell of the Empress and his hour of fame was done.

By that time the whole room was on its feet and Peter turned to his guests, his sword pointed towards the doorway.

"Come," he invited. "Come, ladies and gentle-men. We go to attend a lying-in." He started forward and his entourage followed him in a sudden stampede of pushing, curious men and women, half eager, half horrified by the prospect before them.

As he stepped into the corridor, Peter shouted, and the sentries who ringed his apartments came running at his command.

On the fringe of the crowd, Vorontzov's spy lingered, anxious to see the outcome of his revelation, determined to be within sight of his Czar as a reminder when the climax came.

Peter Feodorovitch glared around him, at the soldiers, obedient to his bidding, at his mistress, whose painted face was twitching nervously, at her uncle, the soft-spoken Vorontzov who had encompassed the downfall of the common enemy, at all his sycophants and courtiers. They pressed about him, eager and excited, with the herd instinct that loses all discrimination at the scent of blood.

For this once he would out-do the barbarians in barbarism, and only when he had plunged his sword up to the hilt into the heart of Catherine Alexeievna would his fear of her be exorcised.

"To my wife's apartments!" he shouted. "Forward, damn you, the Czarina needs us, she is giving birth!"

He raised his weapon and cut viciously at the empty air. "Behold, I bring her the midwife!" he added.

*   *   *

Leo Narychkin was running.

Careless of etiquette or caution, he ran through the interminable corridors and traversed the long staircases so beloved of the architects of imperial palaces, watched by gaping lackeys and the moving eyes of sentries, ignoring the groups of gentlemen and court ladies who sought to detain him and who turned in astonishment at this spectacle of undignified haste.

Time was on Peter's side, and even as he turned in the direction of the Czarina's apartments, Narychkin imagined that the Emperor was already on his way to those same rooms with an escort. What hope had he of saving Catherine, when at that moment she was perhaps in the throes of childbirth, or in the grip of a labour that could not be concealed?

As he reached the end of the passage leading to her rooms, he collided heavily with a tall Guards officer, who had been strolling casually in the vicinity for some time. One glance at the other's profile, hideously scarred, proclaimed the identity of the man who barred his path.

The giant smiled quite amiably, but the hand resting on his sword belied the innocence of his greeting and expression.

"Stay, friend Narychkin! You seem in mighty haste?"

Leo looked at Alexis Orlov, brother of his successful rival. It was Gregory's child that Catherine bore, but necessity vanquished the jealousy and hatred for the family that Narychkin bore them.

"Get out of my way if you value the Czarina's life," he said savagely. "The Czar is on his way here at any moment. She has been betrayed!"

Alexis swore a startled oath. His disfigured face contorted and he stepped aside. It seemed to Narychkin that he resembled nothing so much as a massive Siberian wolf about to spring.

"Go to her!" Alexis said. "Break in the doors if you must, but warn her! As for our good Emperor, I'll spit him on my sword before he takes a step towards her rooms. Hurry, for the love of God!"

Without another word Narychkin raced to the end of the long carpeted corridor, aware as he did so that all was strangely quiet except for the muffled sounds of his own hurrying feet.

He began to beat on the panelled doors with his fists.

Word had spread rapidly through the palace
that the Emperor was about to arrest his wife. The
rumour, current so many times since Peter's accession, had at last the ring of truth, and the experienced at court closed their doors and withdrew
silently from those rooms and corridors where the
Czar was likely to pass.

At such times the wise ones took care not to be
among the uninvited witnesses of doubtful scenes,
and there were many who heard of the Czarina's
downfall with genuine misgiving. Without her all
hopes of release from Peter's Prussian yoke faded
still further, but the traditional apathy of courts
towards the tyrant paralysed and held them.

Revolutions were made by the army, and this
time the Emperor was about to strike first.

The tutor of the Czarevitch Paul stayed only
long enough to hear the report of Peter's advance
with soldiers towards the Czarina's apartments,
before hurrying with the lightfooted speed of all
fat men into the inner sanctum of his room, where
he fastened the door securely and took refuge in
his bed.

His principal feeling was one of quaking fear,
coupled with unhappy reproaches directed at himself and the woman whose secrets would be wrung

301

from her by methods at which the imperial torturers were unequalled throughout the world.

The Czar, possessed by the uncontrolled fury which Count Panin had witnessed so frequently, might kill his erring wife on the spot, if the rumour of childbirth were indeed true. But the vein of national pessimism in his nature counselled Panin that this eventuality was too much to hope for; Vorontzov would stay his ruler's hand until a multitude of incriminating questions had been posed and answered.

Then he, and countless others, would follow the Empress to the scaffold, blackened for all time as conspirators in treason.

The Count drew the bed covers over his head and cursed Catherine Alexeievna for her folly with a fluidity inspired by fear.

Then, as the moments lengthened, he heard the faint tramp of soldiers, and the murmur of excited voices drifted to him through the walls as Peter Feodorovitch passed the Czarevitch's rooms.

Only then did he cease his profanities and begin to pray.

*   *   *

Peter stopped some three yards from the doors of Catherine's suite. He was surrounded by a dozen soldiers and behind him came Elizabeth

302

Vorontzov leaning on her uncle's arm; her astonishment and disbelief of the news had vanished, and only a malice greater even than her triumph remained in her heart. The Chancellor said nothing; his work was done, and if the Emperor chose to murder his wife in circumstances of such flagrant guilt, then none in all Europe or Russia would decry his action. The problem had all but solved itself and within a few moments the Consort's throne would be empty for his niece.

Those who had been at dinner with the Czar crowded the corridor; otherwise the entrance to Catherine's apartments was silent and empty. There was no sign of Alexis Orlov.

Peter addressed himself to the two guardsmen nearest him. "Break in those doors!" he ordered, pointing with his little dress sword.

Without trying the handle, the soldiers flung themselves against the finely ornamented doors, which burst open instantly. The Czar looked into the outer ante-chamber of Catherine's suite; it was occupied only by two startled footmen who shrank back as the guardsmen advanced into the room. A few candles illumined the interior, and the doors leading to the Czarina's bedroom were closed as usual.

Peter strode forward, the weapon shaking in his hand, his whole feeble body shivering with rage and nervous tension. It seemed to him that he must pass through a thousand doors, numberless as in a nightmare, before he came face to face with his enemy.

Surrounded as he was by friends and armed men, he yet hesitated, smitten by the fear of Catherine which had bedevilled him from the hour of their first meeting. She was helpless and caught out in unpardonable crime, but it was not in his power to enter that inner room alone and deal with her as was his right.

He motioned his soldiers forward and fear sharpened his voice to an angry scream.

"Open the doors! And run through any who bar the way."

The guardsmen applied their shoulders to the gilded wood, and the doors swung inwards easily so that the two assailants stumbled and almost fell across the threshold.

Catherine's bedroom was ablaze with light.

For a moment the glare dazzled Peter as he stepped through the portals, and numerous unimportant details presented themselves separately before his eyes, blinding them to the obvious spectacle he sought. Row upon row of candelabra were arranged against the walls, their candle flames reflected in many mirrors; a bright fire burned in the grate and warmed the huge empty bed which stood in the middle of the room, its embroidered covers perfectly arranged.

The Empress of Russia sat in a chair before her dressing-table, a golden mirror lowered into her lap, watching the intruders with cold astonished eyes.

Peter managed a few steps farther into the room, aware that his wife was fully dressed in a silk gown and that Vladyslava stood behind her, setting an arrangement of jewels and feathers in her hair.

There was no sign of disorder anywhere in the room; the scene that met his eyes and those of his followers was the normal one of the Czarina completing her toilette before dining with her household. Even as he watched her, waiting for her enquiry, Peter's brain, excited and strained to breaking point, refused to acknowledge that he had been misinformed.

That chamber and its occupants could not be what they seemed. Somewhere, somehow, Catherine had been bearing a child less than half an hour earlier; this spectacle was a trick, a charade enacted to lull his suspicions.

"Search the rooms!" he yelled, and his voice cracked nervously on the last word.

Catherine Alexeievna rose slowly from her chair and stared in horror at the soldiers who commenced thrusting their swords through the curtains and into the great clothes presses, until they disappeared into the inner rooms of her suite.

"What manner of visit is this, Your Majesty? Of what am I suspected that you send soldiers to destroy the furnishings about my head?"

Peter could not answer her; every moment assured him that his hopes were vain. No woman could have risen from a sick bed and looked and spoken as she was doing. He remembered the agonies of that other birth, when he had attended the long ritual of waiting by the mattress while she tossed sweating and almost unconscious; and among those who watched were many who had followed him into the chamber and now stood staring at her in embarrassment and disbelief.

After a moment Catherine seated herself slowly; still staring at Peter she picked up her fan from the dressing-table and began to sway it deliberately back and forth. The sounds of the soldiers' distant search came nearer, breaking the absolute silence in the room, and some of those in the rear of their Emperor began to drift unobtrusively away.

When the guards appeared once more, it was obvious that they had discovered nothing. Their spokesman coughed nervously as he reported failure, aware that his Czar was staring at him with dilated eyes and that the point of his sword had slit a hole in the carpet upon which he stood. A thin line of foam showed between Peter's lips; he seemed about to strike down the innocent bearer of ill tidings but the Chancellor, recognizing the defeat of their hopes, laid a hand on his arm in counsel and restraint.

Peter Feodorovitch looked at his wife and his chest heaved in a convulsion of disappointment and hate.

"Perhaps this time I have not found you out, Madame," he panted. "But look to yourself! There will be other times!"

Then he turned quickly and stumbled out of the room without another word. One by one his courtiers followed him, bowing low before the silent woman seated in the chair, and there were many among them who cursed their presence in that room, for the sight of their faces would doubtless remain imprinted upon the Czarina's memory for a long time to come.

Her downfall had seemed so assured, but once again, she and not Peter had emerged the victor; who was to say that she would not retain that position in the final denouement?

When the chamber door was closed at last, Vladyslava hurried to her mistress. Catherine leaned back and the fan dropped out of her fingers; not even the hastily applied rouge could hide her sudden pallor, and fine beads of sweat bedewed her face.

The waiting woman fell on her knees beside the chair and began to cry. "Oh, thank God, Madame, thank God! It was only just in time! At any moment I thought that you might faint."

The Czarina smiled wearily at her.

"Dry your tears, my good Vladyslava. The danger is passed; thanks to M. Narychkin and the excellent timing of my son for his birth. Where is he?"

"With Countess Brobinsky, at the other end of the palace, by now. Pray God he leaves this world more peaceably than he came into it. . . ."

But Catherine Alexeievna was not listening; the last desperate reserves of her strength had been exhausted and a merciful unconsciousness received her.

*   *   *

The story of the Emperor's attempted arrest of his wife spread through Petersburg like wildfire, and the Princess Dashkov left a sick bed upon hearing the news and hurried to her friend.

Catherine Alexeievna was in bed recovering, so she explained, from the shock which the affair had caused her, and the devoted Dashkova accepted this lie without question, as she had accepted so many others. The wilful blindness of her partisanship amazed Catherine as she looked at the girl's indignant face, still flushed with fever, and listened to her furious tirade against the Czar.

"He is a devil, Madame," the Princess was saying, "a dangerous madman who should be chained up like any other! Oh, and to think that in your hour of peril I was absent. . . ."

Catherine smiled kindly at her; the Dashkova would never know how thankful her Royal Mistress had been for that absence.

*   *   *

A few days later she received a visit from Panin. He found her dressed, surrounded by papers which she had been signing, and to all appearance in the best of health and spirits.

Catherine greeted him gaily. "My dear Count, how glad I am to see you! Forgive me while I put my signatures to these; my husband still thinks fit to leave tedious affairs of management in my hands. His own time is too occupied with plots!"

Panin did not smile; his mission was a dangerous one and he deplored Catherine's levity. He found it difficult to forgive her for the fright she had occasioned him; the desire to prevent a repetition of that dreadful night had forced his hand at last.

"I have seen and spoken with a great many o
our supporters, Madame, and the disgraceful epi
sode of a few days past has disturbed and dis
tressed us all. Indeed, I come to tell Your Majesty
that if you will accept the advice of myself and
your other friends at court, you will take immedi
ate steps to safeguard yourself and the Czare
vitch!"

Catherine laid down her pen and looked at him.

"What are you suggesting, Count?"

"That the time has come for action. When nex
the Czar takes it into his head to invade you
rooms with soldiers, I fear that you will leave then
as his prisoner. What then will become of you
son? And your friends?" he added.

The Czarina pushed back her chair and cam
towards him. "You think the time has come fo
revolution," she said quietly. The Count wiped hi
face with a lace kerchief; for some reason thi
woman always made him sweat.

"Yes, Madame, I and many others think so!"

Catherine moved to the window and stood
loking out in silence for a moment. It seemed to
Panin that she would never speak.

"Count Orlov thinks as you do," she said softly
"And so do I."

"What of the army, Madame? Can we rely upor

their support? The ministers are with our cause, excepting of course the Vorontzovs. The issuing of manifestos, the Church proclamations—the Church is loyal to you and to the Czarevitch I need hardly add—all these things can be left to me. But who is to arrest the Czar?"

Panin paused. That last contingency could surely be left to the gallant Lieutenant of Guards and his friends who would most likely solve all further problems by butchering their Emperor within the walls of his own apartments.

"The army will certainly rise for me . . . and my son," the Czarina replied. "As to the actual business of proclaiming, we can draw up the drafts of all documents when the time comes. There is no need to trouble about that until my husband has been removed from his throne. As to the manner of that, Count Orlov has a plan of which it is safer to say nothing for the moment. Only that it shall be put into effect within a little while. When the moment comes, be assured my dear Count, that none but myself shall tell you and you will warn the others!"

Catherine held out her hand to him and dismissed him with a charming smile. Whatever the consequences, he and many whom he had enlisted were too far involved in treason to withdraw; for their own safety they wished to expedite the revolution and place the little Czarevitch upon the throne.

On the 10th of June, Peter Feodorovitch gave a banquet. It was in celebration of peace between Prussia, England and Russia, and the great rooms of the Summer Palace were festooned with garlands; golden tablets bearing the names of the monarchs of the three kingdoms were hung upon the walls, a play had been arranged, and the most sumptuous feast which the resources of Imperial Russia could provide was to take place with the German Ambassador as guest of honour.

Within the palace all was preparation. An air of excitement pervaded the court, for this was the first instance of traditional Russian grandeur which the new Czar had ever staged. And it was to be the first public meeting between Peter and his Empress since their encounter in her bedroom, when he had come into his wife's presence brandishing a drawn sword.

There were to be five hundred guests at the banquet, but among the many distinguished officers of the Guards who were invited, the names of Gregory and Alexis Orlov were omitted.

That night Catherine's lover sat moodily in his room in the barracks drinking and talking to his brother. Gregory was anxious, and his usually robust spirits laboured under a feeling of depression which nothing seemed able to remedy.

The Empress had gone to Peter's banquet; she had parted from him only a few hours since, and during that secret rendezvous he had alternately made love to her and entreated her not to go into what he feared might be a trap. He had kissed her and sworn at her, aware that her blue eyes smiled up at him in unshakable determination, and that even as her fingers caressed his face and twined themselves in his hair she rejected his request. She was the Empress, and as such she would take her place that night before the world. It would not do, her soft voice told him, to let Peter think she was afraid.

Gregory sat down on his bed and cursed.

"In the name of God, Alexis, what hour is it? How long before that damned banquet ends? Think of it, there she is, alone in the palace, with the place crawling with Peter's Holsteiners, and none of her friends in a position to protect her!"

"Passek is there, mounting guard," remarked Alexis. "He will tell us what happens if you cannot wait to hear it from the Czarina's own lips."

"How do I know that she will be free to tell me?" roared Gregory. His brother sat up slowly and regarded him with a curious expression in his light eyes.

"If she was in danger, do you suppose that I would be idling here?" he demanded quietly. "Peter will not touch her. And anyway, here, by God, is Passek!"

"Passek! What news?"

The Captain of Guards kicked the door shut behind him and pulled off his sword belt. His gorgeous full dress uniform glittered dully in the candle-light. He was one of the Orlovs' oldest friends and an active member of their conspiracy.

"To-night our gracious Emperor excelled himself!" he said slowly.

In a flash Gregory had leapt to his feet. "I told you!" he shouted. "What has he done, has he harmed her?"

Passek shook his head. "Calm yourself, friend. She is safe . . . and free. I saw her come in, dressed like a goddess. I've never seen so many diamonds in my life. She truly blazed like fire! Every eye was on her; God's death, Gregory, the Emperor looked like a flunkey beside her!" He paused and drank deeply from the wine jug which stood on the table.

"Go on," snarled Gregory. "Go on, damn you! What happened?"

"Nothing much until the feast was half-way done. That drunken fool began proposing toasts, toasts to this German and that German till I could have slit his treacherous throat, shouting in that squeaking cockerel's voice of his and glaring down the table at the Empress. She drank every toast but the last, that to the imperial family. I was watching him and I saw his face turn as red as the wine. Everything was silent, you know how it is at these banquets, no one dares cough while the Emperor speaks. All of a sudden he turned to the Czarina and yelled at the top of his voice. You could hear his words from one end of the hall to the other.

"Get up, damn you! Stand and drink to Mlle Vorontzov. Fool! Slut!"

Passek looked at the two Orlovs. Alexis had slowly risen to his feet and the scar on his face was throbbing and angry.

"It was the most vile insult I've ever heard given to a woman. She's as good as dead or divorced from to-night. None can doubt his intention now," the Captain added. "I hurried to tell you as soon as I was relieved."

"What did she do?" Gregory asked at last.

"Nothing. She only turned and began talking to some nobleman behind her chair. I hear he's been banished for his pains," he concluded.

Gregory Orlov lifted his sword belt down from a hook driven into the wall. Anger had made him cool; anger and the knowledge that Catherine, though humiliated into the dust, was still at liberty.

"I go to spread the word," he said. "Do you do so also, Passek. Tell our officers and brothers what their Czar intends and how he honours his Empress before foreigners. Forget nothing, and perhaps add a little to what your memory cannot supply. Our Emperor will remember this night's work to his sorrow! I think he himself has given the word we have been waiting for."

*　　*　　*

That night the Czar lay in bed with Elizabeth Vorontzov and repeated the scene he had enacted that evening over and over again for her appreciation. Five hundred people had witnessed his treatment of Catherine; he only regretted that it had not been five thousand. Well, now they knew, and within a few days the whole world would know.

Peter was to take to himself a new wife, and the event was planned for the 29th of June, feast of that great Saint after whom he had been named.

At long last Chancellor Vorontzov had agreed to Catherine's arrest; and now that the decision had been made, it was necessary to render her harmless before the Czar left for war against Denmark. The date of his embarkation was fixed for the 30th of June.

316

The night before, a body of Holstein troops would make the Empress prisoner, for neither Peter nor his Chancellor cared to trust Russian soldiers with such a task; and while the whole court celebrated the feast of St. Peter and Paul, Catherine Alexeievna would be hurried away to the Schüsselburg fortress where she could be quietly put to death, and the excuse which the Czar would give his people was the announcement that his wife had been discovered intriguing with the Danish enemy.

With a heart made light by the prospect before him, Peter Feodorovitch left Petersburg for Oranienbaum, that palace where Serge Saltykov had wooed the young and lovely Grand Duchess all those years ago, where Poniatowsky had first seen and fallen in love with her, and where Gregory Orlov had laid siege to her and found that in the midst of victory he had himself been conquered.

A curt order penned by his secretary requested the Empress to retire to Elizabeth's old estate at Peterhof, a small palace which lay within easy reach of Oranienbaum and was yet conveniently isolated. There she was to remain in semi-banishment until the Emperor's Holsteiners arrived to take her prisoner on the evening of the 29th.

Catherine could do nothing but obey; Gregory

had to stay behind in Petersburg, the Princess Dashkov had been given duties which would detain her in the capital, none of her friends or intimates were permitted to accompany her to Peterhof and, despite herself, Catherine Alexeievna felt lonely and afraid. Peter had a reason for separating her so suddenly both from her enemies as well as friends.

Alone with Gregory before she left St. Petersburg, she confided her feelings to him. Orlov lifted her face to his and mocked her gently; there were times when her fearlessness angered him, when her strength of character and will-power challenged his own, times when, despite his love for her, she almost ceased to be a mistress and became a rival. But that day she lay in his embrace, weak and submissive as any other woman, and her doubts gave him the mastery.

"Afraid, my intrepid Catherine? Where is all that boasted coolness in the face of danger? Or is it the ghosts at Peterhof which trouble you?"

Catherine turned away from him in restless impatience.

"The only ghost I fear to meet there is my own! I swear Peter has some intention behind his command to me. Gregory, what if he acts before your plan can be carried out? What if something happens to me at Peterhof, if I am never allowed to return to the capital before he sails for Denmark?"

Orlov looked at her and laughed.

"We have spies everywhere, beloved. Since the night of the banquet our Emperor hasn't a friend among his subjects. I should have the first word of any plan against you. This is just another insult, to banish you from his imperial presence. Trust me, and remain quietly at Peterhof for a few days. Passek, Panin and I are completing our plan for dealing with our gracious Czar. Before the end of June you are to return to Petersburg and your friends. Then you know what will befall!"

"You will assassinate him before he sails for Denmark," Catherine said slowly.

Orlov nodded and laughed grimly. "Shall I not make a handsome Dane?" he enquired. For answer Catherine kissed him, and for the moment his confidence dispelled her doubts.

Obediently she left for Peterhof, taking with her a small retinue of servants, departing with misgivings which deepened during every mile of the journey. Orlov was so contemptuous of her fears; only Princess Dashkov seemed to share them, for her mingled jealousy and intuition suspected the wisdom of leaving matters in the hands of men like Gregory and Alexis without the guiding shrewdness of the Empress to restrain them.

The Dashkova watched the Empress's carriage

speed out of the city and turned from the window with a sigh. How long before the nightmare of waiting and intrigue would end, how long before her life's work of placing Catherine on the throne would be accomplished?

While the Emperor and his court entertained themselves at Oranienbaum and the Empress remained quietly at Peterhof, Gregory and his fellow conspirators set to work preparing the way for Catherine's proclamation immediately Peter's murder should be announced.

Among the most ardent partisans of the plot was Captain Passek, and he repeated, with embellishments, the tale of Peter's conduct at the banquet. He was a man of fiery temper and unbridled tongue, a patriot and a soldier of long service.

It was unfortunate that he was also a drunkard; unfortunate too, that his speeches were delivered one night within the hearing of a soldier who had long borne him a grudge for an old punishment inflicted at his orders.

It was a few hours before midnight on June 27th when Gregory Orlov burst in upon Princess Dashkov and Count Panin with the news.

Passek had been arrested: the Empress's conspiracy had been betrayed.

CHAPTER 13

AT five o'clock on the morning of the 28th June, a shabby hired carriage drove into the grounds of Peterhof Palace, past the avenues of trees with their companies of sleepily twittering birds, past the magnificent façade of the main building, favourite pleasure palace of the dead Elizabeth Petrovna, its wheels furrowing the soft gravel paths, and turned towards the small summer pavilion, where in a window a single candle burned.

It was there, without guards and attended only by a few servants and her waiting-woman, that Catherine Alexeievna spent her days of uneasy retirement, and at that very hour within its flimsy walls the Empress Consort of Russia lay asleep.

Her lady-in-waiting, Mme Chargorodsky, knelt at her devotions, her room lit by the flame of that solitary candle, for she was a pious woman, and the silent oppressive atmosphere of Peterhof seemed to her as if it were heavy with the spirit of the late Empress, as well as weighed down by the ill-concealed nervousness and anxiety of the present Czarina. So the good Madame left her bed and sought the comfort of the ikon before which she was even then prostrated.

So it was that when her door opened softly and a large shadow darkened the floor, creeping towards her on silent feet, she heard nothing until a hand rested on her shoulder and the touch of a knife blade at her throat stilled the scream she had opened her mouth to utter.

"One word and I'll pin you to the wall by the neck," whispered Alexis Orlov and, looking at that devil's mask profile, the lady-in-waiting never doubted his threat.

"Get up! Where is the Empress?"

Mme Chargorodsky nodded weakly towards a door in an alcove.

"Open it and go inside."

The Czarina's bedroom was bathed in grey half-light, and for a moment Orlov hesitated as he approached her couch. She lay sleeping peacefully, her black hair spread over the pillows, and it came to him suddenly that his brother must have often seen her thus, relaxed and stripped of all the trappings of great estate, a lovely woman, vulnerable as any other in the innocence of sleep.

She awoke to the touch of his hands on her, shaking her gently; and in a blinding flash of fear Catherine returned to consciousness and struck at him as she would at any assassin. But his hands held her, firmly and soothingly, despite their terrible strength, and at last in the half-light she saw the scar on his face and gasped in astonishment and relief.

"Alexis! What are you doing here, in God's name?"

"I come to take you back to Petersburg! Passek has been arrested; our plans have been betrayed to the Emperor. Soldiers will be sent to capture you within the next few hours. Hurry, Madame, or by the Virgin, we'll not reach the capital alive!"

Even as he spoke all fear left her.

Too late now for Gregory to assassinate Peter as he had proposed, and for the schemes of Panin to work their tortuous paths. Princess Dashkov had been right: without her presence they had blundered, as men of action always will when tact and cunning is demanded of them. But Fate had intervened, averting her destruction by a few short hours, giving her once more the respite which had saved her at the birth of Orlov's son. This was her chance, ordained those many years ago when the young Princess of Anhalt had taken the first steps towards the Russian throne, wherein she must succeed or perish in the end.

Within ten minutes she was dressed, her hair secured with a few pins, hurrying in Orlov's wake towards the waiting carriage. As he helped her inside she saw that the first red tinge of sunrise was beginning to colour the delicate roofs and

323

colonnades of Peterhof, and every bird in the hundreds of trees had woken and were singing in a jubilant greeting to the coming day. Opposite her sat the white-faced lady-in-waiting, too dangerous to be left behind.

Sitting in his corner, Alexis observed her with admiration and masculine amazement. Despite her beauty, her charm and sensuousness, he saw the contradiction in her that had enslaved and since infuriated Gregory, the deadly force of character which so belied her womanhood, the courage and coolness which made her smile in the very teeth of death and danger. Small wonder that Peter Feodorovitch had known he must kill her in order to be safe.

"Alexis," she said suddenly. "How long since Passek was arrested?"

"Last night, Madame," he answered.

"Then by now news must have reached the Emperor at Oranienbaum. God knows what may not have been forced out of Passek; we must abandon all thought of Gregory's plan. What does he contemplate?"

"A revolution, Madame, but how it is to be achieved I do not know. . . ."

Catherine leant forward and touched his arm.

"Well, friend Alexis, I think that I do! Tell that fool to whip up the horses; the sun is risen and we have no time to lose! If all goes well with me, I shall know how to reward you for your help this day!"

In obedience to her command, the carriage increased its speed, lurching and swaying from side to side so that it's illustrious passenger and her escort were almost flung from their seats.

Catherine clung on, cursing the slowness of the third-rate horses, watching the sky turn lighter.

Just before they entered Petersburg another coach appeared, driven by Gregory Orlov himself, who transferred his mistress from the shabby *calèche* into a vehicle befitting her status; and again Alexis drove.

All Petersburg was still asleep; only the Orlovs and their fellow conspirators knew of the blow that had fallen, and had spent the night in fevered preparations to receive the Empress and do battle for the throne.

Panin had promised to support her in the Senate, the Dashkova had hurried away to inform her intimates that Catherine might be expected in the capital at any hour and that the rising must take place that day.

Listening to Gregory's account, Catherine sensed the panic and confusion which had engulfed her partisans and which not even the iron courage and resourcefulness of her lover had been able to stem. With Alexis and his brother once out of the city, who knew what treacherous forms that fear might not take?

"I see the Ismailov Barracks. . . . Tell Alexis to stop the coach!" Gregory glanced at her in surprise.

"What madness is this? I tell you we have no time to lose. I must lodge you safely in the palace before I can begin to act."

"I am not going to the palace. I am halting here. I have changed the plan, Gregory, I changed it on the journey and I order you to stop the coach!"

For a moment he hesitated, and Catherine thrust her head out of the window and called herself, careless of the anger on his face at her defiance or his resentment at her tone.

Obediently Alexis drew on the rein and jumped down. Catherine opened the door and alighted; then suddenly she turned to Gregory and the hardness had melted from her eyes and mouth.

"Forgive me if I was abrupt, beloved, but my instincts in this tell me that they must be followed. I trust no politician; their ways are not your ways and I fear they might forfeit my life and their promises to me without a qualm. Come, Gregory Gregorovitch, trust me and forgive her who loves you and cannot bear to see you angry! From this moment I am in your hands and in the hands of those who know and follow you!

"Rouse the soldiers of the Ismailovs. Tell them their Empress is in danger and appeals for their protection! As you love me, go!"

*   *   *

The start of Catherine's revolution was a strange scene to the observer; the emergence of half-dressed sleepy soldiers into the street outside their barracks, summoned by a single drummer's echoing beat, a tiny nucleus of moving men beneath the early morning sky who heard the declaration from the lips of their Empress. She, the magnificent Catherine whose health they had drunk and whose beauty they had coveted in the manner of all men, was in danger of her life and stood there pale and dignified, fair as a goddess in her plain black gown, asking the protection of her people.

Simon Goronov, soldier and son of a freed serf, broke the silence that had descended upon them once their Emperor's wife had spoken. For a moment they had hesitated, waiting for someone to take the lead, to speak first in the cause of what they knew in their hearts to be treason, while Catherine's face drained deadly pale and the Orlovs' hands crept to their swords.

No scruples troubled Goronov; he wore upon

his back a Prussian uniform, for months he had drilled endlessly in the hated, unfamiliar German fashion and dreamed day and night of cutting the Czar's throat as reprisal for these humiliations. Now, as by the gift of God, his opportunity had come in the person of the Empress.

He flung his hat in the air and roared with all the power of his great voice.

"Long live our Little Mother Catherine! Death to the German pig!" On the instant that cry was taken up.

Every man among them joined with the giant Goronov, who had fallen to his knees and was kissing the Czarina's hands with tears of rage and emotion running down his leathery face and into his black beard, cursing and swearing eternal loyalty. Catherine found herself surrounded by hundreds of shouting enthusiastic men, struggling to be near, to get a close glimpse of the legendary Catherine Alexeievna, to hear her voice or touch her gown.

It was useless for Gregory and Alexis to thrust and elbow their way into that crowd, for none could have reached her, neither friend nor enemy. The officers of the Ismailovs had begun to mingle with their men, and at last the wildly cheering troops made a pathway for their Colonel, who fell on one knee before Catherine and kissed her hand in homage.

"God be praised, Your Majesty! The Ismailovs will fight for you to the last drop of their blood!"

Dozens of reverent hands lifted the Czarina into her own carriage, and a forest of naked swords surrounded the vehicle as still more soldiers hurried up. Alexis jumped on to the step and his brother sprang into the coach with Catherine. In one corner Mme Chargorodsky crouched silently, her hands clasped in an attitude of prayer. Orlov cast one contemptuous look at the shivering bemused woman and then caught his mistress in his arms. Someone among the crowd peered through the window and set up a mighty, envious cheer at this mark of imperial preference for the army.

Breathless and trembling, Catherine tore herself free.

"Not yet, my Gregory. We are not sure of victory yet. But it is the right beginning. Tell them to move on!"

Someone had fetched the regimental priest to give his blessing to the proceedings, and priest and crucifix were hustled into the front of the procession which began to move slowly forward, hemmed in by its escort of yelling soldiery in the direction of the Semionovsky barracks.

There the troops had been already warned of

Catherine's approach, and a horde of officers and men came running down the street to greet her. Again she ordered the carriage to stop and alighted in the midst of the enthusiastic Semionovsky Regiment, giving her hands to be kissed, unaware that she herself was crying with emotion, knowing only that even if the day ended in her defeat and death she would never forget the love these people had shown her in her hour of greatest need.

But time was short; the streets had begun to fill with civilians who approached this fantastic sight with caution, while the whisper spread throughout St. Petersburg that the Empress had entered the city to raise an army for protection against the Czar.

That rumour reached the Preobrazhensky Barracks deeper in the centre of the town. Among the first to hear the news of Catherine's approach was Elizabeth Vorontzov's brother, who commanded the Grenadiers.

He and several other officers who had received or expected favours at Peter's hands called out their men and reminded them of their oath to obey and succour the Czar against all comers. It was no less their duty to defend his throne against the treacherous onslaught of an unfaithful wife.

Watching Alexis, Catherine sensed a change in

his expression as the vehicle turned into the broad sweep of the Nevsky Prospect. She leant out and pulled at his sleeve.

"What is it, Alexis? What is wrong, we have almost stopped?"

"It is the Preobrazhenskys, Madame, and by the look of them they are come to fight us, not to join our cause!"

By this time the coach had halted, hemmed in on every side by the ranks of the Ismaïlovs and their brothers in the Semionovskys. The long expanse of the Nevsky Prospect was quite silent except for the ominous tread of the third regiment with Count Vorontzov at its head, which advanced with weapons drawn and muskets levelled towards Catherine and her troops.

Gregory leapt out of the carriage, pausing at the window to order Catherine to kneel on the floor when the first shot was fired.

His face was a mask in which his light eyes glittered dangerously; the fighter rejoiced in spite of himself in the chance to do battle. This was his *métier*, the world wherein the sword was arbiter, and the strongest triumphed without mercy over the weak. Until this moment Catherine had given the lead; hers was the victory, won by the strategy of cunning which he would never understand or practise with success. Now his fierce pride saw a chance to prove himself, to win all things for the woman he loved by virtue of sheer valour, and to establish more firmly the domination over her destiny which he had fought so jealously to maintain.

He did not want to win the Preobrazhenskys to her side, when he could annihilate them and cover himself with glory.

In that quick exchange of glances Catherine knew that unless she acted he would give the word to fire, and the earliest stage of her *coup d'état* would end in a welter of her people's blood. She, the liberating Empress who promised to free them from the Prussian yoke, would have begun by engulfing them in civil war.

Without a moment's thought of danger, she opened the door and stood on the coach step within full view of the Preobrazhenskys, and Orlov swore a fearful oath and lowered his pistol.

He swung round and tried to thrust her into the interior of the carriage, cursing and pleading with her to obey.

With his hand upon her arm, she hesitated for a single moment, bracing herself against the lintel of the door, and looked out over the heads of her men to where the serried ranks had halted only a few yards away.

That sight of her and the fanatic shouts of her

supporters broke the spell. Suddenly Count Menshikov remembered that he stood by the side of the hated Elizabeth Vorontzov's brother, that he and his men were about to attack the woman whom he had admired and liked for years, and to shed blood in order to keep Peter Feodorovitch upon a throne he was unfit to occupy.

It was his voice that rose from the ranks of Catherine's enemies, loud and ringing with excitement.

"Long live our Little Mother, the Empress of Russia!"

The next moment there was pandemonium, a shouting, surging chaos in which the Count Vorontzov found himself disarmed and made prisoner by his own men, while the rest of the Guards ran in droves towards that carriage, cheering and brandishing their weapons, fighting to get to the coach and its royal passenger, crying their loyalty and contrition with hundreds of eager voices.

The crisis was past. The army was going over to Catherine Alexeievna, and there in the open city streets they dragged the priest into their midst and knelt in homage, while Peter's wife was proclaimed Empress of all the Russias, and every man among them swore allegiance.

Swelled by thousands of townspeople, the

procession made its way to the very heart of Petersburg, joined by regiment after regiment who hastened to put themselves under the new Empress's command. Gregory Orlov's own troops handed her the keys to the city arsenal, and the historic coach halted finally before the great doors of the Kazan Cathedral, and there where she had stood beside Peter as a bride of sixteen, Catherine Alexeievna took the oath as Empress and Auctocrat of all the Russias.

There, too, she received Nikita Panin who had been hurried to the cathedral by Alexis Orlov, and there she embraced her shrinking son whose throne she was usurping.

Orlov had discovered the Count in his bedroom in the palace, feigning sleep and apparently deaf to the tumult of revolution which was taking place beneath his windows. Panin the conspirator had awoken to find his Czar deposed, and not Paul Petrovitch but the German-born Czarina proclaimed in his stead.

He came to the cathedral, dragging the Czarevitch by the hand, to make obeisance to the woman he had foolishly thought to use for his own ends, but he was wise enough to recognize defeat and bow before her to the ground.

Catherine greeted him with the effusion she knew how to express so well. Panin was powerful still and cunning; at all costs he must be retained among her friends.

"Of all my subjects you are the most welcome, my dear Count! From this day I shall have ever greater need of your counsel and support. Come to me in the Winter Palace when this service is ended."

Panin murmured his gratitude and backed away from her. As usual her grasp of human nature had chosen the exact amount of flattery and promise to decide him in her favour.

When Catherine emerged once more from the church she saw a sea of faces stretching before her, overflowing from the square into the surrounding streets, and for a moment she paused on the steps, waiting as she had done on the day of her wedding all those years ago, to acknowledge the cheers of the people, and they filled the air with the sound of their happiness and acclamation.

That cheering, waving multitude was the reward of twenty years of patience, of her wretched marriage and persecuted youth. With this destiny in mind she had endured and schemed and cheated; for this she had risked her life and come to Petersburg that morning, rather than take the coward's recourse and flee to Sweden while she still had time.

A great flood of feeling overwhelmed her as she

stood on the cathedral steps, a tide of emotion beside which her former loves and fears dwindled to insignificance, the shallow reflexes of a nature as yet unfulfilled.

Her lovers Saltykov, Poniatowsky, even Gregory in all his magnificent sensual power . . . what were they to her compared with this? . . . There in that roaring crowd she saw the symbol of her country; her love for them and their need of her was the true fulfilment of her life, the last gratification of mind and body which no mere man could hope to give her.

Every church bell in the city had begun to peal as she raised her fingers to her lips and blew a kiss to the multitude, before descending once more to enter her carriage.

Catherine's drive to the Winter Palace was a triumphal march, a procession through streets packed tight with people, while the coach travelled at the slowest walking pace. An escort of soldiers protected the new Empress from the enthusiasm of the populace, who thrust and struggled to get a glimpse of the woman bowing and smiling at them through the window. In places the crush was so great that it threatened to strand and perhaps overturn the carriage until the guards began clearing a path with kicks and blows.

Inside the Winter Palace a crowd of excited

courtiers had assembled and the first to run forward and greet Catherine was Princess Dashkov. Crying with happiness, she flung herself into the Empress's arms, too overwhelmed with emotion and relief to remember the dictates of ceremony. For some moments the two women embraced, laughing and talking at once, while the Dashkova held on to her beloved friend and gazed into her face.

Scores of her intimates clustered around Catherine, kissing her hand, showering their congratulations upon her, until among them she saw a familiar face and hurried forward extending both hands to greet him.

He tried to kneel to her, but she would not permit it; she put her arms around him and kissed his cheek before the eyes of the whole court.

"Dear Leo," she said, "my dear, faithful friend. It only needed you to share this day with me and now my cup of happiness is full."

Catherine looked at him and smiled. Now, when the reins of power had passed to her, she would be able to reward with wealth and honours a devotion unlikely to be matched by any other.

Later she supped, ordering the table to be placed by an open window within full view of the crowd still massed in the palace square, and raised her wine glass in acknowledgment of their delighted cheers.

All her innate showmanship and talent for stage management rose to the fore during those early hours of her revolution, so that she studied every word and movement to attain the right effect. No hint of violence, of anything save spontaneity, must reach those crowds who called her name with such enthusiasm. She must appear to them a saviour, placed on the throne by their own wish, while all rightful claimants to the Russian crown still lived. . . .

That afternoon the Senate was assembled and, with Panin at her side, Catherine sat down at her first Council. The oath of loyalty to her was taken at once, and with a unanimity which made her smile behind her fan; she had done well to flatter Panin, for in return he had kept his word. Not a voice was raised against her.

At regular intervals the meeting was interrupted by messages sent back by the guards posted along the roads out of the city, and reports came in from armed boats patrolling the Neva at Catherine's orders.

While the Senate debated the best method of dealing with him, the Empress's soldiers kept watch for the tell-tale cloud of dust which must herald the approach of Peter Feorodovitch and his army, marching on treacherous Petersburg to regain his throne.

★　　★　　★

Catherine and Gregory had closed the roads and placed troops on every bridge leading out of the city, but despite these measures and the speed with which they were enforced, word had reached the Emperor at Oranienbaum that his capital was in the throes of an armed rising.

Deaf to the advice of Chancellor Vorontzov, who counselled him to assemble his private army of Holsteiners and march on Petersburg without delay, Peter wasted precious time in violent ravings and abuse, coupled with the determination to ride not on the mutinous city, but to nearby Peterhof, where no one could persuade him that he would not find Catherine waiting quietly as she had been bidden. Contrary to Orlov's fears, Passek's arrest had not been reported, his captors had delayed until the morning, only to find themselves in the hands of Catherine's troops.

At Peterhof, the Czar declared obstinately, would lie the root and the remedy of all unrest. There they would have his most dangerous enemy in custody, and Peter voiced his intention of having her executed within the hour of their arrival.

With Elizabeth Vorontzov at his side, he made the short journey to the Old Palace, followed by his main force of Holstein troops.

His confidence and rage covered an abyss of foreboding and fear, so deep that he dared not hesitate and recognize it in the sure knowledge that his wavering sanity could never plumb those depths.

Preceded by his guards, he ran into the Monplaisir Pavilion, dragging the Vorontzova by the hand, shouting to Catherine to show herself. Only a scattering of white-faced servants appeared to answer his summons, and to admit that they had not seen the Czarina since the previous night, and that she was nowhere to be found.

Peter paused at last in her bedroom, surveying the unmade bed and heaps of discarded clothing which proclaimed the evidence of flight. He was trembling in every limb and the sweat ran down his disfigured face; for a moment he stood there in silence, swallowing repeatedly as his mouth dried up with terror. He swung round at last, his features distorted out of all semblance of control.

"She's gone!" he yelled. "I tell you she's escaped! Now do you see how right I was! Now do you see that I ought to have killed her long ago! You wouldn't let me, you fool!" he continued, shrieking at the Chancellor, his finger stabbing the air in accusation. "Now God knows where she is; God knows what evil she is working against me!"

The Chancellor coughed, he knew Peter and the punishments he was capable of inflicting when in the grip of frenzy. He moved quickly aside as Marshal Münnich, one of Peter's court and an experienced soldier, hurried into the room.

"Your Majesty, I have news!" The Czar almost sprang at him.

"You have found her?" he demanded.

"No, Sire. A messenger has just reached us from Oranienbaum. The Empress is in Petersburg. The rising is in her name, she has been proclaimed autocrat and the Senate have formally deposed you this afternoon. It is the vilest treason!"

"So she heads a revolution against me, me the rightful ruler! She and the snivelling curs in the Senate depose me, do they? What of the army, Marshal?"

"I fear they have gone over to her cause."

"Then my capital city has betrayed me utterly, my soldiers have proved themselves the swine and cowards I always deemed them. Come now, Chancellor, what do you suggest we do? Has that fertile brain of yours no plan for overcoming all these things?"

Vorontzov shook his head, aware that Peter

mocked him crazily.

"Well I have not been idle in these last moments," the Emperor continued. "I have a plan which should do justice to your talents as my wife's escape does justice to your judgment. We will compose a letter to my wife; we will demand that she and all the other traitors shall surrender. Who knows, they may be lawful at the end, they may read it and submit! What say you, Chancellor?"

Vorontzov shrugged. As well might Peter try to extinguish a fire with spittle, but it would hardly do to argue with him at that moment.

"It is a good plan, Your Majesty!"

"I am glad that you approve." Peter Feodorovitch began to snigger. "For as soon as it is written, I shall commend you to the care of my men for escort and they will set you down at the gates of Petersburg, where you can deliver the message to the gentle Catherine with your own hands. Perchance she will surrender without putting you to death for all the wrongs she owes you in the past."

He watched the colour draining out of his minister's face and began to rock with laughter. "Hurry now and write out my demands! You must proceed without delay."

No sooner had the door closed behind

Vorontzov than Marshal Münnich approached his sovereign.

"I beg Your Majesty to be serious. The position is most grave. We must take action quickly."

Peter faced him, his unsteady humour vanished, his hands tearing nervously at his cravat.

"I am not afraid," he said thickly. "I am a soldier, danger does not frighten me. We Germans are worth a hundred of these Russian dogs. I will fight her. I will stay here with my army and fight to the death!"

Even as he spoke his heart contracted with fear. He spoke of fighting, he who had never fired a shot in anger, even as he talked of death, when his flesh crept with terror at the thought of finality and darkness.

Münnich gestured impatiently.

"That is impossible. Peterhof could never withstand a siege, it was built for pleasure, not for war. We would be annihilated. Take my advice, Sire, and set sail at once for Kronstadt. The navy will be loyal to you, and from there you can make plans to sail down the Neva and attack Petersburg from the river!"

Peter stamped to the window; he was shaking violently and a torrent of confused thoughts raced through his burning brain. Suggestions were pouring in upon him, for others had joined the

Marshal and were adding their pleas to his. He did not know what to do or where to turn. Catherine was within a few miles, gathering an army, taking his crown, alienating his subjects. How could he go to Kronstadt and leave the protection of these walls?

"No," he repeated. "No; I will stay here and fight. I am not afraid. . . ."

It was almost evening when his resistance collapsed, when the atmosphere of terror and confusion which had invaded his supporters destroyed his last reserves of pretence.

Vorontzov had gone, white-faced and speechless, to his doom at Catherine's hands; the court had eaten a makeshift meal, its eyes fixed on the Czar who sat scowling and grimacing vacantly into the empty air, deaf to the entreaties of his mistress to take a little food, holding out his glass at ever shorter intervals for a lackey to refill with wine.

Only then, with the trembling Elizabeth Vorontzov clinging to his arm, did he consent to yield to Münnich's advice and embark on the royal yacht for the imperial naval base at Kronstadt.

Most of the journey he spent in comfortable oblivion, his head in his mistress's lap, the wine fumes dulling fear and consciousness, until the swaying motion of the vessel changed as she dropped anchor and Peter awoke to find the object of the trip was reached at last.

The harbour lay in darkness, a few pinpoints of light glowed faintly from the fortress building, and from the ship's deck a sailor's voice rang out, echoing across the silent water.

"Ahoy there! Open the harbour!"

The answer came from the port's protecting bastion.

"Who goes there!"

Peter had obeyed Münnich's summons and climbed on deck. It was he who answered, his words shrill and quavering as he stood shivering in the chill night air.

"It is I! The Emperor!"

From the watch tower of the bastion he heard a derisive angry yell.

"There is no Emperor! Long live the Empress Catherine! Move off or we fire!"

Peter caught at the rail, his legs giving under him. They were too late. Catherine had got to Kronstadt first and the navy too had betrayed him.

Seeing his distress the Marshal came to his side at once.

"Order them to open the harbour! Command them in the name of their rightful Czar! Show strength, Sire! They will lift the barriers, I swear they will lift them! Then sail in and land, no one will dare to lift their hand against you once they see you face to face!"

Peter Feodorovitch held on to the rail, breathing deeply, shuddering and gasping with fear. He had never wanted to leave Peterhof; he had never wanted to sail to this damnable treacherous place. Now they counselled him to sail in and put foot upon the shore, to deliver himself to his enemies in the belief that the sight of him would suddenly restore their loyalty when he knew them to be horrible and thirsting for his blood, when he had always known better than to trust his people!

"No, no, *no*!" he whimpered, and the last word was a scream of terrified refusal. "I will not go in! They will kill me, they are only waiting to kill me. Out of my way, damn you, let me pass! Draw up the anchor and set sail at once! For God's sake, Marshal, get me back to Oranienbaum where I shall be safe!"

Münnich stood back helplessly, while his sovereign staggered to the companion way and almost fell down the steps in his eagerness to take shelter.

The soldier turned away in disgust and gave orders to move on; delay under such circumstances would only expose them to cannon fire from the garrison at Kronstadt, and they departed with such haste that the anchor chain snapped.

While Münnich and the rest of the Czar's entourage spent the night hours of the return journey pacing the deck, watching the sky growing lighter and the reign of Peter the Third drawing to a close, Peter Feodorovitch remained below, sobbing and cursing with terror, held close in Elizabeth Vorontzov's arms, hidden in the deepest hold of the vessel.

*   *   *

Catherine Alexeievna was in her boudoir in the Winter Palace, holding private counsel with Panin. For the moment her doors were closed against both Gregory and the Princess Dashkov, who persisted in deluging her with contrary advice and confusing the issue by displays of jealousy over the attention which the Empress showed them.

Clearly, even at this early stage, there would not be room for Orlov and the Dashkova among Catherine's intimates, and the prospect of having to separate herself from the princess was a painful one in the light of all her loyalty and devotion.

But that, with many other disagreeable tasks, still lay ahead of her, and Catherine relegated it impatiently into the background; she needed quiet and the counsel of a shrewd friend to guide her, one whose judgment was not influenced by personal relations with herself.

Panin was cunning and impartial; he had managed his part in the revolution with a magnificent regard for his own safety which compelled Catherine's instant respect. On such a man she could rely, now that he had committed himself to her cause without hope of withdrawal.

The Count accepted her invitation to be seated and eased himself into one of her delicate gilt chairs.

"My friend, I have sent for you because I need your help. So far all has gone well for us, better than I had ever hoped, for not a drop of my people's blood has been spilled."

"Not even Vorontzov's," remarked Panin dryly. "How extraordinarily wise and merciful of you to have put him under arrest instead of executing him as no doubt Peter hoped you would!"

"It would be a poor beginning to my reign had I taken the life of one of the greatest nobles in Russia, when by a little prudence and a short memory, I might yet make use of his services. . . ."

Panin smiled in admiration. "Every man hopes to serve under a sovereign such as you will prove to be, Madame, but I confess such qualities in a woman are very seldom found. However, I know that you dislike delay; on what subject do you seek my opinion?"

Catherine got up and began walking the room, she was frowning and her manner betrayed some nervousness.

"The Senate counsels me to wait here; to issue ukases and establish myself by legislation, while a force under the command of a man like Count Gregory Orlov should go out and secure the Czar. Orlov supports this. On the other hand Princess Dashkov, whose views are not to be despised, advises me to assemble my army and ride out to do battle with Peter this very night! Which course do you approve?"

Panin eyed her shrewdly.

"If you wish to be rid of the Czar, Madame, then I support the first idea; I doubt if Count Orlov will deliver him alive. Bear in mind that we cannot possibly permit Peter Feorodovitch to live. But if you wish to avoid the stain of your husband's death in captivity, to appear as a woman prepared to fight and lay down her life to enforce the wishes of the people and remove them from the power of a tyrant, then I agree with the princess. Assemble your troops, place yourself at their head, and set out to engage with Peter in the field. It can be arranged that he shall receive a fatal wound during the combat."

Catherine stood in her favourite position by the

window, her face in deep shadow. No one could have read her expression.

"The last is my view also. It shall be done, Count Panin; send my officers to me, and inform the Senate that I intend to do battle for the crown."

Panin rose immediately and went to the door.

"It shall be done at once, Your Majesty. I applaud your decision."

Catherine's voice interrupted him coldly.

"I would remind you, sir, that you take one matter very much for granted, and I order you never to speak of it in my presence again. I have never said that I intend my husband's death. You may go!"

Within a few hours a force of fourteen thousand men had been gathered in St. Petersburg and a great phalanx of soldiers, regiments which comprised the cream of the Russian army, waited in the palace square.

A path had been made among them, stretching from the entrance of the palace to the distant confines of the vast courtyard, and this lane, cut through a mass of infantry, was lined by soldiers of the Semionovsky, Ismailov, and Preobrazhensky Guards, those who had first risen for the Empress, and each guardsman bore a flaming resin torch. Flambeaux blazed and smoked from the walls of the palace, casting a red glare over the scene, lighting the moonless sky to a false dawn.

The soldiers stood motionless, packed together in tight ranks, the leaping torchlight playing on them. Almost the first order given by Catherine had been the reissuing of the old Czarist uniforms, and the city had witnessed its army stripping itself of the hated Prussian coats and breeches and stamping them into the ground.

Now, with preparations completed, Catherine's army stood outside the palace, formed up ready to march out of the capital. It was said that the Empress intended to lead the troops herself, and every eye was fixed on the entrance, outlined and illumined by the flaring torches.

Suddenly they glimpsed a magnificent dapple grey horse being led to the bottom of the broad stone steps, and a ripple of anticipatory movement passed over the serried ranks of men like a wave running on to the shore. That was the Empress's mount.

Within a few moments she would appear.

When she did come she was greeted by silence; for an instant the men did not recognize the tall figure in the uniform of the Preobrazhensky Guards who paused at the head of the wide stairway, a group of officers at her back. Count Galitzin had lent Catherine the dress, and the masculine attire fitted her perfectly; a soldier's cap entwined with green oak leaves shadowed her face and her black hair hung straight down her back, the tendrils moving in the light summer wind.

The flames of the torches leapt and flickered, framing her beautiful, supple figure in its male garb, lighting her pale, proud features until a tremendous rolling cry told her that she was recognized, and a cheer arose from those waiting thousands which echoed out over the city like thunder.

"Long live the Empress Catherine!"

She began to walk down the steps, swaggering with the easy grace of a young man, the slight, girlish Princess Dashkov following, also dressed in uniform in imitation of her idol.

Catherine mounted as cheers of admiration rocked the palace building to its foundation and her escorts, Orlov, the Dashkova, princes and nobles of Russia rode up behind her. Then she raised her hand for silence, and on the instant the noise ceased.

Catherine looked down at her side and frowned slightly; she had no sword knot; without it her dress was incomplete.

Another saw that glance, another who had watched her fascinated from a distance and who risked his rank and future fortune on the chance to speak to her.

With two strides he had left his place among the guards and stood before his Empress. He was very tall, this impetuous officer, and his shoulders were of Herculean breadth. The face Catherine noted to be ugly rather than handsome, the complexion dark, the eyes black and brilliant. It was an extraordinary countenance, powerful and bold, with a distinctly Oriental cast of feature. Without doubt Tartar blood ran in the man's veins. The badges on his uniform were those of a Lieutenant.

For a moment his eyes met Catherine's and held her gaze without embarrassment. Their expression was almost fanatical; in another, such looks would have been impudence, but in this strange, arrogant young soldier there was no hint of Orlov's ruthless appraisal, before which Catherine's majesty invariably fell away. He looked up at her as if he regarded a divinity which had appeared in female form.

He swept her a magnificent bow, his sleeve brushing the ground, and with a dramatic gesture removed his own sword knot and offered it to her.

"If Your Majesty will do me the honour," he said, and his voice was deep and pleasing. Catherine took the ornament from his hands, aware that his olive skin darkened with colour as their fingers touched.

353

"I thank you, Lieutenant. Your gesture is as gallant as your observation is acute. I am most grateful."

The young officer bowed again and stepped back with perfect precision into the ranks of his fellows. Catherine fastened the sword knot and gestured to Gregory Orlov to approach. He spurred his mount to her side and, at a word from her, the signal to advance was given.

A series of commands rang out over the square as the procession of horses, led by the Empress on her grey, moved to the end of the courtyard, and the great mass of soldiers, cavalry, cannon and supply wagons prepared to move out of Petersburg.

Catherine Alexeievna rode steadily, passing through the city streets, watched by cheering crowds, many of whom recalled the grace and beauty of Elizabeth Petrovna whose habit of reviewing her troops in full Guards dress had become a tradition, and admitted that not even the daughter of Peter the Great had sat her horse with such a magnificent air.

That morning she had passed among them, seated in a plain carriage, surrounded by a yelling rabble of rebellious guards, and the people had welcomed her as the panacea for all the ills which Peter Feodorovitch had brought them. Now for the second time that day they saw her, as a proud, relentless adversary, the victorious sovereign leading her army to do battle. It might well have been Peter who was the usurper, so naturally did his wife fulfil his rôle.

It was a long march and the pace was slow; with Gregory on one side of her and the Dashkova on the other, Catherine conversed at intervals. She asked the name of the officer whose sword knot she wore and nodded upon hearing it, but throughout the long weary hours of their progress towards Peterhof she said little and thought a great deal.

The end was near and she knew it, for she did not believe that Peter Feodorovitch would expose himself in battle for the convenient bullet which Panin had suggested. She did not believe that Peter would come out and fight at all. She had an unhappy premonition that he would surrender, and the words of her Minister repeated themselves many times during that night.

"We cannot possibly permit Peter Feodorovitch to live."

Sometimes the Princess Dashkov questioned her, noting the set expression on her face, the frowning abstraction which possessed her when she should have been afire with confidence and resolution. For the twentieth time she turned to her royal mistress and enquired what ailed her.

They were within sight of Peterhof when Catherine turned to her and the Dashkova saw that the strained look had vanished, and that her blue eyes were blank and clear.

"I have been considering a problem, my little Katrina, and at last I have made my decision. My heart is therefore light once more."

*   *   *

The Empress's spies reported that the Czar had taken refuge in Oranienbaum, and Catherine, who had ridden without sleep or rest, established her headquarters in one of the rooms at Peterhof and decided upon a plan of action. An advance guard must go to Oranienbaum, she declared, test the outer defences and deliver an ultimatum to the Emperor that, unless he surrendered without delay, the imperial army would bombard the palace and blow its buildings and occupants to pieces.

The outposts guarding Oranienbaum were manned by Holstein troops, badly armed and bewildered by the flood of terrified contradictory orders which the Emperor's staff issued every hour. A preliminary skirmish with Orlov and his soldiers sufficed to drive them back into the palace grounds and, under the protection of a promise of safe conduct, General Ismailov, former friend and emissary of Peter's who had deserted to the Empress, entered Oranienbaum with the order to submit and the act of abdication, prepared by Catherine herself, lodged in his pocket.

By midday word reached the Czarina at Peterhof that her husband had surrendered himself and signed the document she had dictated.

*   *   *

Those few miles from Oranienbaum to Peterhof were lined by hundreds of eager, vindictive soldiers, men who had suffered every military humiliation that their Czar had been able to inflict upon them, and the news that he was being escorted as prisoner to the Old Palace brought the guards running to line the route, anxious to avenge themselves, armed with stones and handfuls of filth.

In a plain carriage, Peter the Third, Emperor and Autocrat of all the Russias, whose trembling hand had just signed away his freedom and his birthright, sat huddled in a corner of the vehicle, the tears coursing down his disfigured cheeks, his mouth a little open, staring out at the yelling, cursing soldiery, whose indescribable missiles spattered the walls and windows of the vehicle; panes of glass had been shattered by stones, and

the splinters glittered over the clothes of the passengers.

Peter heard the angry, insulting cries as from a
great distance. His mind had gone almost blank
within the last few hours; the misery of his return
from Kronstadt and the discovery that the
dreaded Catherine was advancing on Oranienbaum at the head of a large army, all these things
had pressed in upon him until he had startled his
mistress by uttering a weird animal cry of pain
and despair, and his meagre court had discovered
their Emperor prostrate on the floor, crying like a
child.

When they lifted him into a chair he had continued to weep and to stare at them, his eyes passing from one to the other, with a terrible childlike
look that caused Marshal Münnich to cease in the
middle of an admonitory sentence. Then he had
held out his arms to Elizabeth Vorontzov and
buried his head in her breast.

He was wandering slightly when they brought
him the act of abdication and repeated
Catherine's threat.

He had looked at them, his weak mouth opening and closing in the effort to speak, struggling to
understand the import of the things they told him,
the written characters on the strange document
dancing before his eyes.

They wished him to surrender; his only chance was to forego his crown, and finally Peter nodded. He had understood. Catherine wanted his throne; she had always wanted it, while he had not, and perhaps if he gave it to her peaceably she might let him return in time to Holstein and live quietly with his Vorontzova. He signed.

He remembered little of the nightmare that followed this simple action, the entry of Alexis Orlov and his men into the room, the rough separation from his mistress who fought and scratched to protect her lover, the contempt and savage enmity of his captors, led by that fearsome officer with the scarred face.

Throughout the journey to Peterhof he never spoke, but gave his hand to Elizabeth Vorontzov, whose pleas to accompany him had been granted, and clung to her until the carriage stopped and Orlov hustled him into the palace.

There they took away his uniform and Panin, who had advised his death, had a last interview with his former Czar. In later years the count was to recall that day with horror, and the spectacle of Peter as the most pitiable of his life. He, the least sentimental of men, shrank from the visible evidence of grandeur fallen to such depths.

By five o'clock that afternoon a heavily shuttered carriage swept out of the drive and sped away from Peterhof. An escort of soldiers galloped alongside. By a window in the palace Catherine Alexeievna watched it go.

$$\ast \quad \ast \quad \ast$$

"Apartments are being made ready for the former Emperor in the Schüsselburg," Panin reported conversationally.

The Empress and her army had returned to Petersburg after a triumphal march through the city, and were in residence at the Winter Palace. Panin had watched her and waited for a private audience. There was something weighing on her, despite her outward show of gaiety.

The fate of Peter Feodorovitch could not be deferred much longer, and had it been any other woman and not Catherine, Panin would have deplored the laxity which lodged such a dangerous prisoner in a mere fortified house like Ropscha instead of burying him in a dungeon at the Schüsselburg.

But the Empress procrastinated and hedged, saying openly that she had no wish to make her husband's lot more miserable than she could help, and that his prison must be fitted comfortably for his needs. Curiously, Panin believed her as devoid of spite as she appeared, but then malice or deliberate cruelty were not among her faults.

One thing alone belied this gentle attitude, and that was the refusal of Peter's last pathetic request for the company of Elizabeth Vorontzov in his banishment. Panin did not believe his royal mistress to be impelled by jealousy, and this single inconsistent act had roused his most acute suspicions. Now he had learnt something which had just confirmed them and brought him hurrying to Catherine's private rooms.

The Empress had sent Alexis Orlov to Ropscha as one of Peter's guards. . . .

Catherine Alexeievna was seated at her desk. Panin noted that her usual brilliant complexion was extremely pale and that she played nervously with a quill pen. She regarded him with eyes dark-ringed with strain and for a moment did not speak. The count continued to watch her, a little careless smile on his fat face.

Suddenly the Empress rose and came round her desk towards him. She held a torn sheet of paper in her hand.

"My good friend. Support me in this dreadful hour! This confession has just reached me!" Panin took the parchment and began to read.

"Christus!" he said slowly. "Is it possible?"

Catherine retrieved the paper and began folding it into thin squares. Her hands trembled slightly.

"It is true. I know it is true. He says he killed him in a quarrel. He says that they were playing cards with Peter and that the Czar accused him of cheating. He says that it was done before he realized. . . . Tell me, Nikita, in God's name what am I to do?"

Panin eyed her narrowly; suddenly she made his flesh creep with fear.

"You can punish Alexis Orlov," he said slowly. "You can execute him for the crime of strangling the former Czar. . . ."

Catherine glared at him in desperation. "That is impossible! I owe everything to him and his brother Gregory. Do you suppose that I dare act against them! I tell you there is nothing I can do. It is abominable! It is a dreadful crime! But as I value my throne and my own life, I dare not punish it. There is no course open to me but to forgive."

"Then I counsel you to do so privately, for whatever bonds exist between you and these Orlovs, the world will not acknowledge them strong enough to protect your husband's murderer. Keep this news secret, and by to-morrow I will have a ukase issued from the Senate. We can say Peter Feodorovitch died a natural death."

That evening the court was received by the Empress as usual, and Catherine danced a minuet with Gregory Orlov before the gaze of an admiring and indulgent crowd, while the Princess Dashkov watched with jealous, uncomprehending eyes these marks of continuous favour by her mistress towards an uncultured boor of lowly ancestry.

All who had witnessed Catherine on that evening agreed later that she had never looked more beautiful or shown greater animation.

Only Panin left the ballroom early, to lie in his bed and ponder the enigma of his sovereign's innocence or guilt.

The following day Petersburg received the news of Peter Feodorovitch's death from an attack of hæmorrhoidal colic.

*   *   *

In the Czarina's bedroom in the Kremlin all was very quiet. Throughout the day those servants who were not employed in decorating and preparing the palace had been able to witness a magnificent spectacle, enacted not once but several times, as the rehearsal of the Empress's coronation was repeated for Her Majesty's satisfaction.

She had spent hour upon hour, weighed down by her heavy robes and immense yellow embroidered cloak, walking under the great canopy, taking measured steps in time to the fanfares and music which had reverberated throughout the ancient halls and galleries of the Old Palace.

In this, as in the smallest detail connected with her realm, only perfection satisfied her.

Now the day was over, the evening's banquet ended and Catherine Alexeievna had retired to her room.

The Kremlin state rooms were small compared with the vast imperial palaces of later design, and the building gloomy despite its ornate magnificence.

The walls of Catherine's bedchamber were very old; they were frescoed in a religious design, and the dim faces of anguished Byzantine saints regarded the Czarina in her beautiful bed. The bed curtains were drawn and a fire burnt in one corner of the room; it cast a flickering red light over the furniture, gleaming on gold and inlay, the work of long dead hands, the treasures of ancient Muscovy Czars.

Here the women of the Tartar lords had passed their time in strict seclusion; Ivan the Terrible had paced this floor, leaning upon his murderous spiked staff. . . .

Catherine Alexeievna lay upon her back, her eyes wide open, looking at the ceiling; she stretched slowly, clasping her hands behind her head. That night, for the first time since her accession, the private door leading to her room would not open to admit Gregory Orlov. This night, he the insatiable lover, whose passion for his mistress assumed aspects of terrifying jealousy, had been forbidden to disturb her, and none but a humble lackey snored on the threshold of her door.

To-morrow she would make the state journey down the Beautiful Staircase, so aptly named, dressed in her gorgeous robes, and then into the Cathedral of the Assumption where every sovereign of Russia had been crowned since Ivan the Third.

There the magnificent crown of diamonds, specially made to her requirements, would be placed upon her head, and her brow anointed with the consecrated oil. There she would receive the outward signs of an authority already firmly in her grasp, and on this, the eve of her greatest public triumph, Catherine had not wanted Gregory. She had not wanted anyone, neither for companionship nor for love.

Catherine Alexeievna lay awake, watching the firelight playing on the walls, looking back over the past.

A procession of images flitted before her brain. . . . Her father and mother, the one dead many years, the other an exile in Paris, living in luxury at the expense of the French king; Elizabeth Petrovna, in the flush of youth and beauty, receiving the blushing Princess Augusta of Zerbst, and again Elizabeth, ageing and sick, bedaubed with paint and glittering with jewels, advising her nephew's wife to take the throne. Peter Feodorovitch. . . .

Quickly Catherine closed her eyes, as if to preserve her sight from a fearful vision, the vision of Alexis Orlov's terrible muscular hands.

Bestujev had returned to court, promptly released from his Siberian prison, but of all the honours she bestowed upon him the Empress Catherine had decided that power should not be among them.

Panin was her chief minister; Panin who had helped her, and who was dangerous to offend . . . and she was stronger than Panin. He could never rule her as his old master had ruled Elizabeth Petrovna.

No man should rule her and no woman either, as the presumptuous Princess Dashkov was already learning.

She had so much to do, so many projects to fulfil, and still find time to love, to be a woman to the man she had loaded with riches, with positions and honours, and whom she knew to be dissatisfied with all but the one reward that she would never give him. She owed him her throne and her life, she owed him a hundred things, and to Alexis she owed something more . . . but she would never marry Gregory.

To-morrow she would be crowned Catherine the Second, Empress and Autocrat of a vast country, ruler of millions of people, owner of incalculable wealth and power. Her childhood dream was about to be made reality for ever. The annals of the history of the world would bear her name, and that was something which belonged to her alone.

Even as Russia belonged to her, and she held that submission in a sacred trust; all those plans with which she had beguiled the long, lonely hours of her marriage, plans for the betterment of her country, for the freeing of the millions of serfs, for building and education—plans lately conceived for conquest and glory, strategies which would enlarge her boundaries. . . .

The days would scarcely be long enough for the great work with which she would immortalize her people and herself.

In return for the crown she was to receive, she would care for her subjects and nurture them as tenderly and fiercely protective as the maternal namesake they had given her.

Mother and mistress she would be to Russia,

and all the waters of the earth and the tumults of the future should never erase the mark or deaden the memory of her name.

The fire was dying slowly and a line of dark shadow crept up the walls. Catherine Alexeievna closed her eyes to sleep and, all unbidden, conjured into consciousness by some fore-shadowing fate, the dark fanatical Lieutenant whose sword knot she still retained among her most treasured mementos of that memorable day recalled himself to her mind, and looked into her face with burning Oriental eyes.

She stirred a little, sinking deeper into the silken pillows, remembering that Orlov had told her the man's name during the course of that night march to Peterhof.

For a moment rest eluded her as she struggled irritably to recall it. Then her lips parted in a faint smile; she recollected it, her memory was always excellent, and she murmured it aloud in satisfaction:

"Gregory Potemkin."

She would not forget again.

Somewhere within the palace a clock in one of the courtyards began to chime the hour; within a while the sun would begin to rise flooding the gilded cupolas and towers of Moscow with morning light, and the citizens of Moscow would stir

368

and hurry to their places in the Kremlin square to glimpse the great procession of the crowning of their Empress.

Meanwhile the last flame of the fire in the royal bedroom grate flickered and died into a glowing ash; within a second this too was extinguished and, in the final darkness before dawn, Catherine Alexeievna fell asleep.

Photoset and printed in Great Britain by
Redwood Burn Limited, Trowbridge, Wiltshire